HAUNTED

THE CHASE RYDER SERIES BOOK 2

JO HO

This book is dedicated to all those out there who are in need of family and love.

Keep searching and never give up.

Thank You to
Matt, for being my love and my rock
and Dawn, for keeping me sane.

Thanks also to my ARC team, many of whom acted as beta readers for this book — you guys are awesome!

SIGN UP TO JO'S NEWSLETTER!

Be the first to hear Jo's news, book releases, and giveaways. Apply for her ARC teams (she has one for ebooks AND one for audiobooks) to get free, advanced copies of her books to read/listen to and review.

Plus, you'll get a free book as a thank you for signing up! What's not to like?

Sign up and join all the cool kids at www.johoscribe.com

PROLOGUE

Acrid smoke filled the air, burning the back of his throat and stinging his eyes.

The Scientist swallowed uncomfortably, pressing a tissue against his nose, though it offered only the faintest respite. Firefighters littered the devastation before him, having battled the blaze long through the night. It had taken a small village to control the fire, and though it would never rage again, there wasn't much left of Sebastien's pride and joy.

The roof of the building that was home to Platinum Industries had collapsed and now lay in a pile of rubble. The once spotless glass windows (which Sebastien, ever the neat freak, had cleaned on a weekly basis) had exploded outward when the temperature had proved too much to bear, showering the ground with their remains.

His loafers kicked at a charred shard, the metal glinting in the afternoon sun.

Stupid fool. All those experiments, all that knowledge. Everything was now lost to the wind.

He had warned him, warned Sebastien that pursuing a selfish

goal would be the end of him. Science — especially a breakthrough like the one his team had discovered — was meant for the world, not just one man, but as usual, Sebastien did as he wanted... and now the world was paying the price.

Having seen enough, he started moving towards his car. Amongst the fire trucks, police vehicles and corporate cars favored by the executives who formed Sebastien's legal representatives, The Scientist's own small hatchback seemed out of place, but he himself did not notice, not having a materialistic bone in his body. It was one of the things Sebastien, who had spent money like it was going out of fashion, liked to mock him for.

Last night, as he was getting ready for bed, he had received news of Sebastien's demise from his assistant Suzanne. Forever paranoid, Sebastien had his men regularly scouring police networks for news, particularly while they were on the hunt for Alpha. It was because of this that they were able to pick up the news of his death long before the police stepped in. The Scientist had gotten dressed and immediately made his way to Platinum Industries, hoping vainly that he would be able to salvage some of Forbes' work. Though he himself was never employed there (The Scientist kept his own lab), he had visited a number of times, so he knew what to expect. Still, it had hurt to see years of research and the billions invested into Sebastien's experiment going up in flames.

Luckily, none of it was his money.

Sebastien had been addicted to fame, luxuriating in the spotlight while The Scientist, a quiet man, was interested in only one thing — to make his mark in history by bringing man the most precious gift of all.

And he was very close to achieving it.

Sebastien's thugs' failure to retrieve Alpha was a terrible setback to his work.

Having seen what damage Alpha's new family had wreaked,

The Scientist knew he had to rethink his plan, particularly as he didn't have vast wealth or cronies of his own to fall back on. Though Sebastien had been funding his secret research, his untimely death ensured his money would now be tied up in legalities. He would have no access to it and as the small-minded bureaucrats holding the public purse had no vision and would deem his work unethical — no matter how important it would be — it meant he could not go that route.

Despite these new setbacks, The Scientist knew this would only be a blip in his plans. Activating his phone, he called up live footage of his lab. The picture was grainy and in black and white, but he could easily make out the large steel tank inside which his experiment grew.

He would wait until his creation was born.

Then nowhere would be safe for Alpha to run.

2

CHASE

I stared out over the green horizon wondering how, even after
six months of living here at the ranch, I hadn't tired of the view
yet.

Thrushes flew across the early morning sky, chirping and
singing a song that I had grown accustomed to in my time here.
Zeb, Sully's dad, was quite the bird watcher, and it turns out, so
was I. We had spent many evenings on the porch identifying our
feathered friends while Bandit tried to memorize them. If you had
told me a year ago, back when I had just left home to take my
chances on the streets, that this would be my life, I'd have laughed
in your face and called the Po Po to come take you away.

But you know what? I was kinda loving it.

I felt a warm breath on the back of my hand and immediately
knew Bandit was with me.

"Hey, Buddy."

He woofed and pawed the ground in his usual greeting to me.
Then he took my sleeve in his mouth and started leading me into
the kitchen. I laughed.

"Wow, OK. I see we're hungry this morning."

He took the iPad that hung around his neck in the pouch Gideon had custom-made for him, set it gently on the ground and proceeded to "speak" using the Speak, Spell and Read app I had downloaded for him. Gingerly taking up the modified stylus into his mouth, he tapped out the words while the app spoke them to me.

"I am hungry every morning."

"We're so alike," I said.

"Like peas in a feather."

"What?" I said, momentarily confused before it sank in. "You mean peas in a pod. The other saying is "birds of a feather.""

Bandit's mouth fell open as he tried to understand it all. He shook his head, looking perplexed.

"Your sayings are confusing."

"Yeah. Must be hard trying to remember them all." I scooped some doggie chow into his bowl and set it before him as I poured myself a giant bowl of cereal.

"Isn't it time you got a job or something before you eat us out of house and home?" came Sully's voice from the doorway. He came in, dressed in the jeans and checked flannel shirt that seemed to form the staple of his wardrobe here. I thought it made him look like a hick but Sam seemed to like it, which I guess was all he cared about.

"You mean, like you?" I shot back, knowing that Sully hadn't worked since we'd been here. Back in Greenwich, Sully had been a veterinarian, but that was before Bandit and I had turned up on his doorstep and changed his life forever.

"Least I have an expertize," he replied. "So do I... professional bum," I retorted. Bandit's tongue hung out of the corner of his mouth in what I now knew was his way of laughing. We did this kind of thing every day. After all, I'm the girl who calls Bandit "Muttface" as a term of endearment. Sully and I taking shots at each other? This was our version of "good morning".

Sully poured himself a cup of coffee and sat by the table as Sam came into the room. She was dressed in her Sheriff's uniform and the ends of her hair were still wet from a recent shower. The two of them had been inseparable since Forbes' death. It was Sam who had made sure no trace of Bandit was mentioned on the paperwork that was filed. It was because of her that we were safe and together today. She smiled at us over the top of Sully's head.

"Hey, you two."

Bandit woofed a greeting as Sam grabbed a donut from the counter and poured coffee into the steel thermos Sully had gotten her as a present. She whistled cheerfully, seemingly super happy. Sam was always chirpy, but she positively glowed this morning. I looked at Sully then back at Sam, staring suspiciously, but Sully flipped open a newspaper, hiding from sight. "Where's Gideon and Zeb?" Sam asked.

"Gid had to be at work early today, he's already gone," I volunteered. "And Zeb's in the barn, getting things set-up." Sam looked suddenly disappointed. It wasn't a big change — she was still smiling — but some of her earlier brightness had faded.

"What's up?" I asked, wondering what had caused the change in her expression. She didn't answer straight away but looked at Sully who shook his head in the tiniest of motions.

"Oh, nothing. Just asking."

If I knew one thing about Sam, it's that she doesn't ask anything without a reason. She wasn't the kind of woman who spoke just to fill in the space (unlike my mom, who would only shut up when she was drunk and passed out on the couch). The hairs raised on the back of my neck, and I felt a tingle of apprehension.

"Seriously, something's up. What is it?" I asked, unable to keep my mouth shut. Sully obviously decided that now wasn't the time to talk about whatever it was they had to say, as he turned a page on his paper. Apparently, it was a riveting read as he wouldn't peel his eyes away from it. "Nothing's up, Chase. You don't have to worry."

He had always been a terrible liar, and this time wasn't any different. Seeing their expressions, however, I knew I wouldn't be getting anything out of them. Narrowing my eyes at them, I took my phone out of my pocket. By now, Bandit had woofed down his meal and was circling around me. Whatever was going on with them didn't seem to have affected him any. I took comfort in that, knowing that if it were terrible news, Bandit would have sensed it. As it was, he was almost tripping me up in his excitement.

"Dude, you need to chill out before you knock me over." He snorted, correcting me. As if I'd do that. He might not have said those words, but I heard it in his response. Sam grabbed a paper towel, dabbing the sugar from her mouth, then hurried out to work.

"Y'all be good now, I'll see you later."

"Bye hon," Sully said. And with that, she was gone. I shot a look at Sully, but he couldn't see my ire behind the newspaper. Annoyed, Bandit and I headed out to the porch where I settled on the swing. Bandit sat on the floor next to me. After everything that's happened, Sully insisted on getting me a phone, even though — outside of the random attack by those soldier types and Forbes — this was literally the safest place on Earth. Here, people didn't lock their doors. Sometimes they didn't even close them. Having lived in NYC for a while, I found this faith in humanity crazy bizarre.

Propping my phone onto a table, I started up a Jeopardy app that we'd discovered a few weeks ago. As soon as I laid my eyes on it, I knew we had to have it. As the intro music sounded, Bandit's tail swished back and forth across the porch floor in excitement. He set his iPad on the ground and took up the modified stylus into his mouth, primed and ready for action. As the voice of the host of the show came on, Bandit and I battled each other in what had

become our post-breakfast ritual. Despite how it might seem friv-
olous, this actually served two purposes: one, it was Bandit's most
favorite thing in the world to do, and two, it was a way for us to
monitor his brain, something which Sully insisted upon as a
precaution against future issues.

Though the operation at Platinum Industries had been
successful, there wasn't any precedent for this and Sully did not
want any more surprises; the two of us were still haunted by the
fits Bandit had previously suffered. Sometimes, I'd wake up in the
middle of the night, desperately afraid that Bandit would be dead.
Whenever that happened, Bandit would wake too and come lie by
my side, putting his head on my chest. He'd chuff at me, letting
me know all was OK, and I'd stroke him until I finally fell asleep
again.

Every morning, Bandit and I would go head-to-head at the
game, and I'd only have to report to Sully if anything seemed off.
So far (touch wood), I'd never had to tell him anything other than
I was pretty sure Bandit cheated. He read voraciously and
retained all the knowledge, so much so that despite my own
photographic memory, most days he won.

It was a strange feeling to know that you were constantly being
bested by a dog.

We did a couple of rounds of questioning when Sully popped
his head out the door at us. "It's time, Fella."

Bandit slid the stylus and iPad into his pouch and went with
Sully to the barn. I watched Sully, noticing he still walked with a
limp. Zeb had been making him do these dance-like exercises
every day. They were supposed to rehab his leg, but Sully always
complained that he was "no damn ballerina." Gid and I were
banned from ever going into the barn where he did them,
however, because of how we'd reacted the first time we had snuck
in. Let's just say you could hear us laughing clear across the state.

Bandit always joined Sully in these sessions, though not to dance, that would be stupid. While Sully worked his muscles, the two of them would do physical checks on Bandit. I watched them go through them all once but they weren't very exciting to see so I usually just left them to it.

As they disappeared into the barn together, I cleared up the dishes in the kitchen, then went back to my room.

3
____

CHASE

After Bandit's physical, we headed into town.

Sully and Sam had been talking about the possibility of me going back to school for a while now, but I really, really didn't want to go. Just picturing myself in a classroom *every day* caused me to panic.

I knew it was stupid, I mean, look what we had gone through already. I'd taken out Forbes and his men. What the heck were teenagers going to do to me?

But I've seen Mean Girls.

I knew I wouldn't fit in. I never have, and the thought of having to try five days a week was getting me down, not least because I'd be away from Bandit so much — it was unthinkable. But whenever I said no, Sam would talk about how important an education was to get further in life. She'd bring up what I wanted to do in the future, asking difficult questions like that.

The reality was, I'd never given any of it any thought.

So much of my life before was just about surviving. I didn't know if I'd see another day. Who had time to worry about the future? I never got further than wondering where my next meal would come from, or if after I went to sleep in someone's doorway, whether I'd wake up again the next day.

I hoped to God that wasn't what the two wanted to discuss this morning. That would suck big time.

Since I was still too young to drive, Sully had gotten me a bicycle. I moaned about it a bit — didn't want him to think I was easy — but secretly; I was thrilled. I'd never had one as a kid and the luxury I felt now, in being able to get about so much further and faster than if I'd been walking was an independence I loved.

Bandit too, adored running beside me, but like most dogs, he never seemed to know how much was too much, so Gideon had built a special dog seat for him that we had attached to the back of the bike. It was Sully who had warned me about this.

Apparently, dogs were so thrilled to play and be with their owners that they wouldn't stop running beside them, but their little bodies weren't built for distance. Some get so overexcited that they won't stop until they become weak and collapse! This is an actual condition!

I figured Bandit to be smarter than that, but even then, I didn't want to risk it. So I always set a timer on my phone when we headed out. I let him run for up to fifteen minutes straight, but then he needs to ride behind me. Bandit had no problem with this and treated it like car rides. His tongue would hang out and he'd look positively blissful. When I'd asked about it before, about what it was that made him so happy, he said it felt like he was swimming in air.

My dog, the poet. *Who'd have thought it?*

We arrived at a garage on the outskirts of town. It wasn't a big production, but Warrey always seemed to have six or so vehicles being worked on. It was one of the reasons he'd hired Gid. Business had been picking up, and he wasn't able to manage on his own. Gid happened to call on him at the right time and when he showed Warrey how handy he was, he was hired on the spot.

Rock blasted out from a stereo — not Gideon's choice I know, since he preferred alternative styles.

Warrey came over from the truck he was inspecting. Grease stains covered his T-shirt, and he had a bandana tied around his head. Sam had commented before on how good-looking Warrey was, I remembered as Sully had scowled for the rest of the day. Seeing me, he waved a wrench in greeting.

"Chase. How's it going?"

"Oh, you know. Boring. How about you?" I asked.

"I could regale you with the excellent work I'm doing on this engine right here, but I figure that's not going to help your mood any."

"You'd be right."

Bandit trotted up to him and gave him a small lick on the hand. Warrey patted him absently on the head as he called out over the music. "Gid, visitors for you."

There was a clang as tools were dropped, then Gideon slid out from beneath the car he was working on. Like Warrey, his shirt was also covered with stains, but where the older man wore a T-shirt, Gideon had only a sleeveless vest, one that showed off his toned arms... which I'd noticed quite a lot recently. He came towards me, one brow raised in question.

"Everything all right?"

"Yeah, we're just visiting. I took Bandit out for a run and we just found ourselves here."

I was about to say something else just as lame when I caught a figure moving from the corner of my eye. It was a guy, older than Sully but younger than Zeb. His long gray hair fell into his face as he struggled to maneuver a removal box up the fire escape outside using a pulley system that Warrey must have rigged up some time ago, judging by the screech that now sounded.

"Who's that?" I asked.

"Erik someone. Warrey finally found a replacement for his old tenant. He works in IT."

"What's an IT guy doing in the middle of nowhere? This town barely has wifi."

Gideon shrugged. "I don't know, didn't ask."

"How come?"

"He doesn't look that exciting to me. If you have questions, you can bother him yourself."

He just finished talking when Erik lost his handhold on the box and its contents crashed down the fire escape causing an almighty ruckus. I went to help him. "You OK up there?"

Erik stared down at me, embarrassed. "I'm all fingers and thumbs today."

I gathered up Erik's belongings, which mostly consisted of computery things as far as I could make out. "Interesting er, stuff," I began. "Gideon said you're into IT."

Erik nodded, wiping sweat from his brow.

"So what are you doing in the middle of nowhere? Most of the folks around here don't even use email." The question popped out before I realized it could be construed as rude. I hoped he would know I was just making conversation, shooting the breeze as Sully would say.

Erik smiled, looking at me with his piercing blue eyes.

"That's actually why I'm here. I lived in the city for twenty years and I'm sick of it now. The slow pace and fresh air will do me the world of good. Besides, city people aren't very friendly. I wanted to be in a place where everyone knew one another."

"Well, you've found it then," Gideon said, having joined us on the fire escape. "I'm Gideon, this is Chase."

"Ah, nice to meet you. Are you two together?" Erik asked. It was an innocent enough question, but I suddenly felt my cheeks turn red.

"No," Gideon replied, "but we do live together."

"As a family," I supplied quickly, "with my dog and some others."

Erik turned his attention to Bandit on the ground, watching up at us.

"That's your dog, I take it? He's a pretty thing."

I nodded. "His name's Bandit. Bandit, say hi," I called down to him, but Bandit made an agitated move and barked. "He's usually pretty friendly, he doesn't like it because he can't come up the ladder."

"Understandable," Erik replied. "Well, thank you both for helping me but I've got quite a bit more to move into the apartment so I should get to it."

"I work in the garage below but if you need a hand with anything, just let me know," Gideon offered.

"Why thank you, young man. So nice to see not all of your generation have lost their manners."

I climbed back down the ladder to Bandit's joy. He bounced up and down like he hadn't seen me in years — the dufus.

"That was nice of you, offering to help him," I said to Gideon.

"Are you kidding? Did you see the way he used that cinch? The guy's going to wreck it then who's Warrey going to get to fix it? Me. I just did that to save myself hassle in the future."

"Smart move."

"Right? They don't call me Three-Steps-Ahead-Dion for nothing."

"No one calls you that, you idiot," I laughed. Bandit barked twice — one bark for yes, two for no — making us both laugh even more.

4

―――――

CHASE

We hung around until Gideon's shift was over and the three of us picked up the list of ingredients he and Sam had prepared last night.

Now that our motley family consisted of six, we took turns at cooking, but while I was the clear winner in the baking department, Gideon and Sam proved themselves amazing cooks. Literally, anything they put on the table was TO DIE FOR, which is why shopping for groceries had become the highlight of my day. I loved to see how these seemingly unrelated ingredients would come together to form a party in my mouth.

"What is all this?" I asked, looking at the endless list I had just unfolded.

"Don't know. Sam's cooking, but she said it's a surprise."

"But look at this. There's bacon, marrow bones — that's got to be for Bandit — shrimp, steak, and scallops. Scallops, Gid!"

"What about it?"

I shoved the list into his face.

"Don't you see? These are all our favorite things! Why is Sam cooking this?"

Gideon looked at me as if I was crazy.

"You just said they're our favorite... why wouldn't she, would be a better question."

"You weren't there this morning, but there was something fishy going on. Sully wouldn't look me in the eye and Sam was being cagey... They're up to something, I'm telling you."

Gideon gestured to the shopping cart laden with food. "Well, if they're going to feed me like this, then I'm a hundred percent behind them."

He took the list out of my hands and moved on, whistling happily as he pulled items off the shelf, but I couldn't shake the hollow feeling in my stomach. I hated surprises, and I knew they were going to spring one on us tonight. The food was clearly being used to butter us up.

I looked down at Bandit, who sat, head tilted up at me in question.

"I've got a bad feeling about this, Boy. I really have."

Feeling my anxiety, he whined at me.

5
<hr>

CHASE

I stared at the spread before me.

Our usual — simple — dining table was covered with a decorative tablecloth that had delicately embroidered flowers on the corners. I'm not sure why, but the sight of them had me gaping. I didn't know things like this existed. Why would anyone think covering a table with a pretty cloth would be a good idea — it was only going to get splattered with food, especially if I got anywhere near it?

The soft light from candles set around the table cast a dreamy glow about the place. *Candles and table cloths? Were we trying to burn the place down?* I took a seat at the table, staring miserably at Sam and Sully in the kitchen as they finished preparing our meal. Bandit sat as he always did, by my feet, as Gideon strolled in pushing Zeb in his wheelchair.

"Wow, what's the occasion?" Gideon said.

I could have kicked him, tried in fact, but couldn't reach him, my legs having become tangled with that stupid tablecloth.

"All in good time," Sully said.

I knew it! They were up to something! But now I had proof, I didn't feel the least bit vindicated. There was just a hollow ache in the pit of my stomach. I glanced at Zeb to see if I could gather any hints from him, but he looked as clueless as I felt.

"What's this all about?" he asked, however, Sully and Sam continued as if neither of them heard him.

"Dinner's ready!" Sam called out suddenly.

She and Sully carried over plates of food for us, but I saw, with some confusion, that each plate contained a different meal. Zeb was served a steak, mashed potatoes, and broccoli. Gideon was given Shrimp Alfredo, a pasta dish. For me, Sam set down a plate of mac and cheese with bacon bits (made from real bacon, not that soy trash you get in a tub) and a burger oozing with cheese. As I'd guessed earlier, Bandit got his marrow bones, which he was already happily chomping away on. Sully's scallops were in another pasta dish, while Sam had made herself a chicken stir fry. Through my misery, even I could see that the two had put an enormous amount of effort into the meal.

It made me sick to my stomach.

They sat down, Sam staring at us expectantly. Sully, I don't know. He looked kinda nervous. He poured himself a glass of water, but some of it splashed out of the glass soiling the table-cloth. *Good! Stupid tablecloth.*

"Well, I know you're all wondering what's going on," she began. "We thought long and hard about what we're going to say and..."

But I couldn't wait to hear any more. Shoving my chair back so that it scraped across the floor, I shot to my feet.

"What is it? What is going on?! Can you stop drawing this out and just spit it out?!"

Four human faces and one canine one all turned to me in shock.

"Stop buttering us up with the food. If you've got something bad to say, just say it!"

My heart was racing and I could hear thumping in my head. It was like someone was pounding on it with a hammer. It was a miracle really that it didn't explode. As my words sank in, the shock suddenly disappeared from Sully's face and his expression turned contrite.

"Oh hell, Chase, I'm sorry. It never crossed my mind you'd be thinking this was something bad."

And now Sam looked apologetic.

"Hon, this isn't bad news. It's good news."

"It is?" I managed to get out.

Sam smiled over at Sully and reached for his hand. "Yes. Sully and I have decided... we're getting married."

Zeb and Gideon must have cheered or something, but I wasn't really sure as the blood was still pounding in my head. I was waiting for the other shoe to drop.

"Wait... that's it?"

Sam shot me a reproachful look. "Well gee Chase, I'd have thought you could show a little more enthusiasm..."

I turned to Sully to get confirmation. "Seriously, that's all you wanted to say?"

Even he seemed put out by my response. "Well, it's a pretty big deal to us."

"I thought you two were going to take off on us or something."

Sully's mouth fell open. "Why on Earth would you think..."

I gestured at the table. "Well, you made all our favorite food. Who does that unless it's an apology or a bribe?"

He trailed off suddenly, understanding shining in his eyes.

"Chase, I told you. We're family. Nothing will ever change that."

I felt the tears pricking at the corners of my eyes. Despite all the time we had been together, a part of me still believed that it was fleeting. That it would go away in a moment and my life would revert back to awful. I guess it would be awhile before I'd feel totally at ease.

Suddenly, the shock wore off and my eyes went wide.

"Wait. So, we're having a wedding?"

Sam nodded, smiling as Sully took her in his arms.

I looked down at Bandit, grabbing his head in my hands. "We're having a wedding Boy!"

He barked and danced around me, picking up on my delight. "There's going to be a white dress and flowers and cake! Oh man, there's going to be so much food! When is it?"

Sully stared across the table at us.

"We're thinking the end of summer. I have a few things I need to sort out before we can get married. That should give me enough time to do them."

Zeb spoke up now, hearing something in his voice. "What things?"

Sully looked at Sam, waiting until she nodded in encouragement before continuing.

"I need to go back to Connecticut. See Florence and Mark. Sort out paperwork..."

And make peace with the dead.

Although Sully didn't say those words, his intention was clear. But me, well now that I knew it wasn't anything to worry about, all I could feel was excitement.

"WE'RE GOING ON A ROAD TRIP!"

Sam smiled at me. "Yes, this way, we'll get it over with before school starts."

And just like that, they managed to put a pin in the bubble of my excitement.

Thanks a lot, guys.

6
____

CHASE

We set off against the rising sun.

I'm not sure what it was about early mornings, but Sully seemed to think it fitting. He said it was a psychological thing: new morning, new beginnings. There was only the faintest hint of sadness when he'd said it, but I knew better than to make a thing of it.

Since our family had grown in the last six months from three to six, transport had become a bit of a problem for us — it wasn't like we could just hitch a ride in the back of Sam's truck (though Gid thought that sounded like fun, and so did Bandit). One of the first things Sully did after Sam moved in was to buy a minivan. No, it wasn't glamorous, but it sure was comfortable. If I'd had one of these when I was on the streets, you would not have heard me complaining.

The greens of Montpelier soon morphed into the grays of the highway as we shot towards Connecticut. I was so excited at the prospect of a road trip that I had hardly slept last night, so I was paying for that this morning. We'd barely been on the road an hour when the rocking motion lulled me to sleep.

When I woke up later, it was to find us passing through New Hampshire. Having read about the place before, I decided some showing off was in order (I had a vain hope that if Sam could see how much knowledge I had up in my head already, she'd drop this whole going-to-school thing).

"Hey, did you guys know that the very first free library was funded right here, in New Hampshire? In a place called Peterborough in 1833. And, the first potato planted in America was also planted in this state."

Sully nodded absently while Sam actually listened to me. "I didn't know either of those things," she said, impressed. Buoyed by this, I continued.

"They also don't have to wear seat belts here, so we could legally remove ours and it wouldn't be a problem, just while we're in this state..."

"Absolutely not," Sam replied quickly. "Law or not, some things are better left to common sense, Chase."

"I was just saying we could, not that we should." But she didn't seem the least bit amused by this. I looked at Gideon hoping for some backup but he had earbuds in and was listening to a loud, emo track by the sounds of it, and Zeb was dozing in his chair, out for the count.

Of course, Bandit was captivated by my random facts. He pressed a paw onto my foot to let me know he wanted me to continue. He loved trivia almost as much as I did. "Let me think, what else do I know about New Hampshire... It holds the first presidential primary election as part of the process to choose a new president every four years."

"Who is a president?"

"Not a, the president. He or she, though it's always been a he so far, is the most powerful person in America. He lives in a famous building called The White House and gets to make laws and stuff."

I could have been a little more eloquent with my explanation, but it probably wouldn't have mattered, Bandit couldn't seem to wrap his head around the fact.

"He controls everything?"

"Yeah."

"Like how much food we eat? And when we eat it?"

"Well, no."

"Does he say when you have to sleep?"

"No, he doesn't do that either."

"What about playtime? Does he say how much you get to play?"

"Er... no."

"Then he isn't in charge. Sully is."

I had to hand it to him. You couldn't fault his logic.

We drove through a drive-in burger joint for lunch. Although there was a banner advertising it as the "Best Burger In Town", it wasn't a patch on the ones Gideon makes so either someone was lying or they didn't have very high standards in this place.

We drove for a few more hours. Zeb continued to snooze while Gideon went through the entire music collection on his phone. Bandit and I entertained ourselves playing I Spy, which he proved to be pretty ingenious at, noticing things the average person wouldn't. When we'd finally exhausted all the possibilities, I pointed at his iPad.

"Wanna watch something?"

"Stranger Things! Oh boy, oh boy, oh boy!"

"We just finished it the other day? Don't you want to try something else?"

"Please, Chase. Stranger Things!"

"OK, OK, but one day you'll have to tell me why you like it so much. I mean, it's a great show and all, but what exactly's your deal with it?"

"Eleven and I are peas in a pod."

I heard the words as his Speak, Spell and Read app voice spoke them, but I wasn't quite sure what he meant. He must have sensed my confusion as he went on to explain.

"I was made in a lab. Bad men wanted me to do things. Then I ran away. Mike saved Eleven, you saved me. And now we are a family."

I felt my heart melt. He leaned into me and I wrapped my arms around him, resting my chin on his head. "Yeah, we are."

Usually, this would be all the comfort he needed, but today, Bandit had something else on his mind. His little body was still tensed. He shifted his weight on his paws, battling with whatever was going on inside him.

"What is it, boy?"

"I do not want to go back. I do not like the cage."

He turned his head to stare at me with those brilliant green eyes of his. I could almost feel the intensity of his words in them.

"We stay together, Chase. We always stay together."

A lump formed in my throat and I found myself unable to answer him with words right away, so I just nodded as I hugged him harder. We'd been separated once before, and that almost killed us both. I was determined that no one would ever get between us again.

"I promise, boy. You'll never spend another day in a cage again."

I had no idea just how badly I would be breaking my promise.

THE SCIENTIST

The Scientist neared his target with the ease of one who was practiced in such maneuvers, though this couldn't be further from the truth.

Like the dog, he had spent most of his life in a lab, but unlike the dog, he had been on the other side of the glass. Where the dog had been the specimen, The Scientist would have been the one to study him had he been privy to Forbes' experiments at the time. Thinking this, a surge of red-hot rage coursed through him.

Once again, he lamented his partner's selfish quest. Science should be available to all, not only the select few.

The front door was in his sights. He crossed the few remaining yards and let himself in with the key he had swiped from the dumb mechanic. Why anyone would trust him with their keys was beyond him. He had kept them in a cabinet with a coded label that even a child could have deciphered.

There was no concern that he would be seen — the family were gone for a few days, on a trip back East. The Scientist knew all about it, actually... people around here really loved to talk. Sullivan was getting remarried and wanted to go to his previous home to bury his past. Of course, no one else knew what had gone on there, how Forbes' men had almost burned the clinic down. They didn't know about the dog or the science he carried within. No, despite all the talking, they knew only the surface story.

Which suited him just fine.

He entered the ranch, closing the door behind him. It looked much as expected. A mediocre home for a mediocre family. He felt a burst of anger that these people were the only thing stopping him from his scientific breakthrough. He missed his work, wanted nothing more than to get back to his lab where he could immerse himself in his experiment, but... his pet project was not finished yet. There was one last thing he needed, and the key lay within the dog. Having seen what was left of Forbes' personal army, however, The Scientist knew he had to be patient, but what he lacked in physicality, he more than made up for in intellect.

When he was a child, he was an avid chess player. It was one of the few things that had brought joy to his life. He was made the captain of the chess team within a month of joining it, angering the other members and their parents, but despite their vocal complaints there was something about his brain, about the way it was always thinking several steps ahead, that meant he was unbeatable at the game. His opponents learned to fear him as would this family, though by the time they would learn of his plan, it would be far too late for any of them.

He was in the girl's room now. Her disgusting clothes were everywhere. Empty food and drink cartons littered the table and floor. It was as if a pig lived here. Though The Scientist wasn't particularly clean himself, even he was taken aback by the mess. Beside the bed, there was a basket for the dog. His hairs covered the cushion, and there were dog toys lying beside it. The Scientist stared at a battered soft toy of a rabbit with half its ear hanging loose. These people were ridiculous to treat him like a child.

He climbed onto the girl's bed and found a perfect place on

the book shelves to hide his camera. He angled it away from the bed — he wasn't a creep, after all; he had no interest or intention on spying on the girl that way — no; he was only interested in the dog. The camera was a slight thing, so small you really had to be searching for it to find it and looking at the state of the room, the girl would not notice it even if it were staring her right in the face.

Satisfied with the placement, he moved into the other rooms, hiding cameras in discreet places until the ranch was full of them. When that was done, he took out a spray bottle filled with a solution that he had created to mask his own scent. Given that dogs have such an acute sense of smell, it wouldn't do for Alpha to learn of his presence before he wanted him to. The Scientist went through the house, spraying every room until the solution was used up.

Satisfied with his mission, he smiled to himself.

The second move was completed.

Check.

8

SULLY

The drive East went by all too soon.

Sure, I had joked with the kids on the journey here, but my heart wasn't in it, my mind on other things. Well, one in particular. My deceased wife, Emma.

Just before Chase had appeared on my doorstep, Bandit near death on that shopping cart, his blood all over her, I had felt as if my world had ended. It was a slog just to get through the day, and let's face it, I hadn't been doing a great job of that as my buddy Mark — who I had flung a lasagna at — would testify. But opening that door to her had opened up a new life for me, one where I found myself in the unlikely position of being in love again.

I glanced at Sam. Her spiral red curls were being blown by the wind. This was not a woman who fussed over having immaculate hair. She wore it loose and natural, and it framed her beautiful face perfectly. An annoyingly upbeat song was playing on the radio and as usual, she sang along with it heartily. The woman was full of life. In the time I had been with her, I had never seen her broken or down. Her sunny personality was what had attracted me to her. It had been the same with Emma until those dark days that had drained any life she'd had left.

I hadn't meant to start a relationship with Sam — as far as I was concerned I wasn't in that place at all, hell, I couldn't even sleep in bed on my own until I tired my body out with my late night runs — but we had hit it off from the moment we met. We just... fit. And the kids loved her, even Zeb. It wasn't easy to leave Emma behind, but I knew it was time. Life had moved on, and she would want me to be happy, but before I could make the final step, there was something I needed to do.

So here we were.

As we turned a corner into my old neighborhood of Ellington, familiar sights came into view. I saw the giant Oak that was so strictly protected from harm that Old Mr. Felner's house had had to be built around it. The car passed by a playground where a group of young preschoolers were up to mischief as their parents watched on, chatting over cups of coffee. A slight pressure built up in my chest as a memory of Emma and me flashed up in my mind.

We used to sit on the swings, chatting about how many kids we were going to have. The number changed on a weekly basis, and the only thing we ever agreed on was that we wanted more than two. I mentally shoved the image away as I always did when Emma's face flashed up in my mind, unable to handle the conflicting emotions. Mentally, I knew I was ready for this next step, though I guess my heart was still confused, having loved only one woman for all those years to suddenly have it replaced with another.

We rounded another corner and suddenly I saw it. The site where my clinic stood before Forbes' mercenaries had set fire to it.

I was relieved to see that much of the ground floor — which still housed a veterinary clinic — remained. Upstairs, however, that was a different matter. My eyes grew wide as I took in how much it had changed. When I lived there, when I had called it home, upstairs was a simple apartment of four rooms, but it had now expanded across one side of the building and the exterior was painted a pale green. No hint of damage from the blaze remained. The entire place had been redecorated. It looked... nice, but it wasn't the home I remembered.

As I slowed the car, the noise died down as the others realized we had arrived at our destination. Seeing the changes, Chase looked as astonished as I. "Wow. They fixed it up a bunch, huh?"

"Well, last time you saw it, it was burning to the ground," I said, wryly, though my heart had started pounding inside my chest. I hoped Sam couldn't hear it. She was staring at the clinic, assessing it with her cool, calm eyes. She didn't say anything but turned to give me an encouraging smile.

"Looks nice. They did a good job," Zeb said. "Nice shingles."

I knew Zeb wasn't interested in buildings, shingles or otherwise, so this last was said for my benefit. The old man was trying to help the turmoil he knew I was going through. I killed the engine and in the silence that suddenly surrounded us, we piled out of the car when a woman in her sixties came hurrying out of the building. As usual, she wore one of the floral dresses that apparently formed the sole contents of her wardrobe.

"Sully?! Oh My God, it's really you?!"

Hearing that familiar voice and all she had meant to Emma and I, I suddenly found myself bounding the few yards to her. Grabbing her in a bear hug, I lifted her clear off her feet. She squealed in delight, though I noticed she seemed much frailer now. Had she always been this thin? I couldn't remember.

Moments later, we followed Florence inside.

9

SULLY

Inside, the clinic looked much the same as it always had.

The same chairs sat in the waiting area, Florence stood behind the same counter where she greeted all new patients and filed their details into the computer. Fact was, there was only one discernible difference to my eyes, and I moved towards the giant pinboard now.

Where once the photographs and postcards littering the board were addressed to me, these now thanked Matt and Izzy, the two vets who had taken over from me. Judging by how many there were, they were doing a better job than I had ever done too. There was a lump in my throat. Since the night when I was forced to flee my own clinic, I hadn't had the luxury of giving this place and my work much thought. Now I found myself missing that simple life and the joy of saving a family's beloved pet.

As if she could sense what I was feeling, Florence's voice came from behind my shoulders. "They're great, but they are not you."

I turned to find her behind me. Tears misted up in her eyes that she didn't bother to hide. "I'm so happy to see you again." She turned to the others, who had followed her into the room.

"And it's wonderful to finally meet all of you. I've heard so much about you."

Chase gave her a shy smile as Sam went to introduce herself. "Hi Florence, I'm Sam."

Unwittingly, I held my breath. In the absence of our own family, Florence had been like a mom to Emma and me, so I found myself nervous of what she would think of Sam. Would she think I was betraying Emma's memory, that I was replacing her too soon? But I shouldn't have worried. Florence gave her a warm smile and cupped her face in her hands.

"So you're the one who has stolen my Sully's heart. I can certainly see why."

Sam smiled and some tension left her shoulders. I hadn't noticed until now, but she must have been feeling some pressure herself. After Forbes' men had attacked the clinic, I had fabricated a story about Chase getting into trouble with a gang while she was living on the streets. They attacked Bandit and when Chase came to me for help, she unwittingly led them to us. When I refused to pay them off, they attacked us and set fire to the clinic as a lesson. I'd explained to Florence that I was going to help Chase and wouldn't be back for a while and that a change of scenery would do me good. She'd bought that part of the story more, but she'd never asked any questions of me. That was the thing about Florence. Even if she knew you weren't telling her the truth, she respected your wishes.

Almost unconsciously, I moved outside the waiting room, to the bottom of the stairs that lead to the private quarters above. The chatter behind me faded as I took in the walls — no longer that sunshine yellow Em had painted them, now replaced with a pale blue. Through the pounding that sounded in my heart, I vaguely heard Florence invite the others to the kitchen for coffee. I knew her well enough to know she wasn't just being a good host

— she was giving me time. Before she joined them, however, she came up to me.

"Matt and Izzy knew you'd want to see your old home, so they told me to tell you it's fine. Go ahead." She shot me a supportive smile before disappearing to the kitchen.

I took the stairs slowly, one at a time.

When I reached the top, what I saw before me was nothing like the home I remembered. Instead of the small kitchen/lounge I expected to see, I found myself in a large living area. Couches lined a whole wall in front of a flat-screen TV. There was a games console, a Playstation. Its controllers sat neatly beside a tower of video games. It seemed that outside of saving animals, the vets here liked to save the world too, judging by the titles of the games. I recognized a few of the names, having heard Chase and Gideon talk about them (they'd been bugging me about getting a console for a while now but I had resisted — call me old-fashioned but I'd had enough of Chase shooting guns, real or otherwise).

Where the kitchen had been, a long dining table now stood. Exotic flowers grew in pots along the window ledge, giving the air a spicy aroma. Several doors lead from the living room, through one, I could see the new, much-expanded kitchen. I wasn't much of a cook — that had been Emma's wheelhouse — so our quaint setup had suited me fine, but this new number came with marble islands and chrome fittings that even I could appreciate. I stopped myself from going inside, however, feeling drawn to the one room that had been our haven.

I stepped into the main bedroom now. A king size bed stood in place of where ours had been, but other than that, the room was unrecognizable. There were plush new carpets and furnishings, even the cream curtains we had made from fabric we had picked up at the local flea market had been replaced with something much more upscale.

With a fresh coat of paint and a drape of designer fabrics, our life had been completely erased.

It was painful and yet a relief at the same time. I couldn't see us in here anymore. This wasn't my home.

And with that realization, there came a sudden lifting of my heart.

10
_____

SULLY

I rejoined the others to find them sitting around the kitchen table in the clinic below, drinking cups of coffee and nibbling at what looked to be a delicious homemade carrot cake. I was touched by how much effort Florence had made ahead of our return and mentally affirmed to eat a slice despite how little appetite I had.

Florence stood up the second she saw me, inclining her head to the office next door. I shot Sam a smile, letting her know everything was fine, and followed her to the other room. She greeted me with a pile of correspondence.

"These came for you after you left. I tossed out the obvious trash, leaflets and such, but these looked personal so I left them here for you."

"Thanks." I took the pile from her, quickly sorting through the envelopes. Most were letters from medical suppliers or final bills from the electric company. Nothing of any interest. I contemplated just throwing the whole pile into the bin when one envelope caught my eye.

It was plain but made from a good quality paper. And unlike

the others, my details were handwritten in a neat, flowing script. I frowned, trying to place the familiar handwriting, but it escaped me so I tore the envelope open. Inside, there was a simple note made of the same stock and weight of the envelope. Only three words were written on it in that same familiar script.

"Always and forever."

Those were the three words that had been inscribed on our wedding rings. And suddenly, I recognized the writing.

It was Emma's.

11

SULLY

I looked up at Florence.

"What is this? Why is this here?" I demanded.

Startled, she leaned across so she could see the note. The color drained from her face as her eyes became muddled. "I'm sorry, I should have checked first."

"Where did this come from?"

She twisted her hands in apology. "I don't know. I thought it came in the mail with the rest of the letters..."

"Well, that's not possible, is it? That's Emma's writing, so you must've gotten this mixed in with the mail." I couldn't keep the anger from my voice. Those written words had hit like a truck, making me feel suddenly guilty over what I was here to do — and that was the last thing I needed. I knew my anger was irrational. It was obviously a simple mistake, but I was unable to rein my feelings in. Florence took the note from my hands.

"Yes, I know. There isn't a stamp on it, so I must have picked this up elsewhere. Let me get rid of it for you... unless you want to keep it?"

Her question hung in the air.

Every muscle in my body was tense. It wasn't that long ago when I couldn't throw a thing of Emma's away, but then that choice was taken from me when her things went up in a cloud of smoke. Now here was something tangible, a physical link to our past. I could feel my hands moving towards the note of their own accord.

"No. I don't want it."

Even as the words came out, I felt sick to my stomach. A part of me wanted to scream at her, that, of course, I wanted to keep it, but it took every ounce of my willpower to let it go.

Maybe this was a test. If so, I was determined to beat it. I pictured Sam's smiling face and forced myself to look away from the note.

"Get rid of it."

She nodded and hurried out of the room with the note.

And I let out the breath I had been holding.

12

CHASE

Something was happening.

One minute we were laughing, drinking coffee, and hearing stories of Sully's animal patient escapades, and the next Sully had returned to the room looking pale and subdued.

Sam had gone to him immediately, but Sully just shook his head. Whatever it was, he wasn't ready to talk about it in front of all of us. Recognizing this, Sam just kissed him on the cheek and gave him a supportive smile. But me, I wasn't respectful like that. I went over to him, Bandit by my side. He must have picked up on my concern as he whined softly at me.

"What happened?" I asked Sully.

He looked at me, weighing up whether he would tell me the truth, but he must have realized it wouldn't do any good to keep things from me, I'd get it out of him, eventually. He filled me in briefly. His voice was flat as if he didn't feel any emotion about the subject, which I knew was just his way of deflecting pain.

"Well, that sucks," was my eloquent answer. "Good job on letting it go though. Must have been tough."

He didn't answer. Finally, Florence came back into the room.

She came up to Sully hesitantly, afraid to make any further mistakes. "We were hoping to surprise you, but under the circumstances, I think it's probably best if I run our plans by you."

"What plans?" Sully said, unable to hide the concern in his eyes.

"Mark is coming by tonight, to surprise you. We're going to throw a barbecue. Matt and Izzy will be joining us too after the clinic closes, but if you want us to cancel, we still have time."

Sully opened his mouth to answer, but then he hesitated. His eyes flicked over to Sam, watching him quietly from a few feet away. She didn't move or say anything, but her presence alone seemed to be enough for Sully to make up his mind. "No, that's fine. Keep it. It'll be fun."

Forgetting himself, Bandit barked once. He *adored* a good barbecue. We all knew he was agreeing with Sully, but Florence didn't. She just thought he was being cute. She bent down to stroke him. "Who's a good doggy? Would you like a treat? I think I've got some in my jar over there?"

It took a moment before I remembered that Florence had no idea how intelligent Bandit was, hence the way she was speaking to him. I could see that the last thing on Bandit's mind was food, but we needed to keep up his cover of "normal dog" so I nodded, silently telling him he should go with her. Faking enthusiasm, his tail swished back and forth as he allowed Florence to lead him away. Sam slipped her hand in Sully's. "So Mark's coming over? That's good, I've been wanting to meet this old friend of yours. The stories he must have..."

"Don't believe everything he says. Guy has a way of exaggerating," Sully said, looking alarmed now that he realized the two would be meeting.

Catching his expression, Sam became amused. "Got some stories you don't want me to know about, huh?"

"There's no need for you to know *everything,* is there? Some mystery is sexy," Sully said, a little desperately, I thought.

Sam laughed. "You're cute when you panic."

And that was my cue to leave. Sully being upset I could handle, but flirting with Sam?

That was just gross.

13

CHASE

The party was happening in the backyard.

A bank of outdoor kennels stood on one side, but they were empty right now, their inhabitants having been moved inside so that the noise and smoke from the grill wouldn't bother them. We sat on a pretty terrace where roses climbed across a trellis and the outdoor grill glowed a cheery orange as the coals heated up.

Sully's friend Mark had arrived with a giant bowl of potato salad and some beef skewer things that had Bandit salivating at the smell. Before Sully could get excited at the prospect of Mark learning how to cook, however, Mark revealed that he had picked up both at his favorite deli. Sully made a joke about that being a first since he usually just got whichever poor soul he was dating to do all the cooking.

I had to admit, Mark wasn't what I was expecting at all. He had slicked back hair that shone from the amount of product he had up in there, thick black-rimmed glasses that I wasn't convinced weren't just for show and was the kind of guy who wore shoes with no socks. He was a hipster and unapologetic about it.

He seemed like a nice enough guy, but I find it hard to trust any man whose nails were so neat. After some badgering, he finally admitted that he had regular manicures. He literally had nothing in common with Sully, but you wouldn't know it to see the two of them laughing and joking around. Sam must have thought their relationship curious too as she asked how they had met. Turns out, it wasn't long after the clinic had opened.

Mark had been dating this girl who had a cat with a sensitive tummy. Unfortunately, he didn't know about that, or how to treat cats in general and had been feeding her milk and all sorts of human food — both of which are no no's since cats are lactose intolerant and human food contains too much salt, something which caused kidney problems in cats. After weeks of toiletry issues, the cat finally decided she'd had enough as she left several protest poops around their bed. When Mark's girlfriend found out he was the cause of her cat's distress, she dumped him, but he became friends with Sully in the process.

He and Sully were knocking back beers now, talking about things I didn't understand, like stock markets and bonds. The current vets, Matt and Izzy, had also joined us. Matt smiled a lot and had a booming and infectious laugh while his girlfriend Izzy was a dainty thing with a wicked sense of humor. They seemed like really good people and I was glad they were the ones running this place now.

Gideon, Zeb, Sam and I sat around the garden table as Florence brought out an old file of hers. "I thought you might like to see some pictures," she began as she showed us a leaflet of Sully opening the clinic to a crowd of well-wishers. "This was our first day here. It was a very proud moment for us," she said.

"You've worked with him since the clinic started?" Zeb asked, surprised.

"Oh yes. I had known the two of them a while. Well, I actually knew Emma first. She was my friend Irene's granddaughter. When they decided to open the clinic, I had recently lost my job to a younger, prettier model. When Irene mentioned this to Emma, she forced Sully to hire me. I suspect I wouldn't have been his first choice for the job, but she just wouldn't hear of it. She was quite the campaigner for justice. Couldn't bear any wrongdoing."

Zeb fell quiet. I suddenly realized how much of Sully's life he had missed since the two had fallen out. He'd never met Emma, so it must be hard to be faced with her memory like this. I remembered how, when we'd first turned up at the ranch, Zeb had blown up at Sully, letting him know that he didn't care to meet her or go to their wedding, as he was angry at Sully for tossing away his promising career as a surgeon. I think he somehow thought she influenced him on this, though anyone who knew him now could see that Sully loved saving animals. I couldn't imagine him doing anything else.

Sam stared at the leaflet. I realized then that this might be the first time she'd ever seen Emma's face. Her expression was stoic so I couldn't tell what she was thinking. She just stared at Emma, taking it all in.

Florence looked up at Sam suddenly, smiling. "I'm so happy Sully found you, my dear. It wasn't that long ago when I thought he would never get over losing her. I'm just so relieved he has found happiness again."

Sam gave her a warm smile. "I'm sure he would have moved on eventually, even if he hadn't met me."

"I don't know about that. Sully couldn't even get rid of Emma's things. Why, it was just before he left when Mark and I tried to help him, that their big fight happened. I felt it was unhealthy to be surrounded by memories of his dead wife like that, so we tried to force his hand. It wasn't just her pictures, you understand? Sully had kept her clothes, toiletries, everything... for a year. We'd tried unsuccessfully many times to help him rid them to no avail when we finally decided enough was enough. But when Sully saw Mark packing up Emma's things, he attacked him and wouldn't speak to him for a long time."

Something about her comment caused Sam's smile to waiver. I saw it, but, caught up in memory lane, the older woman didn't pick up on Sam's emotions. "Wasn't that only six months ago? "

"Why, yes. I guess it was."

"I didn't know that," Sam replied quietly. Her eyes turned thoughtful, but she didn't say anything else. Zeb, too, looked as if he were struggling with his own feelings. He'd lost his wife himself so he, better than anyone, should know what Sully had gone through. I thought about how much time the two had wasted through being mad at each other. If they had both gotten over their issues, they could have supported each other through those painful times. Hindsight, right?

Florence rifled through the file until she came up with another image. It was a newspaper article about a dog Sully had saved from death.

"And this is Sully with the first puppy he delivered. The mom was found dumped in an alley. She had been someone's pet until they decided they didn't want the puppies — probably didn't want the added cost of feeding them — so they just left her to fend for herself instead. Poor thing was starving when a local found her and brought her to us."

I felt anger at the people who could do this to her. "When there are so many shelters and charities that will take your dog for free, why do people still do this?"

Florence sighed. "Because many people are cowards, Chase and they don't want to face up to their responsibilities."

Bandit barked *yes,* but I gave him a sharp look, silently warning him not to do anything else that might reveal his specialness. Despite how Sully felt about Florence and Mark, despite how he trusted them, it was safer all around if we didn't tell them about his abilities. Catching my warning, Bandit lowered onto all fours before settling back down. To anyone else, it might have looked as if he were simply stretching, but I knew he was being submissive and saying sorry.

"Well, people who do that shouldn't be allowed pets in the future," Gideon said. His face was firm, and he had one hand on Bandit. It made me think how much he had changed during our time together. When he had first met Bandit, Gideon hadn't seemed all that interested in him. Then again, he hadn't seemed interested in anything other than Zeb. Florence pulled out some other newspaper clippings now but her face fell and she hesitated, not sure whether she should show them to us.

"What is it?" Zeb asked.

Finally, Florence took out the clipping. I looked down to see images of the nearly destroyed clinic on that fateful night when I had turned up unannounced on Sully's doorstep. The fire had fizzled out, but smoke still curled in the air. The picture must have been taken just hours after the blaze. Gideon had heard the story before, but faced with the pictures, he looked shocked.

"It probably looks worse than it is. I mean, the building didn't fall down and what could be fixed has been rebuilt." I don't know why I said that or why I was trying to make him feel better. It wasn't like he had any experience of it. He wasn't there that night.

"I didn't know it was that bad. I know you told me, but, I didn't really know..." He trailed off. "It must have been terrifying."

"Oh you know, I've been through worse," I shrugged, trying to play it off.

"I sincerely hope not!' Florence said, cutting into our conversation.

Of course, I wasn't going to explain what I had meant by that, but my own words got me thinking of a time I chose to forget. My thoughts went to a place they seldom visited, and a familiar face I tried not to think about flashed up in my mind. I shook my head, trying to erase the picture, but it was no use. Once it was there, it refused to go away.

Mom.

14

CHASE

T hings had gotten heavy there for a moment.

As usual, whenever a situation became uncomfortable, I would get out of there, so I excused myself and made a break for the restroom. I splashed cold water on my face, hoping to feel refreshed, but I couldn't shake the black cloud that now hovered over me.

It was weird. When I usually thought about my mom, I felt only anger. I was mad at how she'd let Tubs into our lives, how she didn't protect me from him, and how she had let that jerk dictate how we lived. Although our lives were far from perfect before him, we had always had each other, but, as soon as she had let him in, it was like this giant Tub-sized wedge had pried us apart.

And suddenly, everything had changed.

I'd thought about leaving for at least a year, but I didn't have any money and there was no one I could run to. And while the beatings at home were bad, he'd mostly left me with only bruises or some missing hair — I'd suffered no broken bones, so I figured I could tolerate it. But then my appearance started to change, and

I found myself growing in places that had been previously flat. When Tubs started noticing me in a different way, I knew I had to get out of there. He loved to drink, and I knew I was one drunken session away from something that would scar me forever.

Maybe it was all the revisiting and talk of old days, but I found myself with the sudden urge to hear my mom's voice. Since I had left home, I hadn't spoken to her, not even once. Hadn't really wanted to either, so this took me by surprise. I wanted to know if she regretted not standing up for me. Was she missing me now I was gone? There was a time — a long time ago, yes, but it happened all the same — when she put ribbons in my hair and bought me ice-cream along the beach. Was there any part of that mom left?

I thought about the many beatings I had endured, all while I waited in vain for her to put a stop to it... and suddenly a new thought occurred. I wondered who he was using as a punching bag if I wasn't there to take the blows. The thought stunned me until I found myself frozen to the spot. I couldn't believe I hadn't thought of this before. What if Tubs was hurting her now he couldn't hurt me?

Part of me was thinking, good, let's see how she liked to be pummeled for no reason, but another part of me, the part that was kind and loved by my new family, felt pity.

Eight months on the street had taught me not to be a rash person, but I shoved away my doubts and found myself wandering the clinic until I reached Sully's old office. A buzz had begun to sound inside my head. I figured it was nerves or a giant alarm, screeching at me to stop what I was about to do, but I ignored it. Like I was experiencing an outer-body moment, I watched myself pick up the phone and dial home.

The call rang and rang and rang.

With every unanswered ring, a coldness grew inside of me. What if she wasn't living there anymore? Maybe she had changed her phone number or moved, in which case I would never be able to find her again. Then my thoughts took a dark turn. What if she wasn't answering because she wasn't *alive* anymore... I was turning numb at the possibility. I ran through the possible places I could check for information when the call was answered by a familiar male voice that instantly caused my body to be flooded with anger and fear.

"Hello?"

It was Tubs, but I could barely hear him over the noise. Trashy music played in the background, and I heard laughing. I recognized the song that was playing as one of Mom's favorites. A crazy thought entered my mind.

Were they having a party?

"Hello? Speak up! I can't hear you!" Tubs yelled into the phone. Unable to help myself, I flinched like I always did when he yelled. Even now, with the many months and miles between us, I hated that he could still have that effect on me.

And suddenly, above the merriment, I heard Mom's voice calling out to him.

"Is it Renny? Tell her she's late and we're still waiting on the pasta bowl!"

My hand tightened into a claw around the phone. I felt like I had been run over by a truck. Not only was she alive, she was *thriving* without me. She didn't care at all that I was gone.

Tears welling in my eyes, I slammed the phone down.

15

CHASE

I didn't know how long I had been standing there, but Gideon's voice shocked me from my dark place.

"What're you doing?"

I wiped the tears from my eyes and spun around to face him. He stood there, drinking a glass of lemonade with a paper umbrella in it. Seeing the ridiculous decoration, a bubble of hysterical laughter burst out of me. The ludicrousness of it, coupled with my experience of just moments ago, had me laughing in disbelief.

"OK," he answered, looking at me as if I needed help.

"There's an umbrella in your drink," I gasped, holding my sides.

"Yeah, it came with it," he replied, still not understanding why it was so funny, which of course, just made me laugh all the harder. He frowned at me and took another sip of his drink while he waited for me to regain my composure. "The others were wondering where you'd gotten to."

I took a deep breath. "I'll be there in a minute."

He continued looking at me, his brilliant eyes scrutinizing my strange behavior. He must have seen through my insane laughter as he suddenly asked, "Is everything OK?"

I bit my lip, wondering if I should tell him. We talked a lot, the two of us, and we were pretty close — at least, I thought we were — but I just wasn't comfortable talking about this. I didn't want him to think I was an idiot for calling her. When he'd learned of my past, he'd had a lot to say about what kind of people he thought they were. I knew his opinion on them, as he'd dubbed them trailer trash. I didn't want him to think less of me now so I figured it'd be best to just keep quiet about my call.

"I'm fine. Just hungry is all."

"Tell me something I don't know. Well, come on, the food's almost done. Those skewer things are amazing by the way, I've already had three. Bandit's been begging Sully, but he won't cave so you'll have to sneak him some." He waited for me to go. I moved past him and lead the way back outside.

"Mark must have stocks in hair gel, don't you think? And who doesn't wear socks in their shoes? Freaking hipsters," he lamented.

I burst out laughing again, but this time it was for real.
Trust Gideon.
He could always make me feel better.

16

SULLY

We chowed down the delicious food and were spread around the terrace now, chatting in groups.

I finished my beer as Mark came up to me brandishing another one that he shook in front of my face. Good with the few I'd already had, I declined.

"Come on, Sul, loosen up."

"I'm not the one who wears suits for a living OK. I'm plenty loose," I retorted. "Anyhow, I don't drink as much as I used to now. My tolerance seems to have lowered as a result."

Mark looked over at Sam, talking to Florence and Zeb. "I'm guessing that's a good woman's influence on you?"

I smiled. "She's the best."

"Very different from Emma, though. She's tougher, though she's no less feminine for it. "

I fake glared at him. "Will you stop checking out my bride-to-be? She's off-bounds."

He rolled his eyes at me. "As if I would go for your seconds. She's not my type, anyway."

"Yeah, nowhere near submissive enough for you," I said.

"There's nothing wrong with an easy life, friend. I get enough excitement with the job as it is, and that was without all your shenanigans."

We stopped ribbing each other, both of us staring at this group of people I called family. Chase laughed at something Gideon had said, while Bandit watched the two of them, his tail wagging. Sam nibbled on a piece of pie as she chatted with Florence, Zeb, and the vets. Mark shook his head, struggling to take it all in. "I can't believe how much your life has changed."

"You and me both. I wouldn't have it any other way now." Even as I said the words, I knew that I meant them. It was a cliche, but time had healed all wounds. Like she could sense what we were talking about, Sam looked over at me and smiled, lighting up the place. God, she was an amazing woman. That I had won this lottery not once, but twice — I knew I was luckier than I had reason to be.

"She'd be happy for you, you know. Emma," Mark said softly. "She wanted you to remarry again."

I looked away from Sam to stare at my friend, startled by this bit of news. "She did? How do you know that?"

"She told me. During one of my last visits with her, back at the hospital." His eyes turned serious as he recalled the moment. "She made me promise that when the time was right, she wanted me to give you her blessing."

Tears pricked at the corners of my eyelids. I felt a huge sense of relief at his words, but there was also confusion. "Why didn't she say any of this to me?"

"Are you serious? You were insane with grief, Sul, and mad at the world. You were in no condition to think about the future, much less the possibility of another woman. She knew that too, which is why she left it to me."

Overwhelmed with feeling, I snatched the bottle from his hand. "You're right, this is a celebration so I should have another."

He slapped me on the shoulder, grinning. "Knock yourself out. Not literally though, I don't want Sam coming after me with her gun."

I laughed, feeling like a weight had been lifted off my shoulders.

17

SULLY

Dawn broke, bringing along with it birdsong that lit up the morning.

We had camped out last night in my old apartment above the clinic. Matt and Izzy, the new vets — and a couple like Emma and I had been — were warm and welcoming hosts, graciously opening their home to us. Mark had said we could stay at his place, a penthouse apartment in the Chelsea district of New York, but we'd already traveled so much, the last thing any of us wanted was to feel the floor moving beneath our feet, even if it would have been the priciest floor the kids would ever have seen.

Despite this, I was surprised by their unwillingness to move until I found them on the Playstation, Chase and Gideon played on that thing well into the night.

Sam hasn't said much to me last night, just that she now knew why leaving here was an even bigger deal than she had imagined — she liked Florence and Mark well enough, but it was their loyalty to me that had brought tears to her eyes. After she had kissed me goodnight, she didn't say anything else. I knew she was giving me space, letting me process my own thoughts back under this roof where I had called home before we had met. I was grateful for her understanding.

I moved out of the bed carefully, not wanting to wake her. Her hair fell in wild abandon over her shoulders as she slept, and she was making that funny little sound she always did, the one that I now couldn't sleep without hearing. I squinted into the still dark room as I climbed over suitcases and shoes to find my workout clothes.

Tugging on a pair of jogging pants and a sweatshirt, I opened the door slowly and snuck outside, stepping over Gideon, sleeping on the floor by Chase. Seeing me, Bandit's ears pricked up as he chuffed in greeting and thumped his tail, but I put a finger to my mouth.

"Shush, don't wake them," I said to him. "Let them sleep." To my surprise, he nodded. I probably shouldn't have been shocked by this, but Bandit's intelligence still caught me off-guard at times. Patting him on the head, I made my way outside.

The air was crisp with the taste that always seemed to follow a recent sunrise. I jogged slowly, enjoying the simple sensation of tarmac beneath my feet. Though my gunshot wound meant I couldn't run like I used to, jogging still brought relief. This was still where I did my best thinking. Alone, out here in the streets, my thoughts could untangle themselves and any pressing concerns usually resolved themselves by the time I returned home.

I took in the familiar streets, drinking in the sight of them as I made my way to my destination. The neighborhood hadn't changed much: immaculate lawns and brightly painted houses with overflowing flower baskets hanging from front porches still greeted me from every angle. The place still looked as if it were straight out of a spread in Better Homes and Gardens. I'm not sure why I thought coming back things would be different. I had changed so much in the last year, I naturally assumed the same would be said of Ellington. Instead, I had to contend with seeing the ghost of Emma around every corner.

My thoughts drifted to Chase, who I noticed was also quiet last night. Several times I had tried to reach her, but whenever I caught her eye, she would give me a small smile and look away. It wasn't until then that I remembered she had her own memories of this place, and none of them good. I planned on talking to her after my run. Until then, she always had Bandit to confide in — many's the night I've walked past her room to hear the two of them conversing fiercely. A kid and their dog was a bond that could never be broken or replicated.

The hard ground changed to grass as I turned a corner into an area of brilliant green. I jogged past two six foot wrought-iron gates into the manicured lawns surrounding neat rows of headstones. Some were elaborate effigies of angels, while others were basic domes of stone. Emma and I had always found the statues too ostentatious and had promised each other that our own would be simple but solid, like our relationship.

When I had lived here, I came to this cemetery once a week, but it had now been half a year since my last visit. I knew it couldn't be helped, but I couldn't stop the sudden pain in my heart all the same.

Never forgotten, always and forever.

Those were the words I had decided for Emma's tombstone. A mix of my feelings and our vows. I took the paths automatically, not paying attention to them. It was as if my feet knew exactly how to get there, and my brain didn't have to do anything at all. I passed by a grove of trees shaped in an arc and steeled myself, knowing I was approaching her resting place. As I grew closer and finally caught sight of her tombstone, I blinked and slowed to a walk, uncertain if what I was seeing was real.

Instead of the neat patch of grass I expected to see, the dirt had *shifted* and clumps of grass lay on top of the grave. I barely processed the idea that it could not have been an Earthquake, not unless they were now a possibility in New England. So this meant only one thing.

Someone had vandalized Emma's grave.

18

SULLY

I was rooted to the spot, unable to take in the sight before me.

There were the remnants of a hole that went down a ways though thankfully not far enough for me to see down to her coffin.

Bile crept up in my throat, but I forced myself to keep it down. *What the hell was going on around here?*

I looked around, eyes scanning the scenery to see if I could spot the culprit of the grave desecrater lurking around, but at this time of the morning, outside of the birds, I was the only visitor.

I didn't know what to do.

Part of me wanted to throw that dirt back and cover up the hole so Emma was safely tucked away beneath... But another part of me, the angry, twisted part was picturing what I would do to the person if I ever discovered who the hateful jerk was. Flushed with rage, I allowed myself the luxury of pummeling him in my head.

I was still picturing myself smashing his head into the dirt when I caught sight of something on the ground. It was small, with a dull brown pattern on it. As I got closer, I realized it was a hair clip, the kind Emma wore every day to keep her hair out of her face. I remembered she called it a banana clip. It stood out in my mind as I had always considered it a ludicrous name, for a ridiculous-looking object. This clip looked exactly like the ones she wore. Bending down, I picked it up to examine it and saw that I was mistaken. That splash of dull color wasn't a brown pattern at all.

It was blood.

My eyes flew open, startled by my discovery. I had never been one to believe in coincidences, but the odds were stacking up. I contemplated calling Sam with my discovery. If there were a logical explanation, Sam would find it. She would be able to make sense of this. Retrieving my phone from my back pocket, I unlocked the home screen when a chime sounded. It was a text message, but it came from a number I never expected to see again. The message flashed up on my screen, bright as day.

"Help me."

It was from Emma's phone.

Blood rushed into my head. I felt hysteria building up inside of me and my breathing begin to constrict. Gasping for air, I clawed at my throat but couldn't get my anxiety to die down. As panic took over, the world spun.

I felt the ground rushing up to meet me until my face landed in the dirt and I was blessedly out for the count.

19
———

CHASE

I knew something was up the instant I woke.

Bandit was prodding my shoulder with his nose, trying to get me to wake. When I asked him what was wrong, he just said, "Sully," with his iPad and circled the floor in agitation. It only took a few minutes for me to realize he wasn't here. I woke Gideon, but we decided against worrying Zeb or Sam — last night had been tough on them, and I didn't get the feeling from Bandit that Sully was in danger. Still, Bandit said he'd been gone a while, and he wasn't particularly happy.

"Can you find him, boy?" Gideon asked.

"Woof." Bandit took off so fast, we had to run to keep up with him. We ran past Sully's old neighborhood. I couldn't help but remember how, on that night we had met Sully, we had run through these streets then, though those circumstances had been life and death. In the bright light of day, I could see it was a decent place. There wasn't a single lawn that wasn't cared for, or a car illegally parked. Not for the first time, I felt bad that I had made him leave his perfect life here.

After a while, I realized Bandit was leading us to the cemetery when I saw the sign looming overhead. I wondered if we shouldn't respect Sully's wish to be alone, but then again, he had been gone a while... I figured he'd just have to be mad at us. We rounded a bend when Bandit barked a warning before tearing off towards something in the distance. I squinted into the horizon before I realized what the slumped mound on the ground was.

"Sully!" I screamed.

We hurried to his side. My heart was racing as I fell to my knees. Bandit was darting around him, sniffing in agitation as Gideon felt for a pulse.

"Is he OK? What's wrong with him?" I cried.

"He has a pulse. It's strong." Gideon examined Sully, checking for obvious wounds. "I can't find anything immediately wrong with him." He was still looking for injuries when Sully groaned and slowly opened his eyes. He looked up at us, glazed and groggy.

"What's going on?"

"We just found you passed out on the ground. Are you OK? What happened?" I couldn't stop the shrillness in my voice, this being the last thing I expected to find. Sully blinked at us, taking in his surroundings. His eyes grew suddenly weary.

"I'm OK. Let's talk about it when we get back."

"What? No! Just tell me, right now!" I demanded.

A haunted expression came over his eyes. He hesitated, whatever it was, bothered him deeply, but he also knew neither Gideon nor I would be dropping this anytime soon. He reached into his pockets but couldn't find what it was he was looking for. Moving quickly onto his knees, he searched the ground around him.

"My phone... can you see my phone?" he asked, his voice unable to mask his panic at being unable to find it. Bandit barked, then came over, carrying the phone gingerly in his mouth. It had been lying a few feet away. Sully took it from him gratefully. "Thanks, boy. It's... the text is in there."

He didn't explain what he meant by that, but I figured it would make sense soon enough. Sully turned the phone over, but we all saw that several cracks now crisscrossed the screen. Concerned, he pressed the home button on his phone, but nothing happened. "Come on... come on..." Sully said, beginning to fall apart. "I need to show you what she said..."

He pressed the button, getting increasingly more desperate until he finally yelled at the thing. "Work Goddamnit!"

Gideon and I said nothing, but shared a look over the top of Sully's head. The guy was falling to pieces, and we had no idea why. Bandit whined unhappily as Sully suddenly took in his immediate surroundings. He was staring in disbelief at the grave. "But... I don't understand, it was disturbed..."

I followed his eye-line to study the grave. Some dirt looked like it was loose, like someone had been digging around but then had put the soil back in place but there wasn't enough to make me think anything in particular. Plus, Sully himself had been lying on it. I'm not saying he dug some of the grave up with his bare hands — that would be loopy — but a quick glance at his fingers and I saw that there was some dirt under his nails. I literally had no idea what was going on.

I looked to Gideon for help. He nodded briefly at me, then took Sully firmly by the arm. "Let's get you up. The others will be getting up soon. Why don't we go back and you can tell us what happened over breakfast?"

His voice was calm and reasonable, like finding Sully freaking out on his dead wife's grave was a regular part of our morning. Glazed, Sully nodded and allowed us to lead him away.

As we left the cemetery, I couldn't help tossing looks over my shoulder. By now, the sun was already shining brightly, casting long black shadows onto the ground. Though I couldn't see anything in those shadows, my senses were in overdrive. Despite all evidence to the contrary, it felt like we were being watched.

Chilled by the thought, I urged the others out of there.

20

CHASE

B y the time we got back to the clinic, everyone was up. Sully wouldn't talk about what happened at the cemetery, despite my hounding him with questions. All he would say was that I needed to wait until he could speak to Sam first. I knew it shouldn't have, but the fact he was shutting me out like this, that he was picking Sam over me, it really hurt. Although I was super concerned about him, it was possible that I may have sulked some on the way back.

Florence had already set the table for breakfast with a spread so lavish, it looked like it had come out of a movie. There were plates of Danish pastries (I only knew what they were as Sully had taught me about them a while back — said New Yorkers were particularly keen on them) and jelly doughnuts. There were also waffles and pancakes and a fruit bowl that was the one concession to health.

I noticed no one touched it. Wasn't that always the case?

We made small talk, even though our hearts weren't in it. We had to keep up the pretense or Florence might notice something was up. When I saw that she had made everything but the

Danishes and doughnuts from scratch, I asked why she didn't take shortcuts. Microwaves were invented for a reason after all, but she waved off the appliance like it was the devil and ranted about how bad they were for not just our health, but also the environment.

She was very proud of the fact that in sixty plus years she had cooked all her meals and would never touch that microwave trash. Sully tried to make a joke of it by saying look what he's had to put up with all these years, but it fell pretty flat. Luckily, busy with the food, Florence didn't notice.

Despite the effort she had put into the meal, the knot in my stomach wouldn't allow me to eat, which was totally unlike me. I picked at the food, feigning interest, impatiently waiting until Florence went downstairs to open the clinic. As soon as she was gone, Sully finally spoke.

"I know how this is going to sound so I need you all to promise that you won't say anything until I finish talking." He looked at me then, somewhat sternly. "Promise me, Chase."

My mouth fell open. "Why am I being singled out?"

Sam would have laughed but for the serious expression on his face. Suddenly concerned, she shot him a curious smile. "What's going on?" she asked quietly.

Zeb lowered the coffee he had been sipping and looked at us. "Speak up, son."

Sully clasped his hands together in front of him, taking a deep breath. "I went to the grave this morning, but it had been disturbed."

Gasps sounded around the room.

"I know how crazy this sounds. I searched the area but couldn't see anyone, but then I found this hair clip, it's exactly the same as the ones Emma used to wear. And it looks like there's blood on it."

He showed us a simple clip. While he was right — that dull red stain did look like dried blood — there wasn't anything else on that clip that would warrant special treatment. Sam must have thought the same as she spoke up.

"That doesn't really mean anything, Sul. Those clips are very common — heck, I've a few at home myself," she said, trying to placate him. "And the blood, well, first of all, we don't know that it is blood. That would need to be confirmed, and if it turned out that it was, it's still not enough to warrant an investigation unless a person has been reported as missing who wore clips like this."

Sully turned his attention to her. I could see he was struggling with his next words.

"That's not everything, Sam. After I found the clip, I was just about to call you when I received a text message... from Emma's phone."

At that, we all gasped. Gideon's eyes were as wide as mine were I'm sure, but somehow, Sam kept her cool. "Can I see the text?"

Sully paused then, looking trapped. "Well, that's the thing. My phone isn't working now. I think it broke when I fell on it."

She frowned, picking up on the one thing that concerned her the most. "You fell? Are you alright?"

Sully shrugged her question off, uncomfortable. "Yeah. It's nothing."

"That's not true though, is it?" Gideon said softly. "When we found him, he was lying on the ground... unconscious."

Sam's eyes flared open in alarm. "What happened?" she demanded. Zeb too couldn't hide his sudden agitation. "Do we need to get you to a doctor?"

"No, I don't need a doctor. I'm fine," Sully replied firmly. "I'd just had a shock is all... I had a panic attack and passed out."

Sam didn't speak for a moment, her mind ticking over everything she had been told. "You panicked because of the grave and the text message?"

"And the blood on the clip," Sully reminded her.

"You're sure that text was from her number? You couldn't be mistaken?" She spoke carefully, like she was treating him with kid gloves. Sully picked up on her tone and replied, his voice peeved.

"I know her number, Sam. She had the same number for ten years. It's not like I'm going to forget it."

Silence blanketed the room. No one wanted to doubt him, no matter how crazy he was sounding.

"I'm sure there's a reasonable explanation for this," came Sam's steady voice. Though she must be shaken, she kept whatever she was feeling out of her voice. It was one of the reasons she made an awesome Sheriff. Nothing seemed to faze her, ever. Not even the return of Sully's dead wife, apparently.

I knew Sully was going through hell. He spoke in clipped sentences and his eyes were glazed over in shock. This trip was meant to be for him to move on, yet how was he going to do that now Emma was back and hanging over his head. I really felt for him, for the two of them.

"We only had friends in this area, at least, I thought we did. It doesn't make sense for anyone to do this to me."

"Unless your trip home fell on someone's radar and they decided to screw with you. Do you have any enemies here? Anyone sick enough to do this?" Sam asked.

Sully shook his head. "I just saved animals, Sam. No one was interested in me until Bandit came along."

The sudden silence suffocated the room. I had been so focused on Sully that the possibility that this could be linked to Bandit hadn't even crossed my mind. I dropped my gaze to look at him now. He came to my side and pressed against me, worried.

"Not even Florence and Mark know about him?" Sam asked.

"Yeah, I didn't want to get them involved, so I left them out of it," Sully replied.

The implication of his answer filled me with terror. While I knew there could be a simple — if twisted — reason for this, we had been through enough that I didn't like loose endings. Especially when they involved someone who was dead and buried for over a year.

"Emma's phone… what did you do with it after she died?" Sam asked, mind already working through this like it was one of her cases.

"Well, that's the thing… After she died, I kept going through her phone just to read her messages. But one night, I'd had too much to drink and must have fallen asleep on the couch. When I woke up, the phone was crushed. I probably trod on it during my stupor. I threw it away months ago before Chase ever turned up at the clinic."

He paused then, for his next words to sink in.

"The phone doesn't exist."

21

SULLY

The second the words left my mouth, I knew there was a simple way to clear this up.

"Sam, let me use your phone."

She handed me her cell even as her eyes grew wide, knowing what I was about to do. I dialed the digits from memory, fully expecting there to be a logical explanation to all this... like I was having a breakdown. Something. I hit enter and waited, gripping the phone so hard, I thought it might shatter in my hand. Sam pinned her eyes on me, love and concern radiating from her. Chase and Gideon flanked my side while Zeb sat by Bandit, neither of them moving. It was as if they thought their proximity would protect me from whatever was happening.

Musical tones sounded from the phone, followed by an automated voice notifying us that this phone number was no longer in use. I couldn't move. Couldn't do anything but stare at the phone. How was this possible when I had only recently received a message from this line?

Sam frowned, but I couldn't tell if it was from concern for me or herself. Somewhere in the back of her mind, she must be doubting my sanity. I couldn't say I wouldn't be doing the same if the shoe were on the other foot. The dead dial tone echoed around the room, loud and ominous.

"What kind of dick pretends to be someone's dead wife?" Gideon finally said, breaking the silence. While the rest of the group seemed stricken by events, Gideon was taking it in his stride. He didn't believe anything out-of-the-norm was happening. He probably thought it was a bunch of basement-dwelling teenagers out for kicks. I still didn't have an answer about what was happening, but I knew one thing, and one thing only.

It wasn't safe to be here anymore.

Whether a simple prank or something more nefarious, I couldn't risk Florence or this clinic again. We had to leave immediately.

"Pack your things, we're going home."

I didn't bother explaining why, and I was relieved when no one questioned my decision. Chase, in particular, had grown pale, probably remembering what happened the last time we were here. I gave her shoulder a squeeze, and she leaped quickly into action, gathering her things. For someone who loved Twenty Questions, she knew when keeping silent was the better course of action. I gave Sam back her phone. She took it, looking contemplative. The others disbanded to prepare for our journey home, but Sam had a thoughtful expression on her face.

"What is it?" I asked.

"Can you pack? I think I'd like to check out the grave site."

My instant reaction was to say no — I didn't like the thought of her being out there alone. As if she sensed my objection, she reached for my hand.

"You know I can handle myself. I'll be careful."

"Still, I'd be happier if you took someone with you."

"That's not necessary, Sully. I won't be long, I promise."

With that she kissed me on the mouth then headed off before I could argue. I knew Sam could take care of herself better than most people, but I wasn't particularly happy about her visiting the grave without me. However, I also knew I was in no fit state to return there.

Looking at the clock, I decided I'd give her twenty minutes then call to check her progress. I was hoping she would find something that would corroborate my story at the very least, something that would make me sound less like a madman.

22

SAM

Sam drove the short distance to the cemetery.

When she had asked Izzy, the vet, if she could borrow her car, the other woman didn't look remotely concerned by the request at all, she only asked if she was going far. It was a testament to the stories Florence must have told about Sully that Sam was immediately deemed trustworthy by extension. When she had revealed that she wanted to pay her respects to Emma, Izzy's eyes had softened, thinking what a wonderful thing she was doing. She even insisted that Sam take the flowers that had just come in from a grateful patient with her. Sam had tried to refuse, but despite her diminutive frame, Izzy was incredibly strong-willed.

So now Sam drove towards the cemetery, a bunch of flowers hastily wrapped in a plastic bag lying on the passenger seat next to her.

Although she hadn't been there before, it wasn't hard to find. Just a few short turns with the car and she was practically there. She probably would have found it even without using Izzy's GPS.

Parking, Sam grabbed the flowers and got out of the car. A breeze whistled through the trees, providing a pleasant soundtrack as she navigated to Emma's grave. A few early morning visitors were dotted around. One elderly couple even nodded to her as she went past. Their eyes were red from tears that they didn't bother to hide. Sam guessed they must have lost a dear one quite recently and lowered her head, respectfully.

She had been going maybe five minutes when she saw the arc of trees that signaled she was approaching her destination. Her pulse sped up even as Sam didn't expect to find anything. If things were as Sully had described, Chase and Gideon would have noticed. As it was, they had been noticeably silent when Sully had explained his sequence of events. Still, Sam had to give him the benefit of doubt.

She knew she had the right tombstone even as her eyes recognized the name inscribed on it. Seeing the words Sully had chosen, conflicting emotions coursed through her: sorrow for the pain Sully had gone through, and though she wasn't proud of it, she also felt envy for the dead woman who still commanded so much of his heart. Yet Sam would never reveal that to Sully, knowing he could never be expected to take on board her own feelings on the subject.

Her eyes traveled down the headstone, to the patch of grass surrounding it. She could see that some of the earth here had been disturbed as Sully had described, but what she saw would be consistent with say a squirrel who decided to dig around while he searched for nuts. Or maybe some maintenance work had gone on in the cemetery.

Either way, it should not have caused Sully to have reacted the way he had.

Trying to quell the anxiousness that was starting to churn in her stomach, Sam bent down to examine one of the spots with her finger. The earth was only loose on the very surface, about two inches deep, adding weight to her squirrel theory. Brow lined with concern, Sam surveyed the area to see if anything suspicious caught her eye, but there were only the rows of tombstones, marking the resting places of other past souls.

What on earth had made Sully react the way he had?

23

SULLY

While I packed, I tried to wrap my head around the phone message. I was sure I had canceled Emma's phone contract shortly after her death, but those were dark days and I had muddled through them medicated by beer and sleeping pills. It was possible, I knew, that I had missed it somehow — I was the man who had been hoarding her things, after all, maybe I had left it deliberately so I could always hear her voicemail.

Sam returned from the cemetery just as we started loading the car. We couldn't talk with others there, not with Florence hovering around us, so the two of us stepped aside. Under the shadow of a tree, several cars away, Sam revealed what she had found.

"I'm sorry, hon. I just didn't find anything that seemed out of place." She had explained her animal theory to me, but that didn't jibe with what I had seen. I didn't understand how this could be. It wasn't in my mind, the message and the holes on the grave, they were real.

"You're sure? Did you check the other graves? If it were an animal, they wouldn't have just hit Emma's."

"I did... there just wasn't anything there." She looked pained, like she wanted to be on my side, but couldn't. A rush of disappointment flooded over me. None of it made any sense.

"We can talk about this later, Sul, once we're home."

I nodded mutely, unable to collect my thoughts. It was almost a relief that I could focus on the manual task of packing. Soon after, everything was together. I made our excuses as Florence stared at me. The women in my life had always been able to see through whatever I was hiding from them, and Florence was no exception. Despite the fact that we were cutting our trip short by several days, she didn't complain, just gave me a hug and asked if she had to worry about me. I said no. To her credit, she didn't even flinch, but we both knew I was lying.

As we piled into the car, Florence slipped her hand through the window and gave mine a squeeze. Her eyes shone with tears as she shot me a small smile.

"Try not to get into any more trouble. My heart can't take another incident."

I kissed her hand and started the engine. As we pulled away, I saw her watching me from the curb, her figure growing smaller and smaller until I could barely make her out anymore.

24

CHASE

For someone who had been initially so excited by the possibility of a road trip, I was so relieved when we pulled up outside the ranch just over four hours later.

Sam and Gideon had taken shifts driving while Sully rested. No one had really discussed doing that, but I guess we decided he needed a break. There wasn't much talk of what had happened at the cemetery and the missing text.

Sam said she'd run the number through the system, but for now, we just had to assume that someone knew Sully would be going home, someone who had something against him and who decided now was the time to get back at him. Sam was absolutely firm in this, refusing to consider any other scenario, but I knew Sully wasn't convinced. I could see it in the way he didn't meet her eyes when he agreed with her. I had a horrible feeling that maybe; he wasn't quite as ready to let Emma go as we had thought.

Sam parked the car as we piled out. Sully went to help Zeb while Gideon flung open the front door and we started trooping inside when Bandit suddenly froze, his ears pricked high. He whimpered and spun around, searching for whatever it was that had gotten his attention. Then he pawed the ground and looked at us. I'd known him long enough to know what he wanted even without the iPad which was still packed in one of our cases.

Follow me.

Confused, I went with him as he led me to the back door. "What is it?" I asked.

He whined at me, pawing at the door. Whatever was going on, Bandit didn't have time to wait for his tablet. He shoved his nose at us urgently, hurrying us to open the door. Frowning, Gideon unlocked the door as Bandit tore off into the long grass, barking and whining until he reached a particular spot and stopped, circling the area, barking at us.

"He's found something," Gideon said concerned, as we hurried out there. He had much longer legs than me plus he could run faster so he got to Bandit before I did. When I finally reached them, panting from the sudden exertion, he waved at me to hang back.

There was a shadow in the long grass.

A shape that was low and *moving*. As Gideon got closer, it whimpered, and I recognized that sound immediately.

It was a dog.

Some kind of mongrel mix. It had the face of a German Shepherd, but its short legs resembled those of a Corgi. I remembered seeing them once and finding them kind of comical looking — I'd read somewhere that the Queen of England had an entire tribe of them.

This dog was short but painfully slim. Her brown eyes were pinned on us in alarm. Her tongue hung out as she panted, terrified.

"Back up," Gideon said. I did as he commanded, gesturing at the others who, having realized something was up, were now coming up behind me, to stay back. Bandit darted around the dog, sniffing like crazy. He whined as if what he could smell concerned him, then he dashed to my side. Seeing how scared the other dog was, however, I figured he wanted us to give her space.

Gideon lowered into a crouch, making himself smaller, then he shuffled closer, making soothing sounds. "Hey, girl. I'm not going to hurt you. I just want to help."

The dog's eyes darted wildly as she took in all of us before settling on him. She bared her teeth in a snarl but couldn't stop the trembling in her body. I knew it was bravado, a show she was putting on to try to warn Gideon away. Still, scared dogs acted irrationally sometimes, attacking without warning, so he had to be careful.

He stopped, reaching slowly into a pocket where he took out the remnants of a Nutter Butter pack. The dog's nose wrinkled as she smelled the cookie. She kept looking at Gideon, but some of her suspicion became overridden by hunger as a great blob of drool suddenly fell from her mouth. Gideon saw this as he snapped a cookie in half and tossed it to her. It landed between her paws, right under her nose. Her jaws lunged forward, and she snapped up the cookie, never taking her eyes off of him. He threw the other half at her. Again, she ate it up. She looked at him, eyes begging for more. Gideon gave her the rest of the pack, which she hovered up in no time.

"I'm sorry girl, if you want more, you'll have to come inside with me. I'm all out," he said, showing her his bare hands and the empty wrapper. The dog looked at him, then his hands, then the empty wrapper. A whine of fear escaped her lips as she tossed a nervous glance at the rest of us, though we were rapidly backing away.

Gideon moved slowly towards her. She whined again but didn't move. Slowly, slowly, he stretched out a hand to touch her. She trembled under his touch but allowed him to pet her. He fussed her for several moments just letting her get used to him when finally her tongue snaked out to lick him. Gideon smiled.

"See, that's not so bad now, is it?"

He stayed with her until he could stand up without her cowering behind him.

"Come on, girl, follow me. We've got lots of food inside."

I wasn't sure whether she understood him or not, but the dog wouldn't move. Gideon tried again.

"No one is going to hurt you. We just want to see if you're alright," he pleaded. Still she wouldn't move. Gideon stopped, not knowing what else to do when Bandit barked beside me. I don't know what he said, but her ears pricked up and she started towards the ranch of her own accord. I stroked the top of his head, marveling once again at him.

"Thanks, boy," I said to him gratefully.

"Woof."

SULLY

Gideon fed the dog, who wolfed down the food like she hadn't eaten in days.

I hadn't been able to get too close to her — she growled every time anyone who wasn't Gideon approached her. I was glad she trusted him, though it made examining her a bit of a pain.

I could see her ribs clearly showing against her side. Her coat was encrusted with dirt and I was pretty sure those black spots were mites in her ears. I'd instructed Bandit to stay away from her until I could clean her up, as I didn't want him to catch anything from her. Bandit seemed all too pleased to comply, which surprised me. I thought he'd like another dog around, but she seemed to put him on edge. He kept sniffing her and staying behind Chase. I'd seen him with dogs before, back at the clinic when Forbes' men had attacked us. Bandit had asked the other dogs for help, so I knew he wasn't afraid of dogs — far from it — so this behavior was a little puzzling. It could just be he was protecting his territory. However, as clever as he was, Bandit was still just a dog.

"Since she trusts you, I'll need you to hold her head and talk to her calmly while I try to get a look at her," I told Gideon. "Now, she may get frightened. The key are her ears. If she lays them flat on her head, she's going to attack, in which case, you back up immediately."

"Got it," Gideon answered.

"Sam, Chase, you guys have this sheet ready. If it looks like she's going to attack, the two of you throw this sheet over her and we'll trap her in it. If she can't see, she won't be able to attack. We use this technique all the time so you should be fine," I said.

I caught Chase staring at me funny. "What?"

"Isn't that only used on cats?" she asked.

"How do you know that?" I said. "Wait, let me guess, you read it somewhere and your brain filed it away for exactly this moment?"

She nodded.

"It'll work on her too." I nodded to them all. "Ready?"

Gideon started stroking the dog as I approached from her side — not her back — I wanted her to see me coming so she wouldn't be startled. At my first touch, her legs shook, and she tossed a few nervous looks at me, but Gideon's voice seemed to have a calming effect on her. She pressed her head into his hands as if she was afraid to look at what was about to happen.

I felt around her torso. Though her ribs were prominent, I couldn't feel any breaks. It was the same for her legs. Looking into her ears, I confirmed my early suspicion — they were plagued by the little suckers. If she'd let me, I could clean out the majority of them, but I'd need drops to get rid of the rest and to deter them from coming back. I'd try that later when she was more at ease with us, but right now, I just wanted to make sure there wasn't anything pressing to contend with.

Bandit whined by Chase, hyper concerned. Hearing him, the

dog shook with fright. We all knew Bandit would never harm her but it seemed she wasn't so sure. I didn't think she would hurt any of us, but I also didn't want to run the risk of her flipping out.

"Bandit, could you stay outside? Your being here seems to be scaring her."

Bandit whined unhappily and shook himself as if to say there was nothing to fear from him, but he trotted out, tossing us a longing look over his shoulders as he went.

"Thanks boy."

Sighing deeply, he left the room. Carefully, I took hold of the dog's mouth, mindful that even in her weakened state, those teeth could do plenty of damage, and what with my face being so close to those jaws... Well, I was being vigilant.

I pried her mouth open. Her teeth weren't too bad — she was younger than I had first thought. Breath was as expected (bad), tongue a decent color. Next, I examined her legs where I could see thick scars that had healed around the bottom of her legs, close to the paws. There was a matching scar around her neck. A red-hot burn of rage started building inside me. These scars were consistent with being chained against her will for an extended period. Shifting her fur, I saw other scars and bruises, some only days old, while others had clearly been there much longer. Unable to hide my feelings, Chase picked up on my anger immediately.

"What's wrong?"

I looked at her. "She's been badly beaten, chained and starved, up until the moment she probably escaped."

Chase drew in her breath sharply while Gideon gripped his fists into balls.

"You think someone did this to her recently?" he asked.

I nodded. "Yeah, but they've had a while, judging by the scars and bruises I've found. Might be that she's always been tortured. We could be the first nice people she's met."

Gideon looked at the dog, with her head in his hands, hiding from the sorry world that had broken her. "I'm sorry, girl, but whoever they were, they won't hurt you again. You're safe now."

She looked up at him with large brown eyes and whimpered.

26

SULLY

It wasn't until I sat on the edge of our bed that I realized how weary I was feeling.

I tugged off my boots, letting them drop to the floor with a thud. Sam moved past into the ensuite bathroom. Moments later, I heard the sound of running water. Steam curled out from the bathroom, fogging the air. I was surprised to see Sam return fully dressed.

"You're not getting in the bath?"

"No, I'm drawing it for you. It's been a long day, figured you could do with some relaxing."

I normally only ever showered, preferring the pounding water to beat down on my body, but the idea of lying in a hot bath didn't seem too bad right now. Maybe a soak would clear the tension from my mind and shoulders. She looked at me and dropped a kiss on my head. If I were a smart man, I would've just gone into that bathroom and let the hot water do its thing, but I wasn't. Frowning, I took her hand.

"You've known me what, six months now. If I'm not sure about something, I don't bring it up, true?" I asked. She looked down at me and nodded.

"I'm not saying you're lying, Sul, it's just... you've been under a lot of stress. I knew going back wouldn't be easy for you, seeing your friends and previous life. I don't even know if you've had time to grieve properly..."

"That's not what this is. I am not making this up because I miss my wife, besides the timing doesn't make sense. Why would I suddenly be doing this?"

She didn't say anything, just continued to look at me with those piercing eyes of hers.

"We have just decided to do something big, Sully, maybe deep down, you're not ready for the changes that might bring about."

I realized then what she was thinking. "This hasn't got anything to do with us getting married. I don't have a problem with that, with moving on."

"I know," she said. "Listen, don't worry about it tonight. I'll look into the calls in the morning when I'm back at work. I'll run a trace, see what I can find out."

Relief surged out of me. Despite how she had said she would do this before, I guess there was a part of me that doubted she would, but if she was going to do that, it meant she was willing to believe me. She didn't think I was the mad man I was beginning to sound like.

She nodded in the direction of the bathroom. "Go on before it gets cold."

She shot me a smile as she opened the suitcase and started to unpack our things from the trip. I gave her shoulder a squeeze as I headed into the ensuite.

"Thanks, Hon."

27

SAM

Sam focused on the clothes in front of her, taking out several armfuls and dumping them onto the bed. The everyday action of folding clothes was bringing a small sense of peace. If she could just sort the mound in front of her, maybe her mind would stop shrieking and sending out its distress signal.

She saw Sully drop his clothes on the floor (something that usually drove her mad, but today the normality of it gave some relief) and lower into the bath. From her position opposite the ensuite, Sully would not be able to see her as he had his back to her.

Exactly the way she wanted it.

Keeping a watchful eye on him, Sam moved to his side of the bed, to where Sully had left his cell phone. Watching to make sure Sully wasn't going to see what she was doing, Sam picked up his phone, unclipped the battery and slipped out the SIM card which she quickly put into her own phone.

When Sully had been giving his explanation of events at the cemetery, he had caught her off-guard and Sam had not remembered that a phone's log wasn't actually saved on the device itself, but on the phone's SIM card. It wasn't until they were on the drive home that this had come to her attention. Sam knew she could have mentioned this to Sully earlier, but the truth was, she wanted to check this out herself.

She turned her phone on and waited impatiently, tossing a look at Sully to make sure he couldn't see what she was up to. Sam wasn't an insecure person and had never had reason to go through her man's phone before. The boyfriends she'd had before Sully had all been decent guys, but the relationships had ended when the romance had fizzled out. She was still friends with a few of them, though their new wives weren't that keen on Sam being in the picture, so she had respected their wishes and disappeared out of their lives. Having to deploy this duplicity now hurt Sam almost as much as it would Sully, but she had to know.

The logo for the phone appeared, followed by Sully's home screen, and Sam was in!

Scrolling quickly through the menu, she came to the text message log, but she could find no mention of the text Sully claimed to have received — there were just the usual texts sent from each of them.

She swiped through until she reached his text messages. Nothing seemed out of the ordinary, just the usual texts sent from each of them. There was one from Sam, asking when they wanted to do their big reveal dinner, a few from Gideon with basic house-keeping questions. Chase had sent Sully some funny memes. The sight of them made Sam's lips curve into a smile. What was it about Chase and memes? The kid was always trawling through the net to find them, or she'd be laughing at her phone reading 9Gag. Trying to explain the joke to Bandit usually resulted in more laughter, as the dog just did not understand the concept of humor. Thinking of them, of her family, the smile left her face as Sam felt another pang of unease that she couldn't shake. They were so happy before this trip. Why did this have to happen?

Finding nothing in the inbox, Sam clicked on the sent folder. There were only three texts, but what she read was enough to send chills down her spine.

"Who is this?" read the first text. The next asked, "Why are you doing this?" The last text, consisting of only one word, had the biggest impact on Sam.

"Emma?"

Sam looked over at the man she loved, relaxing in the bath.

Her eyes dark with worry.

28

CHASE

It took a while, but Sully was finally happy that he'd done all he could for the dog.

Not that he expected to find a missing report on her, but Sully ran through the usual sites all the same. She wasn't an expensive dog, wasn't used for breeding. It looked like it was a clear case of neglect and abuse. Though I wasn't happy about this, I had to admit it was easier to focus on her, rather than what had happened with Sully at the cemetery. We'd retreated into our own rooms, but I was sure Sam and Sully were having more conversations about it all.

Bandit and I were having a big discussion of our own. He sat with me on the bed, asking questions about the other dog. I was trying my best to explain, but it wasn't like I had many answers myself.

"She doesn't like me."

Hearing his iPad say those words, I shook my head and scratched behind his ears on the favorite spot of his. "Not true, Muttface. She doesn't know you is all. She needs time before she'll trust us."

"Except Gideon. She likes Gideon."

"Well, yeah, she does seem to be into him."

An image of him flashed up in my mind. Gideon, making comforting sounds as the dog shivered in his hands. I hadn't wanted to make a big deal of it at the time, or even now I guess, but something about the way he took care of her, how he was genuinely concerned for her... it had made me feel kinda warm inside. Like I'd drank a mug of coffee or something, but then my thoughts drifted to Sully's predicament and I found myself turning cold.

"Chase what is wrong?"

"This whole Emma thing is freaking me out. Why would Sully think she texted him?"

"Maybe it is a mistake?"

"Has to be, right? Sully can't really be thinking that his wife is back from the dead, not after all this time. Things like that don't happen."

A knock sounded on my door. I looked up to see Gideon, the other dog trailing behind him like his shadow. Seeing us, she stopped dead.

"Hey girl," I called out to her. "Do you want to come inside?"

The dog whimpered and backed up until her rump was against the far wall, very clearly not wanting to come in. Gideon reached down and patted her on the head, trying to reassure her. I was surprised to see that she didn't cringe away from him.

"Wow, she's really taken to you," I said.

"I've been bribing her with food for hours, so yeah, it hasn't gone to waste," he replied. "Can't get her to go near anyone else though, even Sully, and you know animals usually love him."

"She just needs time. Of course, now she's decided to adopt you, you know you're responsible for her," I grinned, liking his trapped expression.

"She follows me everywhere. Even to the bathroom. I was

taking a leak when I realized she was standing between my feet. It was pretty disconcerting."

I laughed, "I'd love to have seen that." I said it without thinking, but the minute the words were out of my mouth, I blushed furiously. Idiot! I wanted the floor to open up and swallow me whole. "What I meant was..." I didn't need to finish though as Gideon was shaking his head.

"Yeah, I know. Let's forget you said anything and move on."

"Please."

Bandit walked up to Gideon and nuzzled his hand, but as soon as he got to him, we heard growling from the door. The dog was watching us and didn't like Gideon petting another dog. Bandit stopped, tilting his head to listen to her.

"She does not like me."

"No, Boy, she's just jealous and insecure. And you're another dog, I'm sure this is normal behavior," Gideon explained. "But since she is so flighty and attached to me, maybe it's best if I stay away from you for a while. Just so she feels a little more at ease around here."

Bandit sighed, green eyes looking impossibly sad as he moved away from Gideon and came to sit beside me. I tried to placate him with a hug and felt him lick my ear in return, which felt totally gross but, not wanting to upset him any further, I took it like a trooper. *The things we do for our dogs.*

"Have you come up with a name?" I asked.

"I have, just not sure whether I should name her yet..." He trailed off, looking uncertain.

"You're worried you'll name her then her real owners will find her?"

He nodded.

"You saw the condition she was in. Look at her, she won't even come into the room when Bandit and I are clearly nice. No one is looking for her. If anything, they're probably running scared that we'll find out who they are and sue the living crap out of them — which would be totally worth it. We should so do that."

A smile flashed over his face. I tried not to think about how that made me feel and stuck my face in Bandit's fur. "So what is it, what's her name?"

"Pixie," he said.

I grinned at him. "That suits her perfectly."

I turned to Bandit. "What do you say, can you introduce yourself to Pixie nicely? Maybe you could loan her one of your toys? She's probably never had one."

Bandit barked, then trotted over to his bed where several toys sat around it. His nose hovered over his Frumpy Rabbit soft toy, but I knew Pixie would never get that. It was his absolute favorite thing outside of his iPad. He nudged Frumpy out of the way, then picked up another soft toy — a cat with a long tail — and moving to the doorway, he stopped a few feet from Pixie. A low, warning growl rumbled in the back of her throat. She might only be a tiny thing, but she sure didn't seem to know it.

Respecting her wishes, Bandit laid the toy on the floor gently. Pixie kept growling even as she tried to meld herself further into the wall. It upset me, if I'm honest. Here was Bandit, literally the nicest, smartest dog in the world, offering her one of his toys, and she was just going to yell at him.

Bandit took a step back, watching her. Pixie stared back at him, eyes wide, ears turned towards the back but not yet flattened onto her head. Gently, gently, he nudged the toy. It rolled towards her until it bumped against her paws. Still, she didn't move, didn't even glance down at her feet.

"She's really scared of Bandit for some reason," Gideon said. Hearing this, Bandit whined, then backed all the way back into the room. When he was back with me, Pixie suddenly leaped forward and snatched the toy into her mouth.

"One small step for dogkind I guess. I'd better take her to her room, get her settled."

"She's not staying with you?" I asked, surprised.

"Sully doesn't think that's smart since we've only just met her. He's not sure she won't harm me yet, so she's going to be spending the night in the den."

"Right. Sensible plan."

Gideon clicked his tongue at Pixie and started walking away when I stopped him with a call. "Gid...?"

He turned back to me.

"What do you think is going on with Sully?"

His brow creased with concern as his eyes grew dark with worry. "I don't know, but Sam will figure it out." With that, he went away, Pixie following close behind as she tossed Bandit one last look.

29

THE SCIENTIST

Staring into the live feed of the ranch, The Scientist watched the proceedings in the girl's room with interest. So the boy was bonding with the new dog while Sullivan was showing signs of post-traumatic stress disorder.

People were so predictable, it was boring.

Take the girl. Despite all that had happened to her — and The Scientist had managed to find out quite a bit about her life thanks to Forbes' soldier monkey — she was ordinary street scum, trailer trash. To think this was the girl who had wrecked his partner's life... It was unfathomable.

And the vet... so he'd received a text message from his dead wife's phone, and that was enough to unravel him. The Scientist almost felt sorry for the Sheriff, if that were an emotion he allowed himself to feel. Here she was, thinking that she was going to get married soon when clearly her husband-to-be hadn't gotten over his previous wife. He mulled over the complexity of feelings and how they were the downfall of man — he himself had learned this the hard way. He tensed as a memory clawed its way up from the darkest pit of his mind.

He saw himself as a young boy, a talented boy who wanted nothing but for his parents to acknowledge him, however, they were too busy with their work and social lives, and he was nothing more than a nuisance they kept fed. Occasionally, they would trot him out like a pet to showcase. Their friends loved to see how bright, yet how deeply awkward he was. They would coo at his brain, then laugh when they saw him trip over his own clumsy feet. In their eyes, he was nothing but a clown. But he would show them.

He would show them all.

Looking at the girl now, at how she conversed with the dog over her concerns for Sullivan, he saw she was just a child and a very insecure one at that. The dog, however... he was such a specimen! And it wasn't only his intellect or the way his brain had physically altered itself... the dog seemed like he had genuine feelings.

Human emotions.

It would be almost a shame to do what he had to, but that was the way of science. The groundbreakers were the ones who took risks — even unpleasant ones — in order to get the result they needed. What was that saying he was so fond of?

A genius is one who shoots for something others can't see... and hits it.

Well, he was already a genius, that much was obvious. He only had to wait for the world to see it.

He looked down at his experiment, at the rise and fall of its chest, and smiled.

Soon, my lovely. Soon.

30

CHASE

The sun streamed in, bathing my face in warm light.

I woke and stretched as Bandit snuck a morning lick at me. I'd told him a million times to leave my face alone, but he seemed to think I didn't mean it, plus I got the feeling it amused him. I suppose there were worse things to wake up to, so I usually tried not to make a deal of it.

"Hey, we should go check on Pixie. See how she's doing this morning."

"I hope she liked my cat."

I climbed off my bed, tugging on a thin sweater. Fall was still a month or so away, but there was a definite chill in the air when I woke now. I flung open the curtains, enjoying the scenery outside. Trees stretched out across the horizon as far as the eye could see. It's funny how I didn't miss the busyness of New York one bit. Yeah, it was laid back and quiet here, but I'd had enough excitement to last me a lifetime already. I was looking forward to the day I could sit on the porch and yell at kids to get off my lawn.

Yes, I know I sound old, but I don't care.

We went down the hall, towards the den where I knew Gid had

set up a private corner for Pixie. He'd pushed a few tables onto their side and created a sort of table fort for her that he'd covered with blankets for privacy. We had tried to keep her contained in a room at first, but she'd panicked like crazy when we'd shut the door on her. Sully thought this way was better. She'd be contained but wouldn't feel like she was being caged.

Pixie seemed a tiny bit happier this morning, though the blanket we had given her to sleep on was ripped and bitten to shreds, as were the ones we'd used to drape over the tables. Bite marks punctured what was left of Bandit's cat — chunks of it were spread all around her like roadkill. She must have been gnawing at the thing most the night to kill it like this. Horrified, Bandit took in the sight of his mutilated friend and tried to paw all the pieces into a pile that he picked up gently into his mouth. I felt like a total heel since it had been my suggestion to loan the toy to her. I shot Bandit an apologetic look.

"Sorry, Boy, I didn't know she'd do that. We'll try to fix this one OK, and if I can't, I'll get you a replacement cat, an even better one!"

He woofed in agreement, but hung his head sadly. Those big green eyes of his looked almost as if they were tearing up. Then again, he was always very sensitive. I guess it would be awhile before he'd get over his loss. Feeling awful, I focused my attention on Pixie, hoping she would distract me from my guilty conscience.

"Hey, Girl. How're you this morning?"

She looked at me, eyes wide. Her legs shook a bit, but she didn't otherwise move or growl. Well, this was progress. I smiled at her. Bandit came closer for his own look, but as soon as she saw him, she bared her teeth and whimpered at the same time.

"Sully's never seen that reaction before," came Sam's voice from behind me.

I looked over my shoulder to find her there. She was already dressed for work but seemed a little down this morning. Dark shadows rimmed her eyes, and her smile wasn't as bright as it usually was.

"He checked on her last night, when he couldn't sleep. Bandit must've heard him as he went to join him, but Pixie did the same thing then when she saw him. Sully said it's a double reaction that he's never seen before — usually it's one or the other — but not both. He's pretty confused by it."

"She is strange."

The words came from Bandit. We looked at him.

"Well, she's had a tough life. She's bound to have some scars," Sam explained. But Bandit whined and continued.

"She killed my cat."

Sam laughed then and scratched his ears.

"Oh buddy, we'll get you another one."

"But it won't smell the same."

Gideon came up from behind us, looking bright-eyed and well, completely put together. I tugged my sweater down self-consciously, wishing I'd showered before I left my room. Why did he always look like he'd just stepped out of a catalog?

"How's she doing?" he asked.

"Better, I think, though she killed Felix and the blankets, and she still doesn't seem keen on Bandit," I answered, watching as he went over to her slowly, offering his hand so she could sniff him first. Amazingly, she stopped trembling and allowed him to pet her.

"She really does like you." I was super impressed by how she trusted him.

"Got good taste obviously," he replied, smug.

"Or she's been so badly tortured, she's lost all sense," I retorted, rolling my eyes.

Sam had been listening to us, but now her face became serious. "Guys, I need to speak to you about something, but not here. I need Zeb as well. Sully's going to pick some things up for Pixie after breakfast, so can you stick around? I won't be long, but it's important I speak with you all."

She said all, but I noticed she was omitting Sully.

"Sure," I answered, while Gideon just nodded, his eyes mirroring my concern.

31

CHASE

Breakfast was a tense affair.

Gideon had cooked bacon and eggs but hardly anyone ate. Sully just drank coffee while he checked over Pixie. She seemed a little happier with us today and had yet to growl at anyone, though she watched us like a hawk, only stopping when Gid put a bowl heaped with doggie chow in front of her face. She wolfed down the lot of it like how Bandit used to when we'd first had him. I knew how she felt. I knew what it was to be starving with hunger. I made a mental note to get her some extra treats when I popped into town later.

Since Sam had mentioned that she wanted to speak to us without Sully, the whole thing had been hanging over my head. It must have been bothering Gid too, as he was unusually quiet. Thoughts on his own mind, Sully didn't seem to notice how troubled we were all feeling today. Only Zeb seemed oblivious, doing a crossword while Bandit watched, fascinated. Though he was pretty hot stuff with the Jeopardy app, crosswords he just couldn't get his head around. Something to do with the phrasing of the questions had him super confused. He couldn't answer even the simplest ones, so he thought Zeb was a God whenever he finished one. I pushed cereal around in my bowl until Sully left.

Pouring a glass of OJ, Sam sat in her usual seat beside Sully's empty chair, at the head of the table. She cleared her throat and looked at us.

"I know none of us want to be talking without Sully here, but there are some things I feel it's important for us to discuss, particularly after recent events," she began. Gideon put his fork on the table while Zeb, who never ate much in the morning anyway, watched her, eyes dark and inscrutable.

"I've been looking into grief counseling. I think Sully's stressed and the trip East raised unresolved issues that he still has regarding Emma's death."

"It's been a year and a half though," Gideon said. "Surely he's moved on by now."

Sam shrugged. "It takes some people longer to get over the death of their partner. There is no time limit to this."

"I'm not over losing my wife, and it's been quite a bit longer for me," Zeb said, backing her up, his brows furrowed with concern.

I looked at Sam, not wanting to say anything yet feeling compelled to. "But, you guys are getting married..." I let my sentence trail off, not sure how to finish.

Sam nodded and gave me a reassuring smile that didn't quite manage to reach her eyes. "Yes, we are. But I think the thought of a wedding — no matter how small — is causing memories of his previous wedding with Emma to surface, and with that, his mind is panicking."

"You think he's cracking up?" Gideon asked, worry emanating from him in spades.

"I don't think it's helpful to label it," Sam said, a little sternly.

"I agree," Zeb said. "Probably best just to keep an eye on him, make sure he's looking after himself."

"Yes, we need to look after him. And it isn't helpful to doubt what he thinks."

"You mean the text?" I asked.

"The thing is, whatever is going on, Sully believes it, so we just have to stand by him for now. Let's just give him some time. I'm sure he'll sort himself out."

Bandit pawed the ground and shook himself, which actually meant he was in fierce agreement.

"But you're going to look into it, right? Just in case?" I said.

"You betcha," Sam said, her eyes turning hard.

Relief flooded through me. If someone was messing with Sully, Sam would find them. Sam wouldn't let them get away with it.

32

CHASE

I went through the rest of the morning aimlessly.

After Sam and Gid went to work, Zeb retreated to his room to read. He said it was a perk of being old that he could just laze away his time, but I was young and needed a schedule. It was partly his insistence that made me the de facto grocery shopper for our clan. Carrying an empty shopping basket, I stared up at the endless shelves, mind blank by the options available to me. Who were the people who decided we needed so many versions of the same thing? How different could canned tuna taste? They were even priced the same. I wasn't sure how long I'd been looking at a brand of beans when Bandit's wet nose touched my hand. I shook my head, clearing myself from my daze, and looked down at him.

"Sorry, Bud, just have a lot on my mind, you know?"

He woofed once. *Yes, I know* I translated his answer, sure that was what he meant even without the iPad. One of the perks of living in a small town was how everyone knew one another. At first, this had made me super nervous of being here. I just wasn't used to people knowing my name or my business but, it did have its positives, like being allowed to bring Bandit inside the grocery store, even though the owners knew he wasn't a service dog. Zeb had been shopping here close to forty years now, and the owners were old friends. I was pretty relieved. The last few times I'd had to fake anything, it hadn't gone down too well.

Unbidden, a painful memory surfaced from six months ago.

It was during our visit to Atlantic City when Sully was treating us to the biggest feast I'd ever had at Caesar's Palace. It was a buffet about a block long and would have been the best day in my life if Bandit hadn't suffered his first seizure there. Seeing his eyes roll into the back of his head and his mouth foaming, I had to fight to stave off a shudder. Even though I knew he was fine now, just remembering that moment had me feeling all kinds of terror.

As if he could feel it (which, I'm sure he could — probably smelled it on me or something), Bandit took hold of my sleeve in his mouth and gingerly started leading me to the bread aisle. *That's right, we needed bread.* I found a loaf, then scanned through my list and started grabbing the items. Ten or so minutes and a bagful of groceries later, I checked out and was walking towards the exit when one of the owners, a man with a bad comb-over and puffy cheeks, stopped me. Despite his lack of a clue on all things concerning appearance, Mr. Wellis was a nice guy and never had a bad word to say about anyone.

"Hey, Chase." He stooped down to pat Bandit on the head before slipping him a dog biscuit that he kept in his pocket for such occasions. Bandit took it gratefully and gave him a lick of thanks.

"Hi, Mr. Wellis." I hoisted the heavy shopping bag up against my stomach, wondering briefly if I'd maybe bought too much to fit onto my bike.

"Did you manage to find your friend?" he asked.

I blinked at him, confused. "No, what friend?"

"Oh. A lady. She was asking about you. You must have just missed her."

My mind was a jumble of confusion. I couldn't think who he meant.

"You're sure she was asking for me and not someone else?" I asked. We pretty much knew the same people, so this was pretty weird. I felt a slight twinge of apprehension but quickly shook it off. Mr. Wellis wasn't exactly great at getting facts right. Trying to get him to pass on a message was like playing Chinese Whispers. A couple of weeks ago, I'd asked him to let me know when the chorizo was back in stock (Sully was a big fan), but when he'd finally found me to let me know, he'd lead me to avocado section. Not sure how chorizo had become avocado in his head, but there you go.

Mr. Wellis shook his head. "No, she was definitely asking for you. Wonder where she could have gotten to?" He stared out the window, out into the street, but couldn't find her. My apprehension suddenly grew into the beginnings of panic. Who could be looking for me when no one knew I was here?

"I gotta get going, this bag's getting kinda heavy." I wasn't exactly lying either, the bag had suddenly become a dead weight in my arms. Beside me, Bandit didn't make a sound, but he shifted his weight between his legs back and forth, a clear sign of his agitation.

Mr. Wellis stepped out of my way. "Sure. If I see her again, I'll let her know I spoke to you. You want me to give her Zeb's number?"

"Um, no, can you just take down hers? I can always call her back." Once a suspicious New Yorker, always a suspicious New Yorker, even if I had lived there less than a year.

"No problem, see you tomorrow. You too, Bandit." He patted him on the head once more, then went back to work. I shot Bandit a look and inclined my head to him, telling him to follow me outside. He came immediately, staying close, intelligent eyes scanning the street for signs of this mysterious woman. We arrived at my bike. I swung the bag up, trying to set it into the front basket when someone CRASHED into me. The bag was knocked clean from my hands and food went rolling every which way.

"Oh jeez," I said, looking at the loaf of fresh bread, now lying dirty on the ground.

"Chase! I didn't see you there," came a voice from behind me. It was a familiar voice, made husky from the many cigarettes she smoked on a daily basis, and one I didn't think I'd ever hear again in my life.

I spun around to see the woman standing before me.

"Mom," I gasped, unable to believe my eyes.

33

CHASE

She hadn't changed at all.

Her bleached blonde hair was still dry and tucked into an untidy ponytail, and her eyes were heavy with the thick layers of mascara she liked to wear. She was dressed in jeans and a cheap blouse that she had buttoned up wrong. I wasn't sure what it was about that fact that almost undid me.

How had she found me?

"What're you doing here?" I gasped. Hearing the shakiness in my voice, Bandit pressed against me, looking at her, not understanding the situation but prepared to support me all the same.

"I came to find you," she said. Her eyes started watering with tears and she reached out to hug me, but I stepped away from her. Bandit whined, unsure what to do.

"But how did you know where I was?"

"Does it matter, Chase? Don't you care how far I've come to find you?" she asked, somewhat desperately.

"I don't know why you're here or who told you, but I don't want anything to do with you," I said harshly. "Go home." She flinched, but I didn't care.

"Come on, can't we just talk? Let me buy you a root beer float. They have them in the diner across the road. I know how much you love them." She touched my arm, but I shook her off.

"That's where you're wrong. I hate root beer, Mom. Always have. It's coke floats I like."

She blinked, confused for a moment. I could see her literally racking her brain.

"You're sure? Could have sworn that's what you liked..."

"I guess that's too much for you to remember isn't it, what with you always so focused on pleasing Tubs." I spat the words out, relieved I was finally able to say the things to her that I never could before. Not if I didn't want to be beaten for it. Saying his name caused a flicker of fear to rise through me. I suddenly realized she might not have come alone. My eyes scanned the street left and right, looking for any sign of his hulking shape. Bandit moved in front of me, ready to protect me from the danger he could sense I was fearing. Despite everything else, I felt a surge of love towards him. My buddy would never let me down. Not like Mom.

Realizing I was looking for him, she spoke. "I came alone. He doesn't know I'm here."

"Well, that's one smart thing you've managed to do in your life. Congratulations."

I didn't care that I might sound like a jerk right now to anyone passing by. They had no idea what life was like with this woman. What I'd had to put up with in the last few years. Shooting her a look of disgust, I picked up whatever groceries I could salvage off the ground. Sensing I wasn't in any immediate danger, Bandit grabbed a can of soup, carrying it gently between his teeth. His action caught her attention and she must have finally noticed him as she gave him a look of disgust.

"You got a dog."

She'd never liked animals, and I'd only been lucky enough to get a baby duckling from her after she'd been given it from a neighbor who worked on a farm. I figured I didn't have to answer to her anymore, so I chose not to answer that question. She didn't deserve to know anything about me, and I was furious that she was even here.

"It's none of your business, what I do and don't have. Just go away and leave me alone." I shoved the groceries into the basket, taking the can from Bandit. She grabbed my arm, trying to get my attention.

"Please, let's just talk…" she began, but I'd already had enough of her being here. I shook her off again and grabbed hold of my bike.

"GO AWAY!" I yelled, suddenly having lost all control. My voice carried out into the street, causing startled faces to look my way in concern. Mr. Wellis came out of the store then, and for the first time since I've known him, he wasn't smiling. He called over to me.

"You OK, Chase? Is there a problem here?"

Though his words were directed at me, he was looking at her, and by his stance, I could see that he just needed the word and he would come deal with her himself. I felt so overwhelmed by his support, I felt tears prick at the edges of my eyes.

Mom must have seen he meant business too as she raised both hands in front of her and backed off. "No, no. No problem here. I'm going," she said, walking briskly away.

Angrily, I wiped the tears from my eyes as Mr. Wellis' expression turned sympathetic. "You want to come inside, tell me what she wanted? I can call Sully or Sam for you?"

I shook my head, mad at myself for letting her get to me. "No, I'm good. I'm just going to head to Warrey's to see Gideon. Thanks, Mr. Wellis. Thanks for helping."

"You're welcome, Chase. You take care now."

I took off on my bike, Bandit following close behind. Once I was a little distance away, I tossed a look over my shoulder, but she was long gone.

34

CHASE

I reached Warrey's in five minutes flat.

I knew I could have gone home, but it was a longer ride and I felt I would be safer in town, with Gid, rather than out in the fields on my own. I didn't know what my mom wanted, or whether it was true that she was here without Tubs. The whole thing was bizarre and not in a fun way.

Luckily Warrey wasn't around, but I could see Gideon's head peeking out from behind the wheel of a 4x4. Without Warrey around, the radio was tuned to a local station, and the volume was low as Gid didn't really have it on to listen to. He was just never able to deal with silence despite living in the middle of nowhere.

Hearing my tires crunch onto the gravel drive, he looked up, surprised to see me. I guess I wasn't able to hide how I was feeling as he knew immediately that something had gone down. Throwing down a wrench, he marched towards me.

"What's wrong?"

I told him quickly, trying all the while not to give in to my panic. When I was done, his eyes looked as wide as mine. Wiping the grease stains onto his jeans, he took out his phone.

"We need to tell Sully."

I nodded in agreement. I'd actually wanted to call Sully immediately, but I couldn't do it in front of Mr. Wellis or my mom. Now we were safely away from prying eyes, I was desperate to hear Sully's take on it. He would know what to do. I rested my hand on Bandit's head, getting comfort from the feel of him there. He leaned against me, tongue snaking out to lick my hand now and then.

Gideon put his phone on speaker and he called Sully. The call rang and rang, but he didn't pick up. When it cut to voicemail, Gideon spoke into the phone. "Sul, it's Gid. We've got a big problem. Can you call me when you get this?" He hung up and looked at me. "How did she find you? Did she say?"

"No," I replied miserably. An unwanted thought was beginning to creep up on me and it was one I didn't want to face or own up to, but I knew I had to. "But... I did call her."

"What? When?" he demanded, arms folded across his chest.

I stared down at the ground. "When we were in Connecticut. But I called them from Sully's clinic and I didn't say a word! So she can't have known it was me, can she?" My eyes grew round at the possibility.

"That doesn't make any sense. Even if she figured out it was you and looked up the area code, it would have led her there, not here. She must've found you another way, but how?"

"I don't know."

"Did she say what she wanted?"

"To talk. But I didn't give her a chance," I said. And suddenly I felt so stupid. Here we were, trying to second guess her appearance when if I hadn't been acting like an emo kid, I could have just asked her what she wanted. Neither of us had the answers, but one thing was clear: I wasn't getting a good feeling about any of this.

Where was Sully?
Why didn't he call us back?

35
____

SULLY

I could see my destination just ahead of me.

All morning I had run around town, grabbing basic items we'd need for Pixie. It was clear that her distrust of Bandit wasn't going to go anytime soon, so it was double of everything. Not just food bowls and a bed, but also brushes and blankets. Pixie wouldn't like anything that would smell of him.

As I sped through my to-do list eager to have it done with so I could get onto what I really came out here for, I realized it felt good to be on my own. All night, I had struggled with my "problem" as I was fast calling it. Sam was a trooper, but she clearly didn't believe me and I honestly couldn't blame her. I'd racked my brain until it was ready to explode, but I was still to find a logical explanation; how had that text vanished into thin air? While the others thought I was suffering from stress — and it was entirely possible that I was — I was convinced that the message had been real. I knew I had received it, which meant *someone had sent it to me*.

And I was determined to find out who.

I pulled into the parking lot of the wood-clad building and killed the engine. As I climbed out of the truck, my phone started vibrating in my pocket, but I had already drawn the attention of the man in front of me, who was approaching with a friendly wave. Around my age and fit from the many days spent patrolling the area on foot, he wore an olive green shirt, the same style as Sam's though, being a higher rank, her uniform usually consisted of a white shirt — which she was happy about since the green clashed with her hair apparently (I wouldn't know as she looked pretty fantastic in anything, but I had it on her good authority that was the case and I had learned long ago not to argue with the women in my life).

I glanced down at the phone to see "Gideon calling" flashing up on the display. If I answered, I'd run the risk that he'd hear Brad's greeting. It was best if I just called him back later so he couldn't figure out where I was. The last thing I needed were more skeptical faces staring at me. I flipped the phone to silent, slipped it back into my pocket, and forced a smile.

"Hey, Brad, how're you?"

"Good, good. Wife tried a new recipe last night, her Asian style, secret recipe beef. No idea what was in it, if that's the real name or just something she made up, but that may have been the best steak I've ever had in my life." He patted his stomach fondly, happy from the memory of his dinner.

"Nice. Sam'll have to see if she can pry it from your wife," I said, only half my attention on the conversation. Though I knew what I was about to do wasn't bad per se, my heart raced and I felt like I was going behind Sam's back.

"She can try, but I'm guessing she'll get no joy. Woman seems to think she's going to bottle and sell it." He inclined his head inside. "Sam's out on patrol right now, you want me to radio her?"

I already knew she was out, having discreetly enquired as to her schedule today. It wasn't Sam I needed to see.

What I was about to do, I didn't want her to know about.

"Actually, Brad, I'm hoping you might be able to help me out with something."

36

SULLY

B rad looked at me curiously.

"Sure thing, Sully. You want to go inside?" he asked.

I nodded and followed him into the reception area. Lana, a blonde with a neat updo, smiled at me over her glasses as she tapped into a computer with brightly painted nails.

"Hey, Sul," she greeted me.

"Lana," I nodded at her, careful not to ask how she was. Lana loved to talk and needed only the slightest encouragement before torturing her victim with an intricate blow-by-blow of her day, which usually began with a description of her latest ailment. As I didn't want to run the risk of Sam getting back while I was still here, I averted my eyes and walked quickly past her station. Even without looking at her directly, I could sense her shoulders slump in disappointment and knew I had made a quick escape.

Brad walked over to a drinks station and grabbed a mug. "Coffee?" he asked, but I shook my head, keen to get moving. He must have sensed this as he set the mug down and moved into his office. I followed him inside.

I'd been here a few times before, though always while Sam was around. Usually, we'd shoot the breeze while I waited for her to finish her shift. Today was different, however, and I found myself taking in the room with new eyes. Framed photographs lined every surface. There was Brad with his missus and their five kids, ranging from toddler to surly teenager. And another of their wedding day. Then one of each kid as they went through kindergarten through to middle school where the oldest ones now were. Brad was quite the family man, it seemed. I wasn't sure if that bode well for me.

"Brad, this is a bit of a delicate matter, so I would appreciate it if you wouldn't talk about this to anyone else, not even Sam," I began. What the hell, might as well go in guns blazing.

His eyes went a little wider, but other than that, he kept his face stoic, though I noticed he now clasped his hands on the desk in front of him. It was probably a position he took when dealing with the public, and it was very possible he didn't realize he had subtly shifted his stance with me. "Oh," he said. "How can I help?"

"Are you able to track a phone number for me?"

Whatever Brad had been steeling himself for, that wasn't it. His shoulders visibly relaxed.

"Do you know whose number it is?"

I had known this question was coming and had toyed with several possible answers. Had even considered telling the truth, but I knew that would open up a whole kettle of fish that would end badly for me.

"No," I replied as I shifted uncomfortably in my seat. The lie stuck in my throat, and it was all I could do not to clear it. "I need to know who messaged me from this number and if you pinpoint their location. I've been getting abusive messages from them, and I need to know if I should be taking them seriously."

"Alright." He slid a notebook to me. "Write down the phone number and I'll see what I can do."

I scrawled Emma's number onto his pad but didn't give it back to him. He studied me, a questioning expression on his face.

"Is there anything else?"

"I also found something and I want it examined."

Carefully, I took out the banana clip which I had placed into a plastic bag. I knew my fingerprints were already on it, but I was hopeful that by doing so I would preserve any other identifying information.

"I found this near... my ex-wife's place. There's blood on it, I want to know if it's hers," I replied. It took a few moments for the words to sink in. When they did, he couldn't hide his shock.

"I apologize if what I'm about to ask sounds indelicate, but, I was under the impression that your ex had passed away?"

I cringed inwardly. *Damn these small towns.* Somehow, I had thought I'd get a break, that Brad wouldn't know about Emma, but of course, I wasn't that lucky. "She has, but I still need to know about this."

His eyes suddenly widened. "You're suspecting foul play?"

I didn't know how I could answer his question without going into the whole sordid thing so I lied again, then waited for lightning to strike me down. "Yeah. But don't bring this up with Sam, please. It's a touchy subject between us."

"No kidding," Brad replied.

I had to hand it to him. He was taking this far better than I thought he would.

"Is it possible? Can you identify her using dried blood?"

Brad shrugged. "I have a friend who works in forensics. She was just telling me the other day that researchers for a new study have developed a way of determining a person's age range from blood samples left at a crime scene. The test works by measuring levels of an enzyme called alkaline phosphatase, which change in the body between childhood and adulthood. Other than that, the blood should be able to give an indication to sex and race, but I'm not sure it can identify her completely, however."

"Why not?" I asked.

"We'd have to compare the DNA profile we come up with what exists of your ex. We can only conclude it is her blood if the profiles match," he explained patiently.

"So, you'd need a pre-existing profile of my ex?"

Brad nodded. "Yes. We might be able to compare the findings with medical records, I'm assuming she had those?"

Memories of numerous hospital visits and treatments flashed up in my mind, more than I ever cared to remember. I tried to push the unwanted thoughts away.

"Yes."

"Go ahead and write down her name, date of birth and place of birth. I'll look into it."

I scribbled down the information and handed the notebook back to him.

"Thanks for doing this, Brad. I know I've put you in a difficult position."

Brad studied me silently, thoughts going back and forth in his head. Then he sighed.

"Yeah, but this sounds serious so I'll do it."

He took the bag with the clip inside and called up a form on his computer. Realizing he meant to get to it now, I pushed back my chair and stood up.

"Thank you," I said simply.

"I'll call you when the results come back."

I left quickly before he could reconsider.

37

SULLY

I drove home in a daze.

While I had succeeded in getting Brad's help, I now had the added concern that maybe he wouldn't keep his promise to me. Sam was his boss, after all. It was very possible that she would find out. My hands tightened on the wheel. *Dammit, Sully!* I should have thought this through, but what with last night's restlessness, coupled with the stress of the past few days... I wasn't firing on all cylinders. I tortured myself, going back and forth with my thoughts until I pulled up outside the ranch. Grabbing the items I had purchased for Pixie, I barely made it to the door before it was thrown open by Chase, looking wild and upset.

"You didn't call us back!" Chase cried.

I was momentarily thrown before I remembered Gideon's missed call.

"I was in the middle of something. What's going on?" Even as I said the words, I noticed that the room was heavy with tension. Gideon sat by Zeb, the two looking like they'd just had a serious discussion. A ways away, Pixie lay on a mat. She seemed to be resting, but her eyes kept searching for Gideon, reassured by his presence. Bandit kept darting towards me, then Chase, not sure who to go to. I went inside, closing the door behind me and dumped the bags onto a table.

"I think we may have a problem," came my dad's voice. I was about to ask him what when the front door opened and in came Sam. Seeing us congregated there with our serious expressions, the smile of greeting froze on her face.

"Is something wrong?" she asked.

"The two of you need to take a seat," Zeb said seriously. Sam looked firstly at me, then the others, before coming to settle by my side. We sat on the sofa, waiting expectantly.

Moments later, we'd been given the whole story. I looked at my dad, trying to keep my face bland even as my stomach began to churn. "But how could she know that Chase was here?"

I felt Sam tense beside me and turned to her, surprised to find a guilty expression on her face.

"I think... that might be down to me," she said hesitantly.

Shocked, four faces turned to look at her.

"I'm sorry. I never thought she would come here in a million years." She turned to Chase, eyes pleading. "I'd have warned you if that was the case, Chase. You know I would."

"You called her?" Chase said in disbelief. "Why would you do that?" She didn't bother to hide the accusation from her voice.

"I knew you wouldn't like it, but I'm a sheriff. I have to uphold the law. Although she was terrible to you, you are still a minor and I am legally bound to inform your parent that you are safe. I only called to tell her that you were with us so she wouldn't worry. I was trying to protect us," Sam said, a touch desperately.

Though her words made sense, I was feeling betrayed, so I couldn't imagine how Chase was feeling right now.

"And you kept this from me?" I asked her. She looked at me, eyes pained.

"I didn't want to, but I also didn't want you to have to keep this from Chase. I thought it was better if it was on my shoulders. If you want to blame anyone, then you should blame me."

"Oh don't worry, I will!" Chase cried before storming off to her room. Bandit whined, running after her. Gideon and Zeb sat there, shocked, neither of them knowing what to do. Torn up inside, Sam made a move to follow Chase, but I stopped her.

"Don't. I'll go. You've done enough."

She flinched at my words, and though I felt a jerk for saying them, my mind was on Chase. I hurried after her, ignoring Sam, calling my name.

38

CHASE

Tears pricked at my eyes as I stormed into my room.

I let Bandit in, then slammed the door behind me, every cell in my body raging. I couldn't believe Sam had betrayed my trust like that. This whole time we'd been living together, and she had kept this from me. How could she do that? And now Mom was here to do God knows what. A chill ran through me as I realized that legally, she could take this to the courts if she wanted. If she were twisted enough, she could try to get me back.

I sat on the bed, the room swimming before me as images flashed up in my mind. Images of court cases and interviews and being dragged away from Bandit (she'd never allow me to keep him). And Sully, staring at my empty room.

A whimper sounded.

I thought it was Bandit before I realized it had come from me. Bandit jumped up, placing his paws on my knees, and tucked his head under my chin, trying to comfort me. I wrapped my arms around him and buried my face in his fur.

"No matter what happens Bandit, we'll never be separated, OK? We'll always be together."

He woofed into my armpit, which ordinarily would make me laugh, but today, I just felt like crying. A knock sounded on my door. Angrily, I grabbed a pillow and flung it at the door.

"Go away, Sam! I don't want to talk to you!" I cried.

But the door opened anyway. Sully stuck his face in the gap, concern marring his features. "It's me."

Seeing him, I sniffed and nodded, letting him know it was OK to enter. He came in, shutting the door behind him. Silently, he sat beside me on the bed. We stared straight ahead, neither of us knowing what to say.

"I didn't know, kiddo. Sam didn't tell me," he began.

"I figured. There's no way you would have kept this from me."

"Yeah," he replied dully, looking as shocked as I felt. "What did she want, your mom?"

I stared blankly ahead. "I don't know. Forgiveness? She said she was sorry."

"And did you... forgive her?" he asked tentatively.

My head spun around to him. "Of course not! I told her to go away! I don't want anything to do with her. There's no apology big enough in the world that will make me forget all the crap they put me through."

He nodded, accepting my answer. I wasn't sure, but I thought he looked relieved. "We need to think about what to do if she comes here," Sully began. "What do you want us to do?"

I blinked, startled. "Why would she come here?"

"She's already turned up in town, and it's not difficult to find out where we live. I'm sorry, Chase. I know it's hard, but you have to face up to the fact that she'll probably turn up on our doorstep at some point."

"She can say whatever she wants to, but there's no way I'm going back, that's all I know." I expected Sully to back me up on this, but he stayed silent. Another chill ran through me as a different, far more worrying thought took hold. "She can't *make* me go back... *can she?*"

Sully stared me dead in the eyes. "Let's not worry about maybes... We'll get Sam to look into the legalities and go from there."

He threw his arm over my shoulders and drew me close. I stared down at Bandit's face, even as my vision blurred over with tears.

39

CHASE

It was a while before I was able to leave my room.

I knew Sam wanted to talk to me, but I just couldn't face her. Sully must've said as much as she gave me a wide berth. Zeb came by a while ago with a tray of food for Bandit and I. He'd brought a bone for Bandit and a bowl of chili with some crusty bread (someone must have made an additional shopping trip since my bread was still lying out on the street). He looked like he wanted to say something to me, but then thought better of it. Patting my hand, he gave me the food and left. One thing I was learning about Zeb, he wasn't one for empty words. It was one of the things I loved most about him.

Hearing a sound outside, I looked out of the window to see Gideon and Pixie outside. He was rolling a ball by his feet. Pixie watched his every move but didn't chase after the ball. She sat on her haunches, looking like she wanted to pounce each time the ball rolled past her nose, but something stopped her. I was amazed to see how patient he was with her. He never badgered her or forced her to do anything. He just sat there, rolling and re-rolling that ball.

A few minutes later, I went outside to join them, Bandit by my side. Gideon looked up on our approach. Because of this, he missed catching the ball, and it flew past Pixie. Bandit ran after it, caught it in his mouth, then brought it back to Gideon. As soon as he got to him, however, Pixie growled at him.

"Bandit's our friend, Pixie. We don't growl at friends," Gideon told her patiently but firmly. It was like Pixie didn't understand him, however (which she probably didn't). The growling slid low down her throat until it turned into a fierce rumble. Bandit whined, trying to let her know he wasn't a threat, but that just seemed to egg her on as she went CRAZY. She started barking, dancing behind Gideon for safety.

"Shh... it's OK girl..." He called out, trying to calm her, but Pixie continued. Bandit whined again and backed behind me. Unable to calm her, Gideon shot Bandit a pleading look.

"Can you go back inside? I'm sorry, boy, but she is just too scared of you."

Bandit looked at me, asking for my command. I nodded apologetically. "It's only until she gets used to you. It won't be long, I'm sure."

Bandit woofed unhappily but started back inside. When he was a few yards from the house, I saw him toss a sad look over his shoulder, but he continued to go. He cut such a lonely figure, I felt awful for him. In the entire time we'd been together, we'd barely been separated, yet here I was, sending him away every time I decided to spend some time with Pixie.

As soon as he was out of sight, Pixie stopped barking and her breathing returned to normal. It really made no sense why she was so scared of him. Bandit was the gentlest dog in the world. "You think another dog attacked her before? One that reminds her of Bandit? Her reaction to him just isn't normal," I said.

"Maybe? I don't know, but she does only freak out when he's

here. It's probably best that we keep him away from her until she gets over whatever it is."

I nodded, agreeing as I lowered down to my knees. Sully had told me a while ago that when a dog is threatened, it helps to make yourself as physically small as possible. Pixie hadn't shown any animosity towards me, but I didn't want anything else to set her off, so I moved slowly, trying to be as dainty as possible.

Then something amazing happened.

Pixie came over and gave me an all over cautious sniff. Suddenly, without warning, she laid down next to me and put her head on my knee. Gideon's mouth fell open. I had to force myself not to laugh at his expression.

"She hasn't even done that to me yet," he said, unable to hide his annoyance. I know I shouldn't have, but I shot him a smug grin.

"Clearly, I've got the magic touch."

I lowered my hand to her head and started to pet her, cautious that she could decide she didn't like me again at any moment. But she just closed her eyes, enjoying the fuss. Gideon blinked at me.

"OK. I don't feel the least betrayed. Thanks, Pixie."

We both watched as she relaxed and started falling asleep. Gideon sat down beside me, still playing with the ball absently. We stared out at the field, watching trees sway in the breeze.

"Sam's feeling awful," he began. "She wants to apologize to you."

I'd had some time to deal with my anger now, which wasn't the red hot burn it had been earlier. Now there was just a dullness. "I know. I'll talk to her later."

He nodded. We sat there quietly, when we heard the front door slam and a car roar away, burning rubber, leaving a cloud of dust in its wake. It was Sam's truck.

"I'm guessing they must've had words," Gideon said.

I nodded, feeling torn. On the one hand, I was glad Sully had spoken to her. On the other, Sam had meant well, and I really liked her. I liked how they were together.

I wasn't to know that things would only get worse from here on in.

40

CHASE

Seems none of us slept great last night.

Dark shadows ringed Sully and Sam's eyes. I knew mine hadn't fared much better. Their body language wasn't as easy as it usually was either. They kept avoiding each other, dancing around each other in the kitchen as they got their breakfast ready. I fed Bandit, but even he didn't seem interested in his food, pushing it around the plate with his nose. Poor guy really wasn't happy with the way Pixie was with him. We'd talked about it last night. I'd told him that it wasn't anything he had done, but he didn't believe me. He genuinely believed the dog had something against him.

Who'd have thought Bandit would be so sensitive? I guess he'd never experienced being unliked before. Even back in the lab where he escaped from, they had celebrated his cleverness, so he wasn't tortured like the rest of the dogs were. But Bandit heard their cries, watched them trembling in their cages. Though he himself hadn't been hurt, he had hurt for them, so whatever Pixie had gone through, Bandit would get it. Of all dogs, he would understand. I told him that when she finally was able to be calm in his presence, he should just tell her all that. He seemed happier after our talk now that we had a plan.

Sam was in civilian clothes this morning, which meant she wasn't working today. She stood by the toaster, waiting for her toast to be done, but I saw how she purposely didn't look my way — giving me the space I had asked for yesterday. I felt like a heel suddenly, for causing all the tension around the place, so I poured a glass of juice and looked at her.

"You want some OJ?" I asked. She looked up at me, surprised, then her eyes softened gratefully.

"Yeah. That'd be great, thanks, Chase."

I poured her a glass, handing it to her and suddenly we were friends again. I knew I could have done a whole big spiel, but truth was, I'd missed talking to her, and avoiding her was both awkward and impractical. The toast finally popped up from the toaster. She took two of the slices, put them on a plate and offered them to me. I took the plate and dumped a great glob of peanut butter onto it when there came a knock on the front door. Immediately Bandit started whining and pawing at me. We'd left his iPad in my room so I couldn't figure out what he wanted. Moments later, Gideon came inside, a sick look on his face.

"Chase... your mom's at the door."

And just like that, the relief I was feeling was ripped out of me.

41

CHASE

"What do you want me to tell her?" asked Gideon.

When the rushing sound faded from my ears, I looked at Sully, speechless. His brow had creased into a worried line, but his expression was resolute.

"I guess she's not going away, so we'll have to deal with this sometime. Might as well be now." He looked at me as he spoke, waiting for my response. Despite his words, if I disagreed and said I wasn't ready, I knew he would have told her to go away, but seeing Sam's guilty expression, I knew my small family couldn't keep going through this every day, so I steeled myself.

"It's fine. Let her in."

Moments later, we were all in the living room, watching as my mom came in. She'd changed her clothes since yesterday and was now wearing a yellow skirt, white t-shirt and flip-flops that showed the chipped blue polish on her toes. Despite that, and the stain on her shirt, she looked more presentable than she'd been throughout my life, when her outfits usually consisted of the skimpy leopard-print mini-skirts Tubs liked her to wear.

I didn't know what to think. This mom clashed so much with

the one I remembered. Even her hair was clean, as if she were truly making an effort. For some reason, this made me super uncomfortable. I would actually have preferred it if she looked the way I expected her to.

Across the room, Sully stared at her. He had yet to speak, but I could see he was thinking the same things I was. Having heard all the stories about what she was really like, I'll bet he was wondering how that monster could be hiding under such a boring appearance.

Mom tossed a quick look around the room, giving them all a timid smile before she focused her attention on me. I watched the corners of her mouth turn up even more as she took a hesitant step towards me.

"Chase..." Her voice cracked, and she seemed to struggle for words. She reached out a hand towards me, but I took a step back. It wasn't even conscious. I just didn't understand what she was doing here, and being so close to her physically was filling me with all kinds of unpleasant emotions. Picking up on my feelings, Sully moved to stand in front of me. He was being protective. Bandit must have picked up on our vibes too as he went to join his side.

"I'm Sully. Chase has been living with me for these past six months."

Mom's hands fidgeted by her side. I think she was debating whether to offer it to Sully to shake, but she must have decided against it. They stayed clenched down by her side.

"I'm Tracey. Tracey Blueman. Thanks for looking after Chase for me."

Sully didn't reply, not knowing what to say. An awkward silence blanketed the room until Zeb wheeled forward, offering his hand.

"I'm Sully's father, Zebediah. It's good to meet you, would you like a drink?" He was being purposely pleasant, like this was a normal visit from a friend, popping in from out of town.

"Have you got soda? Something sweet?"

"Yeah, we have it." This was from Gideon. He was staring at her with eyes that were hard with hate, unable to hide his loathing for this woman. Seeing him come to my defense like that filled my heart with love. Gideon didn't always show what he was really feeling, so this was a bit of a surprise. Zeb frowned at Gideon, shaking his head reproachfully.

"Gideon," he said. "That's not how we treat guests."

"Well, she hasn't exactly been invited, has she? Let's not pretend anyone wants her here."

"Gideon!" Zeb snapped sharply. His angry tone shocked me. I had never heard Zeb reprimand anyone before.

"I don't wanna cause any trouble," Mom said. "He's right. You must be hella surprised, but I swear I don't mean any harm. I just wanted to see my little girl."

"Why don't we sit down in the living room. There's a lot to catch up on. Come on through," said Sam, surprising everyone. No one moved. Sam sighed. "Look, clearly there is a lot to talk about, it's silly for us all to stand here. Go inside and sit."

Realizing no one would move before I did, I nodded and let Sully lead the way. I sat on the couch, Sully and Gideon flanking my side as Bandit sat in front of my feet. I was in a triangle of protection, yet despite being surrounded on all sides, I was still feeling super vulnerable and this made me mad. She couldn't do anything to hurt me now. She was just one person and Tubs wasn't anywhere in sight. So why was I feeling so scared? Why was there a chill in the pit of my stomach?

Sam pulled out a chair and Mom perched on it. She sat opposite me, clasping her hands in her lap. "You're Sam?" Mom asked. "You're the one who called?"

Sam nodded. "It wasn't my intention that you come here like

this. I only called you, woman-to-woman, to let you know your child was safe with us. I had no idea you would come here like this. I really wish you had phoned first and given us a heads up."

A flush crept up across Mom's face. "I was afraid none of you would be here if I called first."

"Well, we are," said Sully. "So what is it that you want exactly? What's your purpose for turning up like this?" Now Zeb turned his frown on Sully, but Sully just ignored him. "You may be her legal parent but you are no longer her guardian."

It was impossible to miss the challenge in his voice. He was daring my mom to say something different.

"I only want to spend time with her. I wanted to see her face myself is all, not just take a stranger's word for it."

After she spoke, the relief from Sully was palpable. I myself felt the tension leave my shoulders and Bandit relaxed against my legs. She wasn't here to drag me back home. There would be no court case. Zeb smiled.

"Well, let's get Tracey a drink and we can catch her up on the last year or so of Chase's life."

CHASE

After we had gotten over the shock of my mom's appearance, we spoke for a while, letting her know how Sully, Bandit, and I had first met. Of course, we left out any reference to Bandit's super intelligence, and we changed Forbes' men to criminals, but we kept most of the story the same.

Mom had listened to it all without saying a word, letting out just the occasional gasp or so. I left out our whole confrontation with Forbes and anything about Platinum Industries and ended simply by saying that Sam and Sully had met and now we all lived together. Mom had asked a few questions here and there, like where did Gideon come in? But that was about it. Occasionally I caught her staring at Bandit but she'd never been very keen on animals so I figured she was just keeping a wary eye out on him.

Once Sully and the others realized that she really was just here to talk, they relaxed and left us alone. We now sat on the porch while Bandit snored softly by my feet. There were things I wanted to say but hadn't yet broached. I stared out into the distant green horizon, letting the sounds I loved wash over me. When I finally worked up the nerve, I voiced the question I'd been meaning to ask since her arrival here.

"Where's Tubs?" I asked, deliberately keeping my voice as emotionless as possible.

"Home. He... he doesn't know I'm here," she replied.

"He doesn't?"

"No. I didn't say where I was going, he would only have stopped me. He hasn't gotten over all the money you took."

I looked at her and saw the way her hands tightened in her lap and lines creased her forehead. She was worried, thinking of the reception she might receive when she finally went home.

"If he doesn't know you're here, where does he think you are?"

"I didn't tell him. I left a note and said I was going out of town but would call when I could." A normal person might think she was being respectful to my wishes to stay here anonymously, but I knew she was too scared to tell him the truth — that she was coming to find me. Although Tubs had never liked me, I think he liked having power over me, liked having his own personal punch-bag, but after I had taken off, the only one left for him to rule was my mom, so her disappearing like this? He must be furious.

We sat there silently for a while, neither of us saying anything. My mind was a mess of emotions and I just didn't know what to think. One thing struck me about her being here, though — I had never seen her so calm. Then again, I had never seen her without Tubs all these years. He had always been by her side or behind her, towering over her like an immovable mountain. Without him, she seemed almost happier. It made me wonder for the millionth time why she didn't just leave him, but I wasn't going to say anything about that. I didn't want her to think that I cared.

"You really ate food from the trash?" She frowned, unable to comprehend it all.

I nodded and shrugged. "The first weeks were the hardest. It takes a while before you get used to sleeping on hard ground and the first few times you look for food in a dumpster, the smells make you vomit, but after a while, the hunger takes over everything else so you don't even smell the rottenness or taste it anymore."

She looked down at the ground at my words. "It's good you have these people now, they seem like good folk."

"They're the best," I said.

She looked down at Bandit. "And you have a dog too. You've always wanted a pet."

At the word pet, Bandit pricked his ears towards her even as he kept his eyes closed, snoozing. "Yeah, he's much more than a pet though. He's my best friend and family."

"Well," she said. "He's just an animal, don't go humanizing him."

It was on the tip of my tongue to correct her but I knew there wasn't anything I could say that wouldn't reveal Bandit's secret so I bit down on my tongue and refrained from replying.

We'd been out there on the porch for a while before I was suddenly aware of noises coming from inside the ranch. The others were getting ready to go out. Sully suddenly popped his head around the door.

"We're going into town. You wanna come with us or stay talking with your mom?" Though it was a question, Sully didn't look too comfortable asking it. I was pretty sure Sam had put him up to it. My mom shot me a hopeful look, but I really didn't want to be left alone with her. Despite how much nicer she seemed suddenly, there was a wall around my heart and it wasn't coming down anytime soon. I jumped up to my feet.

"I'm coming with. We're done here."

Sully nodded, looking relieved. Mom got to her feet awkwardly, knowing that she was being dismissed.

"I'm only here a few days. Can I come back to see you?" This, she directed at me. I couldn't answer. My throat constricted, and it felt dry and uncomfortable. They both waited for an answer, but all I could manage was a shrug. She smiled, grateful for the crumb I had given her.

"Thanks, Chase." She turned to Sully next. "You too. For all you've done for her."

As Sully escorted her to the door, I didn't move. I stood there watching until she disappeared out of sight.

43

CHASE

A little while later, Sully, Sam, Bandit, and I were at the Four Seasons Mall. It was an hour out of town, and we generally only came here on special occasions, when we couldn't pick up what we wanted in our local stores. Sam and I liked to do our clothes shopping here as there was so much more variety. Also bonus, there was a Starbucks! I guess this trip was her way of apologizing to me because it certainly hadn't been planned.

On the drive here, Sam had tried to make basic chitchat, and I had responded, not because I was particularly interested in what she had to say but because I wanted her to know that I wasn't mad at her anymore. I had gotten over the initial shock of seeing my mom, and though we'd only spoken a little on the porch, some of my bitterness had faded. I was relieved to see that she and Sully also seemed to have fixed whatever issue had been going on between them, or at least they were pretending to in front of me. They seemed almost normal. I say seemed because it was all a little forced.

The bright colors and sounds of the mall were blinding. I couldn't get used to the sudden noise as chatter and music exploded in my ears. Although I had come from New York, which was so much louder with its sirens and traffic, Montpelier was only a small town with just 10 or so shops on its high street. Noise to me nowadays was an owl hooting outside my window at night.

We made a beeline for the pet store, which was around ten times bigger than the one back home. We always came here first, to allow Bandit to choose a toy for himself. It was here where he had picked up his Frumpy Rabbit. Sully went to the same section where we had found Bandit's though all the rabbits were sold out, there were only cats and fish left. He picked up a cat to show Bandit.

"This is to replace the one Pixie destroyed. And let's get her a fish so she can have one of her own," he said to him. He probably expected Bandit to agree, but he only whined instead. We grabbed basic provisions for the dogs before the three of us went into a J. C. Penney. Fall was approaching and with it, the air had become distinctively cooler. I needed a few sweaters, so I grabbed some that were on sale and paid for them with my allowance. Sully and Sam had gone off to get him a new phone since his old one was still not working. It was hugely frustrating for him, as he was desperate to show us that phone message.

When I was done, I finally found them wandering around in the baby section. Holding onto a baby grow, Sam's eyes had misted over and she was smiling at Sully. The weariness he had been wearing for days left and he too seemed suddenly wistful. And the thought hit me like a punch in the gut.

They wanted a baby.

I felt shaken to the core. Why had I never considered this before? Now that they were getting married, a baby was obviously in their future. For some reason, the thought filled me with dread. I was happy with the way things were, I didn't need a screaming baby in the picture, and I was ashamed to admit that I was afraid. If they had their own child, would they still want me? Especially now my mom had turned up.

I must have moved and caught Sam's attention because her eyes suddenly drifted over to me. She set down the baby growth and smiled at me. "Hey Chase, you done?"

"Yeah," I said. "What're you guys looking at?"

"Nothing," Sully said. "Just looking."

He tried not to make a thing of it, but I could see he was caught out. "I'm parched, let's go get a Frappuccino."

Ordinarily, I would have whooped at the thought of that sweet and creamy coffee goodness.

As it was, I silently followed them as I felt like my whole world was falling down.

44

SULLY

We came back from the shopping trip with Sam happy, feeling that she had mended some of her issues with Chase, but I still had residual issues I needed to face. The visit from Chase's mom had left me on an uneven keel that even now, hours later, I was still reeling from.

Alone in our bedroom, I could hear Sam and the others cooking in the kitchen. They had only just started, but Sam was determined to make her infamous lasagna tonight. It was a favorite of all of ours; she had gotten it from a celebrity chef's recipe book. From start to finish, the entire process took three-and-a-half hours, but it was well worth it. I excused myself from kitchen duty, but the others didn't seem to mind, knowing I had things on my mind.

I shut the door. My laptop sat as it always did on a small desk by the window with a view looking out across the fields of green. I pulled the chair away from the desk, sat down, and turned on the laptop. Since my visit to the deputy's office, I had tried my best to not think about the messages I had received from beyond the grave. Though I had done a pretty good job not speaking about it to anyone, every night when my head hit that pillow and I closed my eyes, the words would appear one-by-one searing into my eyelids, followed by an image of that hair clip.

I was back to not sleeping again.

More than anything, I wished I could go for a night run, but I knew Sam would know what was bothering me if I did, and I couldn't stomach another fight with her. I'd been wanting some time when I could collate my thoughts, but now that I was finally alone, I found they were a mess.

Sighing, I activated Google. Almost without my meaning to, I typed in "possible reasons for a disturbed grave". I wasn't expecting to find much, but several hits came up. There was a report from the UK of badgers, digging around a cemetery who accidentally unearthed human remains. I guess an animal could have dislodged dirt on Emma's grave, like Sam had mentioned, but that wouldn't explain the clip or the text. Other reports talked of grave robbing and superstitious beliefs. Another mentioned the retrieval of mementos buried with the body. Frankly, the longer I read, the more the possibilities grew even more far-fetched. I probably should have stopped when a related article of people seemingly coming back from the dead was suggested to me, but I was too far gone and had to see this thing through. Of course, I knew how crazy that sounded, but I was living with a super intelligent dog so I was willing to suspend some disbelief.

I found some fifty or so cases of people who were declared dead only to spring back to life — sometimes in their own graves, other times in the morgue — the stories were unbelievable but apparently true. I found myself rereading one account in particular, of a woman who had died of cancer only to come back to life inside her coffin after being buried. Passer-bys had heard her screams, but by the time she was rescued, she had died of suffocation. Every case had a similar fact, one that I couldn't hide away from — the survivors were all recently declared dead. Unsurprisingly, I could not find stories of people waking up from the dead a year later.

I could see in Sam's eyes, in the way that she had become so gentle with me of late, that she was treating me with kid gloves and it infuriated me. I wasn't going insane, and I was determined to prove it. For the millionth time, I glanced at my new phone, hoping for a missed call or message from Brad — who I'd given my new number to almost the second that I'd activated the phone — but the screen stayed stubbornly blank. I carried on with my research, finding more and more elaborate tales of ordinary people coming back from the dead.

I had no idea how long I had been reading. My mind was agog with facts and possibilities, but I hadn't come up with any concrete evidence that would help explain my situation. I was still researching when there came a knock on the door, followed by Sam's appearance. Seeing that I was hunched over the computer, Sam looked surprised.

"I thought you were napping?"

Quickly, I exited Google and closed the laptop. "No, just needed some alone time. Wanted to process today is all."

She looked over my shoulder at the laptop. "What have you been up to?"

I ran my hand through my hair, trying to keep as natural as possible. "Nothing much, just seeing what I could find out about Chase's mom."

Sam looked surprised. "You know I ran a check on her before I called, right? But there was nothing of interest, nothing that we didn't already know."

"I figured as much still, no harm in trying."

I stood up and tucked the chair back under the desk, then

made my way over to her, sniffing the air appreciatively. "Thanks for cooking tonight."

"Sure. Dinner is ready."

"Okay," I agreed and went past her to the kitchen, relieved that she wasn't going to plague me with many more questions.

45

SAM

Sam watched Sully walk down the hall, but she didn't follow him.

Despite how the air smelled so tantalizingly of her food, Sam found herself without much appetite and wasn't in any hurry to eat. She waited until he disappeared around a corner before going into the bedroom.

When Sam had appeared at the door, she'd seen how quickly Sully had snapped the laptop shut. She recognized that guilty expression on his face; it was the same one her perps wore whenever she'd catch them in an embarrassing act. All Sam wanted now was to see what Sully had been up to for the past few hours.

She opened his laptop and looked through the recent hits. Seeing the hundreds of searches he had made in the past few hours, Sam felt a mixture of fear and anger. They had talked about this. She thought he was over the Emma-texting-from-the-grave-scenario, but clearly, he had been lying to her.

Feeling duped but knowing now wasn't the time to bring this up, Sam went to the kitchen where she sat down at her place at the table. She tried her best to seem normal, especially for Chase's sake — God knows the girl had been through enough today — but the only way she could get through the meal without exploding was by not looking at Sully. She felt so betrayed, so hurt, she could not look him in the face.

Sully, for his part, didn't notice or was dealing with unresolved issues of his own. He made appreciative sounds over his food but didn't say much otherwise. In fact, they were all quieter than usual.

Looking at Sully over the top of her glass of water, Sam steeled herself for what was to come.

Tonight, Sam thought.

Tonight she would resolve this once and for all.

46

SULLY

Dinner went down like a pile of rocks.

Despite this being a favorite meal, the pasta clung to my throat, and I found it difficult to swallow. Even the spicy tomato sauce that usually had my tastebuds doing a dance seemed overly sweet tonight, giving it a sickly taste. As Sam had spent three hours in the kitchen making this, I did my best for her benefit, but I was pretty sure she could see through my act. Even Chase, who was usually able to eat anything, spent most of the meal pushing the food around her plate.

To think it was only three days ago when everything was fine.

If Zeb noticed our moods, he didn't show it, keeping up a decent level of conversation. He even mentioned Chase's mom. While he didn't go as far as to say she seemed nice, he managed to convey that he didn't find her a monster either. Gideon, however, could not be swayed. He didn't like her and made no qualms about it. He didn't believe people could change, and there was nothing any of us could say that would make him think differently.

Picking up on our vibes, Bandit had spent the entire meal

under the dining table running between each of us, pressing his nose into our hands. He was doing the rounds to check on us, making sure we were all okay. Poor thing was working overtime. Pixie, who had still not warmed to him, stayed in the den while we ate. Gideon wasn't happy with this arrangement as he wanted Pixie with us at all times, but I explained that it was better to let her have some space so she could come to us of her own accord.

I took a sip of my water and noticed that Sam was watching me. When I caught her eyes, however, she looked away from me. I knew from experience this wasn't a good sign. Something was up and I didn't think it was the visit we had had from Chase's mom.

When the meal was finally, blessedly over, I went to do the dishes as was normal whenever Sam cooked, however, tonight she came up beside me as I was setting the dishes in the sink.

"Hey, you think we could chat about something?" It wasn't really a question, and her tone implied that.

"Sure," I said. I tapped Gideon on the shoulder. "Can you guys finish up here?"

Gideon shot me a long-suffering look. "Oh, I see what's going on here. Eat and run. That's nice."

I gave him a distracted smile. "You know me." But my eyes were already following Sam, who was heading into our bedroom. I went after her, dragging my feet a little. A sixth sense told me I was about to get a scalding and I wasn't looking forward to it.

A few seconds later, I joined her in the room. "What's up?" I asked.

"Can you close the door behind you?" she replied.

I did as requested and went to join her on the bed where she was sitting. She turned to me, eyes searching my face.

"Sully, I'm not sure how else to say this so I'm just going to come out and say it. I need you to be silent and just listen to me, okay?"

Baffled by what was happening, I nodded.

"I know you've been keeping things from me. Ever since the day you visited Emma's grave, you have not been the same. Now, I know you said you received a text message from her phone but there isn't any proof of that, however, despite how you were behaving I was willing to let things lie, but you're still fixated on this thing and I think it's a really big problem."

I was actually relieved she was bringing this up. The two of us had been tiptoeing around each other for days now and the pressure had been mounting. Now at least we could talk about this.

"I didn't mean to keep things from you, but I know how crazy it sounds. I knew you didn't believe me. I was just trying to find some proof that I could show you, or at least an explanation for what might have happened."

She didn't answer, moving instead to her bag, which hung on a hook on the wall. She took something out of it, a sheet of paper.

"The thing is, I know that's not all you did. You went behind my back and asked my deputy for help."

"Well, he wasn't supposed to tell you that." I couldn't help feeling angered by Brad's betrayal. So this was why he hadn't called back, the little snitch.

"He didn't. He covered for you, but I figured things out when Lana mentioned you had dropped by."

Of course, Lana and her big mouth. I should have known.

"What were you thinking Sully, dragging them into your madness?"

My eyes hardened. "So you finally admit you don't believe me?"

She threw up her hands, exasperated. "How am I supposed to believe you, do you know how this sounds? You passed out on her grave, Sully! She's dead! How can you keep ignoring this fact? Have you any idea how scared Chase was when she found you?"

"You don't get to ask me that. I know better than anyone how Chase feels."

"That's crap and you know it. You've been so fixated on that supposed text you've barely been there for her at all."

"What about that clip then? That's something, but you keep conveniently ignoring that!" I didn't want to sound like a jerk, but she was getting me riled up something fierce.

She laid the piece of paper she had fished out of her bag onto the bed. The logo across the header announced it as a forensics lab in Baltimore. Brad's friend must have come good after all. I raked my eyes over the page, but the results were as good as gobbledygook. It made no sense at all.

"What does it say?"

"It says that the blood is inconclusive as it is more than two days old," Sam replied. "For the study Brad mentioned to work, the blood needs to be fresh. What it did reveal is that the owner of the blood was a woman with an 'O' blood type."

"That was Emma's blood type!" I said excitedly, more loudly than I had intended to.

"So does something like forty-seven percent of the world, Sully. It's the most common blood-type there is," she answered warily.

"You're going to find fault with whatever I say, aren't you?" I shot at her at my wit's end. "Fine, the clip is inconclusive. I don't know how many times I have to explain it to you, but that text was real. The message was real. I actually think the bigger problem is how you won't believe me."

Sam opened her mouth to argue, then must have thought better of it as she stayed quiet. Suddenly her eyes teared up, and she looked at me, broken.

"The problem isn't whether the text is real. The problem is you're still hung up over your dead wife and you are not ready to marry me."

I scowled, wondering where she was getting this from. ""No, that's not what's happening here."

She nodded fiercely. "Yes, it is. You think it's a coincidence that this all started after we decided to get married? We were fine, then you proposed, and I said yes. All this started happening immediately after."

"It started happening because we went back so I could tell my friends of our good news. I went back to make peace with the dead, as you damn well know. If anything, this should prove how much I love you, how ready I am to get married."

She shook her head at me sadly. "I really think you believe that."

"I do," I said emphatically.

"Then you need to do something for me. You need to see someone."

"You mean, like a shrink?" I asked, incredulous. She nodded. "No way am I seeing some quack."

Sam jumped onto her feet, suddenly furious. "Then you obviously don't care about this as much as you say you do."

With that, she stormed out of the room, slamming the door behind her.

47

CHASE

I had just finished the dishes and was going to my room when I saw Sam heading out of their bedroom and into the back porch. She sat on the swing, looking lost and alone, while Sully sat on the edge of the bed, not faring much better.

I'd been meaning to talk to him all day, but there never seemed to be a chance. My head was a whirlwind of emotions and I didn't know what to do with my mom. I really needed Sully's help, so I was relieved to find him finally alone. I went up to him and knocked on the door.

"Sul?" I said.

He looked up at me but didn't say anything, so I continued. "I kind of need to talk to you." But Sully wasn't really looking at me. He stared past me, his eyes dazed.

"Sully?" I asked again.

"Yeah," he answered distracted. "What did you want to talk about?"

Although he had asked me the question, I could see his heart and attention wasn't in it. Whatever was going on between him and Sam had taken everything he had. There was no point talking to him now, that much was obvious, so I just shrugged. "You know what? It can wait."

He finally looked at me. "You sure?" He couldn't hide the hopefulness in his voice. Knowing he couldn't wait to get rid of me, I felt an insecure pang in my chest.

"Yeah. I'll find you later," I said, already backing away. Sully didn't even respond, thoughts already somewhere else.

I went out to the front yard and found myself walking towards the vegetable plot. Tending to it had become one of my responsibilities since Gideon now worked at Warrey's most of the time. Originally Zeb's pride and joy, he now relied on us to look after the upkeep as he couldn't do it easily from his wheelchair. We had planted some cool weather loving veggies a little while back, so now our patch was thriving with kale, spinach, peas, and beets. Seeing some weeds sprouting up between the radishes, I kneeled down onto the grass and absently began to pluck them. I was so focused on the task at hand, I didn't hear the whir of Zeb's wheelchair until he was almost upon me.

"I was just coming out here to check on the plot myself. How is it looking?"

"Good. I'm getting rid of the few weeds that seemed to have grown overnight."

He wheeled to a stop opposite me. "That's the thing with weeds, leave them alone for just a second and they grow back, bigger and stronger than ever. It's the way with most unwanted things, unfortunately. That is why it is best to cull them before the unwanted effect takes root."

I stopped to look at him, wondering if he had a second meaning, but I couldn't tell by his face.

"How are you coping anyway, Chase? Lots going on today."

I nodded, not trusting myself to speak straight away. With horror, I found that my eyes were tearing up, and I had no idea why. I focused on the weeds as if there were suddenly something of the utmost importance tangled inside them. I took a breath, then when I spoke again, I was relieved to find my voice held steady.

"I don't know how to feel. I've been so angry with my mom, you know? But then she turns up, looking so unthreatening, so pathetic that I almost feel sorry for her, which then makes me furious! I mean, how can I feel sorry for her after all the things she's done? The things she allowed Tubs to do?"

I fell silent then, done with my enraged outburst. Zeb surprised me by taking it all in his stride. "You feel sorry for her precisely because she is a pathetic person. She has been with an abusive drunk for years, letting him berate not only you but her. All that time spent with him would have eroded any confidence that she had. She is only a husk of a person now, but you, you are kind and strong and loving, despite what she has done to you. You should feel proud of yourself for being that way, Chase. You know better even when your own mother doesn't. That takes real character."

I blinked back my tears, touched by his words.

"You shouldn't worry about how you are feeling. It is what it is. You are going through what you need to in order to get to the other side. The only thing you need to remember is that you are not alone. We are all here for you. Got that?" he grinned, suddenly.

I smiled, unable to be miserable any longer.

"There you go, there's that smile. Gideon thinks you're pretty when you smile, did you know that?"

"What?" I managed to blurt out ungraciously.

"It's true, he told me," Zeb said. Smiling wickedly, he winked at me then headed back into the ranch, leaving me wondering at what he meant by that last comment.

48

___

BANDIT

No matter where he went, the air was filled with tension.

Dinner was usually the happiest time for Bandit, but tonight he had exhausted himself from constantly having to check up on everyone. Though nobody said anything, Bandit knew they were all desperately unhappy. He could smell their misery like it was a dirty pair of Gideon's socks.

Chase had been very quiet since the visit from her mother. She had already explained about her past, so Bandit knew Chase was very confused over her mother's appearance. Wanting to cheer her up, Bandit went to his bed and fetched Frumpy Rabbit, meaning to give it to Chase to cuddle. Maybe if she had Frumpy, she wouldn't be so sad. He had it in his mouth when he suddenly smelled Pixie's undeniable scent behind him. He spun around to find the other dog standing in the doorway. She didn't do anything, just stared at him in that unnerving way of hers. Bandit sniffed the air once again, not liking her smell. He didn't know what it was that disturbed him, but something about it wasn't right. He wished that the others would believe him, even though Bandit wasn't able to explain it himself.

He whined at the other dog now hoping that she would speak to him. Back where he was from, he was always able to get along with the other dogs. They knew he was special, and though he hardly ever saw them, on the odd occasion when he did, they would clamor around him, wanting his favor, so Pixie's dislike of him was extreme. The other dog kept staring at him eerily. She didn't blink or move until Bandit found himself suddenly afraid. If she didn't move away from the doorway, he was trapped in this room.

He whined, wagging his tail at her in a show of friendship. He was hoping the gesture would be echoed, but Pixie's tail stayed frozen like the rest of her. Suddenly there came a low growl in her throat. Pixie flattened her ears on top of her head and bared her teeth at him. She took one step towards him into the room.

Bandit stopped wagging his tail. He stood frozen, worried, and concerned, as Pixie advanced, snarling and growling threateningly. Bandit dropped his toy and braced himself. Everything about her screamed danger. Though he hadn't done anything to cause her to become so angry, Bandit knew that Pixie was seconds away from attacking him.

The other dog advanced, getting closer and closer, until she was within leaping distance of Bandit. Feeling suddenly territorial, Bandit bared his own teeth in warning. Though he didn't like to fight, it didn't mean he wouldn't protect his home if push came to shove. This was his special space that he shared with Chase, and Pixie had to learn that she couldn't bully him away from it.

Like he had fired a starter's pistol, Pixie flew towards Bandit, snapping her jaws at his face. Bandit spun so that her jaws narrowly missed him, chewing only on air. He twisted his body, throwing it at her using the full weight of himself to knock her off balance. She fell down, but sprung back onto her paws almost immediately. Circling him, Pixie tried to find a vulnerable spot.

Sensing her tactic, Bandit spun around, but he was slower

than the smaller dog. Pixie sank her teeth into his rump, causing pain to explode in his body. Howling with rage, and driven only by the animal instinct to survive, Bandit bit her on the only place he could reach — her neck. Pixie screamed as Bandit held on to her neck. She let go of his rump, unable to focus on her own attack now that she was hurting.

Through the commotion, Bandit suddenly heard Chase's voice. She had arrived in the doorway, eyes wide with horror at the sight before her. Bandit was thrilled! Now Pixie would learn that she couldn't attack him without consequence. Chase ran into the room, but instead of dragging Pixie away as he expected, she pulled *him* off the other dog!

"Bandit, NO! What are you doing?" she yelled at him.

Bandit was so shocked his jaws loosened around Pixie and he backed away. No one had ever yelled at him before, especially not Chase. As soon as she had appeared, Pixie stopped fighting and now she curled into a ball and whimpered pathetically. Bandit was stunned by the change in her. A minute ago she had been willing to tear him to pieces, but in one breath she had changed into this cowering, pitiful pup. Bandit wished he had his iPad so he could explain, but he had left it outside in the living room. He moved to Chase now, but she waved him away angrily.

"No, boy! Bad dog! I can't believe you would fight Pixie! She's so much smaller than you. You should know better!"

Bandit whined, desperate to explain himself, but Chase was furious with him. "No! I don't want to hear it. Get out! I don't want you in here!"

Bandit was heartbroken. But they were best friends. How could she tell him to go? Couldn't she see that Pixie was pretending? Even now, as Chase fussed over the other dog, Bandit could see Pixie throwing evil looks his way when Chase wasn't watching. Bandit was terrified of leaving Chase alone with her. What if

Pixie hurt Chase while Bandit wasn't here? He barked, trying to warn Chase of this, but she misunderstood his intention.

"Are you arguing with me? Get out, Bandit, I mean it! You are not sleeping here tonight!"

With that, Chase slammed the door in Bandit's face. The last thing he saw was Chase comforting Pixie in her arms, like she usually fussed him.

Desperately unhappy, Bandit whined at the closed door, hoping Chase would open it again. She must have heard him, however, as she shouted through it. "Go away, Bandit! I mean it! You don't fight other dogs, especially ones smaller than you!"

Full of despair, Bandit turned around and slunk away to spend his first night without Chase.

Unfortunately, it would not be his last.

49

BANDIT

It had been a terrible night.

Doing as Chase had commanded, Bandit had stayed in the living room while she and Pixie slept in the bedroom. After the fight, Pixie hadn't wanted to leave Chase's side, so being kind, she had decided to let her stay in their room.

It was every dog's worst nightmare.

Since the day Bandit had met Chase, they had spent every single night together, so it had taken him a very long time before he could fall asleep without her. And even then, he kept waking up throughout the night, concerned about her well-being until eventually he had given up and gone outside her room. There, outside the closed door, he had lain on the ground with his nose in the gap between the floor and the door. By doing this, he was able to smell Chase and reassure himself of her safety. He tried to ignore Pixie's scent every time it wafted into his nose. Knowing that the other dog was so close to Chase filled Bandit with anxiety. He knew the others thought he was just jealous, but that wasn't it at all. Bandit knew Pixie was dangerous, and he was determined to prove it to the others until then, however, he would keep a watchful eye on her. He had to protect his family.

At exactly seven 'o'clock Chase woke up. Bandit knew because she woke at this time every day. Chase had taught him the meaning of time so Bandit understood that this was no coincidence. He heard her rustling in her bed and petting Pixie. He whined and scratched at the door, unhappy that he wasn't in there with her. She must have heard him as she got off the bed and padded barefoot to the door. Suddenly the door opened and Chase was standing there. Unable to quell the surge of joy Bandit felt at seeing her, he launched himself at her, bathing her face with his tongue.

"Ew," she exclaimed. "What do I say about licking my face?"

Bandit jumped down, tail wagging from side to side with such ferocity that it almost threw him off balance. He followed her into the room, happy that he was allowed back in only to find Pixie still sitting on Chase's bed. Bandit stopped dead. As the other dog started shaking with fright again, Bandit sniffed and scanned the room to make sure everything was as it should be. Other than Pixie's strange smell, everything seemed the same until his eyes fell on his bed, which lay beside Chase's. There, torn into a million pieces, was Bandit's beloved Frumpy Rabbit. Pixie had mauled him to death.

Bandit was horrified.

He ran to the basket, to his rabbit, lifted his snout to the ceiling and howled in despair. Startled by his reaction, Chase ran over to see what was wrong. When she saw what was left of the rabbit, she bent down and threw her arms around Bandit, hugging him close.

"I'm so sorry. She must have done that while I was sleeping."

Footsteps thundered down the hallway as Gideon ran inside, clutching a baseball bat. "What is it, what's wrong?" he demanded.

Chase pointed to the rabbit as Bandit's howl receded into a whimper.

"Damn, Pixie did that?"

Bandit barked once, strongly and accusingly.

"Don't worry Boy, we'll get you another."

However, Bandit knew no other toy would ever be the same again.

50

CHASE

I felt so bad about Bandit's rabbit.

It was the first toy I'd gotten him, and it was his favorite. He's slept with that thing every night since I've known him, so I can't believe Pixie did that. She must have destroyed it while I was fast asleep because I didn't hear a thing. I can't believe I woke to find her sleeping at the end of my bed looking angelic when she had completely killed Bandit's rabbit. It made me feel even worse about asking him to sleep outside, but I had never seen Bandit fight a dog before. Maybe I was too hard on him — I never even gave him a chance to explain, just took Pixie's side because she wasn't as smart or as big as him.

I grabbed my bag, shoving Bandit's iPad inside (he obviously couldn't wear it when we went out, but I always kept it on me, in case he wanted to speak) and went to retrieve my phone but I was annoyed to find it wasn't plugged into the charger. I had definitely plugged it in last night when I had set my alarm clock, but the cable wasn't in the phone now, having fallen behind the bedside table. Looking at the battery icon, I could see that I only had a little charge left, but I didn't want to wait to head into town. I wanted to replace Bandit's toy so he could quit walking around like a lost puppy.

I was glad it was just the two of us as we headed out on our daily shopping trip. I had a lot to make up for and I was determined to do it, starting right now. What with Sully being preoccupied, Gideon spending so much time with Pixie, and Sam who seemed permanently angry lately, it made me realize just how much I needed my buddy. I couldn't take him for granted again.

We were approaching the grocery store when Bandit snapped to attention, sniffing the air with interest. He shot a look over his shoulder at me, chuffed, then moved a few feet away.

"What is it, boy?"

Of course, he couldn't answer me out here, so I just followed him as he obviously wanted me to. He led me to a battered old car parked by the side of the road. I frowned, wondering what he was up to when something moved inside the car. It was a person. They were huddled into a ball and fast asleep. It took a few moments before I recognized the untidy brown hair.

"Mom, what're you doing here?" I asked, tapping on the window.

The figure inside woke with a start, blinking confused eyes at me. "Chase..." She seemed momentarily disoriented, looking around her until she finally remembered what she was doing. "Sleeping, obviously."

"But, you can't just do that. There are laws about this kind of thing!"

"There are?" she replied, genuinely perplexed.

I didn't answer, too busy wondering why she didn't stay in a motel. There was a Motel 6 only a few blocks away. She could hardly have missed it. And then the answer came to me. "You don't have any money, do you?"

She didn't immediately reply, but a red flush appeared on her cheeks. She looked caught out, embarrassed. "It's not like it's cheap coming all the way here. Besides, it's free to sleep in the car."

I don't know why the thought of her sleeping in her car affected me like it did, but I suddenly felt a pang of sympathy for her and it made me real mad. I didn't care about her so I sure didn't care where she was sleeping. I cycled quickly through my anger until I came to another emotion — concern.

"I hope you're not here to ask us for money because that's not going to happen," I warned, suddenly tense.

She blinked at me, her eyes growing hard. "I told you why I'm here already! I don't need your money!" This, she snapped as I had obviously hit upon a sore subject. I didn't reply. We stared at each other in silence, both of us weighing the other one up. Finally, she sat up, pulling a cardigan around her. "Where are you going?" she asked pleasantly, as if we did this sort of thing all the time.

I gave her a look. "That's none of your business," I said sharply. If I were back home, this kind of response would have gotten me a slap, as it was she just looked at me evenly.

"You're right. I only asked to make conversation."

Her reasonable tone made me feel like a heel. What was going on around here? How was I the one feeling bad? Deciding I didn't have anything more to say to her this morning, I got back on my bike.

"You shouldn't park there like that, it's illegal in this state," I said before taking off with Bandit. I didn't give her another look as the two of us continued through town until we got to the pet store. Once inside, I let Bandit choose whatever he wanted. Though we searched the entire store, there wasn't a replacement for his rabbit — they only had a small selection of stock. In the end, Bandit picked a panda. He had told me before that he liked how round and happy they looked, like a ball made out of fluff. I went to the checkout, paid, and put panda in my basket. I was deliberating over whether I should stop for some flowers, maybe surprise the others with fresh pastries when I heard a shout. Turning, I saw my mom jump out of her car. She was yelling at a guy, running fast into the distance.

"Someone help me! He just stole my bag!"

Stunned, I didn't immediately react, but Bandit started barking as he bolted after the thief. Concerned for him, I went after him on my bike. No way was I going to let Bandit deal with this guy alone.

Bandit swerved around the corner as I pedaled after him. He was going so fast I had to force myself to keep up. My legs were already screaming with pain, but I kept up the momentum and shot after him, navigating past the back alleys that we now found ourselves in. He ran left then right, following smells or sounds that my human nose and ears could not make out.

Finally, I caught sight of the thief in front of us. He was a skinny guy with mousy- colored hair and an awkward manner about him. He ran up to a waiting vehicle — a black Prius — and jumped into the car. I couldn't make out the driver except to see that he had hair that he wore in a ponytail. As Bandit and I neared them, the driver gunned the engine, and the car took off, leaving a cloud of dust in its wake.

There was no way I would be able to catch up to that car now. I stopped, summoning Bandit to my side. "Bandit! Heel!"

He came back to me after tossing a longing look over his shoulder at the fast retreating car. His body language seemed to say that he thought he could catch them, but I knew it was fruit-less and I didn't want him to exhaust himself; he was already panting heavily. We returned to the main street to find my mom waiting for us.

She hurried over, concern etched over her face. "Why did you do that? You shouldn't have chased him! What if he was dangerous?"

I was surprised to see how worried she seemed to be. It was almost as if she were truly afraid that I had almost caught that guy.

"I can handle myself and so can Bandit," I said more harshly than I intended. I don't know what it was but I couldn't seem to be my usual cheerful self around her.

"I know, you scared me is all."

I looked into her car, into her home-away-from-home, and saw how sparse it was. Other than a few empty cartons of food, there was just a blanket and a hairbrush. "What was in the bag?" I asked.

"My purse, some make-up. All my cards." She raked her hand through her hair, the only outward sign of her turmoil. I sighed inwardly. I wanted to leave, but I knew it was the wrong thing to do. Despite everything that had happened between us, I couldn't just leave her stranded with no money. Of all people, I knew how that felt.

"I guess you'd better come with me to Sam," I said reluctantly.

"Sam? Sully's girlfriend? Why?" she asked.

"You don't know? I thought we'd told you. Sam's a sheriff."

For a brief second, I thought she looked alarmed before her expression quickly changed to one of surprise. "No, none of you mentioned that. She doesn't look anything like one."

"Sheriffs only look like sheriffs when they're wearing the uniform and when you turned up yesterday, it was her day off." Seeing the strange expression on her face again, I wondered what was up with her. "Why, you have a problem with sheriffs?"

She shook her head quickly. "I've never much believed in the law is all."

I thought about the times the neighbors had called the cops on her and Tubs after another one of their epic drunken fights. The cops had never liked either of them and had made it obvious how little they thought of them both, so it made sense why she wasn't particularly keen on them back. "Well, Sam is different. She will be able to help you."

But Mom shook her head. "I don't wanna drag her into this. I've already barged into her private life, how about we leave the professional one alone?"

I frowned in consternation, putting my hands on either side of my hips. "So you're just going to let that guy get away with stealing your purse?"

"Of course not. I'll report him, just not to your substitute mom. I don't wanna ask for her help."

"So this is a pride thing?" I asked, shaking my head in disbelief.

"Look, can we not do this? I've been awake less than five minutes. Most of my money's gone and I don't know what I'm going to do about that. How about you give me a break?" she said this a little desperately causing me to feel suddenly ashamed. I fell silent, kicking at a stone on the street. Bandit looked at her, then me, waiting patiently for me to decide our next course of action. Looking over her shoulder at Denny's Diner, I came up with an idea begrudgingly.

"Denny's has a phone you can use to report the robbery. We can grab some drinks there too... I have enough to cover us for those," I offered.

She smiled at me gratefully. "Sounds like a plan."

I crossed over the street to Denny's and chained up my bike outside. Zeb had laughed before, when he saw me do this once. Crime wasn't rife in Montpelier, he'd said. Apparently the last time an incident had occurred was several years ago, and that had involved some out-of-towners, but I'd rather be cautious and not sorry even if it meant incurring ridicule, especially after what had just happened to my mom.

I looped the lock around a lamppost, and the three of us headed inside.

51

CHASE

Denny's was a simple place without any airs or graces. The only decoration they utilized were the cheerful checked curtains hanging on the front window, but other than that the place was, as Sully liked to call it, utilitarian. For my own personal taste, I had always liked how honest they seemed in here — it was the same with the food. Nothing fancy, just good simple comfort food. I lead Mom and Bandit to my favorite corner booth, where Bandit jumped up onto the seat next to me. Like the grocery store, they were used to seeing us together, and no one minded his presence.

Although it was breakfast time, neither one of us wanted to eat much, so I ordered two Coke floats. Our waitress, a slim woman in her 30s who had served me many times before, set the drinks down in front of us with a smile. "Let me know if there's anything else I can get you." She patted Bandit, then left, leaving us to our business.

Mom stood up. "Guess I should make that call."

I pointed across the room. "The payphone is over there. I'd let you use mine, but it's almost out of charge."

She nodded and disappeared to use the phone. I took a sip of my drink, letting the sweet liquid slide down my throat. Bandit nosed forward, sniffing hopefully at my glass, but I shook my head. "Sorry bud, but this isn't for you. Sully would have a fit if you had this much sugar."

He looked at me in disappointment but backed away from the glass. I stared outside blankly, draining my soda until Mom returned moments later.

"That was quick," I said.

She slid back into her seat. "Wasn't much I could tell them. They said they'd get back if they had any news."

I frowned at her. "That's it? What're you supposed to do in the meantime?"

She shrugged thin shoulders. "Wait, they said."

I pushed my empty drink away, annoyed. "What're you supposed to do for money until then?"

Mom played with the straw on her own drink but didn't drink any of it. "Don't think they care. Not like they have a pot of cash that they give out to callers."

I knew she was right, but it just seemed unhelpful.

"Thanks for trying to catch that guy," she said, giving me a grateful smile.

I shrugged like it was no big deal. "You should thank Bandit, he was the one who went after him. I just followed to make sure he was safe."

Hearing his name, Bandit's tail thumped on the seat next to me. His tongue was hanging out in that goofy grin of his. Mom looked at him uncertainly.

"Right. Thanks, Bandit."

He woofed, pleased with himself. Though she gave him a small smile, I could see it didn't quite reach her eyes. Even though she could see how good he was, she still didn't like him. I would never in a million years understand how that could be, how some folks just didn't like animals. People who were allergic or scared because they had been attacked by a dog when they were a kid? That I understood, but not liking them without a reason? That made about as much sense as a vegetarian who ate fish.

We sat there for a while as she continued to play with her drink. I watched as the ice cream melted into a layer of vanilla foam, fidgeting in my seat. The silence made me uncomfortable — we weren't just a normal mother and daughter after all — so I forced myself to break it.

"So, what's new back home?"

She looked at me over the top of her glass. "I'm still working part time in the bar, and Tubs is still driving trucks. A bunch of new people moved into the park, but I haven't met any of them yet. Let me think, what else... oh, I did see Miss. Hannah, a while back, bumped into her at Subway. She asked about you."

Miss. Hannah was my head teacher. She was a tiny thing and had to wear crazy high heels just to reach my chest, but she made up for that with her booming voice. She was a stern woman who had a habit of sneaking up on you when you least expected it: most of the kids were scared of her. I always thought I got on her nerves because I messed around a lot in class, so this was a surprise. "What did she say?"

"She just wanted to know if I had heard from you."

"That's nice. I thought she hated me."

"Well, she doesn't."

This was certainly stimulating conversation, not. I figured we could sit here making awkward chit chat all day or I could just say the things that have been on my mind for so long. With nothing left to lose, I decided to bite the bullet.

"Why are you still with him?" she blinked, taken aback by my direct question. Hesitating, she fumbled for an answer.

"It's complicated..." She finally began, but I interrupted her.

"No, it's not. He's an abusive jerk and you should have left him long ago." I retorted angrily.

She lay her hands palm down on either side of the glass, pushing down on the table for strength. "It's not that simple, I can't just leave. That's my home."

"It's a tin can. It's worthless and you can get another — equally worthless — someplace else. Someplace where he isn't there." My words were becoming clipped the angrier I got. Concerned for my spiraling mood, Bandit snuck his head onto my lap to comfort me. He sighed a big, long doggie sigh.

"And who's gonna take care of me if I did that? If I left him, who's gonna pay my bills or the rent, you tell me that?"

She was getting angry now too. Her mouth was set into a tight line, and she folded her arms across her chest.

"What are you talking about? Why does somebody have to look after you? You're a grown woman, why can't you look after yourself? Look at me! I spent eight months by myself on the streets and I was fine... and I'm fourteen!"

She looked at me, shaking her head sadly.

"You don't get it, do you? I'm not like you. You've always been able to take care of yourself, but I can't do that. I'm not built that way."

I was stunned.

I couldn't believe she actually believed that. Is this why she had never looked after me when I was growing up? Had she always thought I was so capable that she just never bothered to be my mother? My heart ached as I felt suddenly deeply sad for the little girl I had been, the one who had needed her mother to protect her from harm. After all this time, I finally understood why my life had been the way it was.

She couldn't stop thinking about herself, not even for one minute.

"Other people deal with crap everyday Mom, and yet they

manage fine. You need to stop feeling sorry for yourself. Stop being a victim."

I thought my words would put her on the defensive. Instead, her eyes turned bright. She sat up a little taller and her arms unfolded. "Actually, I have something planned and when it works out, I'll be able to get myself straight."

"Good," I replied, "but is this something you can still have if Tubs is in the picture?"

"No," she said quietly, looking down into her drink. Her shoulders drooped, and she looked suddenly resigned. "It's been so long, I don't know who I am anymore..." She looked up at me, but now I saw something other than the despair she wore around her — it was hope. "But these few days without him, even though I've been sleeping in my car, I've felt better than I have in years."

She smiled then. "I'd forgotten what it feels like when you don't have to answer to anyone but yourself." She looked almost young again when she smiled like that. "I like it."

"So you know what to do," I said.

She nodded, suddenly vulnerable. "Will you help me?"

I started, startled by her request. "Help you, how?"

"Well, that guy took off with my bag. Everything I had was in there..."

My eyes hardened. "I already told you, if you're asking for money..."

She raised her hands at me. "No, no. I'll still have a little on me. I'm saying if I went for help, would you come with me?"

I didn't answer straight away, not knowing what it was that she wanted. I snuck a sideways look at Bandit, but he seemed as confused as I was. "Come with you where, exactly?"

She took out a printout of a website from her pocket to show me. It was a place called Pinewood and was some sort of woman's charity from what I could make out. "There's a shelter for women like me. It's about an hours drive from here. I found the information yesterday and have been thinking about it ever since."

My eyes narrowed. "Wait, you found this out yesterday? But you let me go on about leaving Tubs when you've already half decided to?"

She sighed at me to stop. "It gets a lot easier to realize what you should do when you're away, Chase. But just because I know what I should do, it doesn't make it any easier for me."

I bit my lip to stop from telling her off any further. She was right. Since I'd been away from them, my head had gotten much clearer and I had certainly become happier.

"Please? Would you just come with me for support? It shouldn't take long."

She seemed so desperate that against my better judgment I found myself caving. "Let me call Sully and tell him where we're going."

She nodded. "I'll use the restroom while you call."

She got up and left the table. I took out my cell and dialed his number. It rang for five rings, but he didn't pick up. I let out an exasperated breath. What was with Sully and his inability to pick up the phone these days? I left a quick voicemail telling him that I was going to accompany my mom to the women's shelter in Pinewood, then stroked Bandit.

"You think I'm doing the right thing?" I asked him. He made a sound that was half whine, half chuff. I figured he agreed although, like me, he wasn't particularly happy about it. We sat for what must have been five minutes before mom returned to the table. She had a paper bag in her hands and I could smell the undeniable scent of sausage and egg muffins wafting up.

"Splashed out on breakfast with the last of the cash I had on me. My way of saying thanks. Why don't you guys eat on the way? I want to make sure we get there early, I've heard they give out beds on a first-come basis."

She left the diner as Bandit and I followed her outside. I went to grab my bike, but she stopped me.

"That's not going to fit in my car."

I looked at her small car, then my bike, and I knew she was right. I felt my forehead crease into a frown. I wanted to bring it with me, just in case something happened and I needed to find my own way home, but I could see that it just wasn't going to happen.

"Ok," I said reluctantly. Making sure the bike was securely locked, we got into her car. I took the passenger seat while Bandit climbed into the back. He was already looking out of the window, excited by the idea of a ride. Like other dogs, he loved to hang his head out of it, while his tongue lapped up bugs, air, and dirt. Not for the first time, I wondered why this was a thing with them: you'd never catch a cat doing that. Mom handed us the muffins.

"Thanks," I said as I unwrapped mine, but I stopped her when she went to help Bandit with his. "That much salt isn't good for him," I said.

She shook her head and laughed. "Come on, one isn't going to hurt is it?"

Bandit paced the seat, anxious for the food. He was practically drooling by this point, so I figured it would be really cruel if he wasn't allowed one. "Fine," I said to him. "But we can't tell Sully, okay?"

Bandit woofed, yes.

I noticed that she wasn't eating. "You're not having one?"

"You know I can't eat in the morning," she replied, which was true. All the time growing up, I maybe saw her eat breakfast only a few times. "Besides, it means they're more for you two." She shook the bag and I could see that there were still some muffins left inside.

Happily, the two of us chowed down on our muffins as my mom started the engine and drove us out of town.

52

SULLY

After our fight last night, Sam and I had barely spoken and when I woke this morning, it was to find a note on the bedside table asking me to meet her at "our place."

This was a secluded spot in the nearby woods where Sam and I loved to hike along the nature trail. We'd had many a picnic there, and this was the one place we retreated to when we needed a timeout from the rest of the clan, much as we could get to within ten minutes, anyway.

The sun shone brightly, though it wasn't enough to compete with the morning cold. Buttoning up my flannel shirt, I jumped out of my truck and grabbed Sam's thermos, which I had found draining on the sink. She'd forgotten to take it, so I filled it up with coffee. I'd brought mugs and donuts with me too, as food always seemed much nicer when enjoyed outdoors. I was trying to make amends, and this seemed the least I could do for the woman I loved.

Leaves and twigs snapped underfoot as I hiked briskly, enjoying the crisp air. These hikes were the one thing I had missed when I lived in Ellington. Deep down, I wasn't a city person, and the lack of greenery and mountains had hit me hard, but it was what Em had wanted. She'd had friends and family there, and it didn't make sense for us to be anywhere else.

I had only been going a few minutes when I saw Sam's figure ahead of me. She was sitting on the grass, her back against a towering oak. Although she wasn't wearing anything fancy — just jeans and a sweater — my breath caught at the sight of her. Her cheeks were red from the cold and her eyes bright. Her glossy curls spilled down her back like a velvet curtain. Thoughts of our fight last night flew straight out of my mind.

At my arrival, she stood up. I leaned forward to kiss her, but she ducked out of the way. Seeing her serious expression, butter-flies did a dance inside my stomach.

"Hey."

"Hey," she answered softly, keeping her eyes on the ground.

This definitely wasn't good. She couldn't smile at me, could barely look at me. And her confident, normal manner was nowhere to be found.

"Thanks for joining me up here," she started. "I know we didn't have a restful night."

"Do you want to sit down? I brought us breakfast..."

I held up the food, but she shook her head, disinterested. "Sully, look. I need you to listen to me without interruption."

An alarm sounded deep within my head as a thousand objec-tions flooded my mind. However, respectful of her wishes, I nodded. She shoved her hands into her pockets and continued.

"This isn't working for me. I was ready to move ahead with you, but it's become clear to me now that you're not in the same place, and as much as I hate to say this, as much as I hate to do this to you, Chase and the others, I think it's best if we took a break."

Of all the things I expected her to say, that wasn't it. I felt the smile freeze on my face as I stood there, motionless. "I know I've been distracted with everything that's happened, but don't you think this is extreme?"

She shook her head sadly. "No, I don't. You asked me to marry you, and then you freaked out as soon as you saw your ex-wife's grave. I don't need to be a shrink to see that this is a big, big problem."

I set down the food and grabbed her hands. "I didn't freak out when I saw her grave, Sam, I freaked out when I saw that it had been disturbed, and then there was the comb and the phone message. Please don't make this out to be something it's not."

She pulled away from me. "I'm not going to talk about all that again — we just keep going round in circles when, the truth is, we might not ever know where the message came from, if it came at all. I did run a trace on that number, Sully, but it came back with nothing. There has been no activity on that line since Emma's death. And the contract ended a few months after she died. You canceled it yourself."

I tried to hide my feelings on the subject, but I was reeling from her revelations. "Well, I said, I probably had… I just didn't remember. You can't hold that against me, I was dealing with the loss of my wife!"

Sam paused, taking a breath. "It's not just that… when we met, you gave me the impression that you were long over Emma, but when we were at the clinic, Florence told me how you were holding onto Emma's things for a year Sully - you couldn't even get rid of her toiletries. We only got together a month or two later. How could you have gone from one extreme to the other?"

"Because I did!" I yelled, unable to help myself. "I fell in love with you, and I moved on."

Sam shook her head sadly. "No. You're not over her. In fact, I think you haven't grieved properly and you may be suffering from a form of depression that can cause hallucinations. Which means you really did see that message, if only in your head."

I blinked, unbelievably. "Are you serious?"

Her voice became earnest. "Yes. I've been looking into the different forms of grief and your symptoms fit. It's why I wanted you to get help. Think about everything you've gone through, Sully. Emma's cancer, her death. Then, while you were clinging onto whatever you could of hers, you were attacked by Forbes' men who destroyed everything you had — they essentially destroyed her all over again for you."

I heard her words, but I couldn't take them in. She was wrong. "That's not what happened. I'm fine, dammit! The only thing that would cause me to feel grief again is you breaking up with me!"

Her eyes filled with tears. "I don't want to, but I can't stand by and watch you get worse. I've waited a long time to find my husband, and I'm not about to rush that now, especially if you're not ready. I care about you too much to do this to you."

"That doesn't even make sense. You care about me too much to marry me?"

Among the thick cloud of confusion and panic that had fallen over me, I realized that my pocket was vibrating. Someone was calling me, but I ignored it.

"One day you'll understand, Sully. When this is all over, and you are finally over your ex, you will know why I did this."

And with that, she ran off.

I wanted to chase after her. Wanted to grab her by the shoulders and shake her until sense returned, but I remained frozen, rooted to the spot.

I could do nothing but watch the woman I loved walk out of my life.

53

CHASE

I inhaled that muffin and the next like my life depended on it. Since I'd lived here, I'd gotten used to having breakfast, so today when I skipped it, it had seemed like a really big deal. Usually, we had toast or cereal, though occasionally Gid would whip up some eggs and bacon. Those times didn't happen as much, now that he was a working man, so those muffins felt like a real treat. Bandit had chowed his down in two bites and was now licking his chops and making happy noises in the backseat.

I wiped my mouth on a napkin and looked out at the scenery. Trees and buildings blurred past as we drove away from the town, hitting country within moments. Fields of wheat and barley shimmered under the morning sun. The sky was a brilliant blue, and it was only the slight chill in the air that revealed summer had passed. I shot a sideways look at my mom, but she seemed intensely focused on driving. She sat stiffly and her hands gripped the steering wheel real tight. I guessed she was nervous about what we would find ahead of us.

I checked my phone to see if Sully had messaged — he hadn't and I was annoyed to find that the battery was now blinking at me. Figures that the moment I left town, my phone would be dying.

"Do you have a car charger?" I asked my Mom.

She shot me an apologetic look. "Yes, but it was in my bag."

Of course it was. Just my luck.

I fell silent as we continued on our journey. We didn't talk, which was good in a way, as now we were in this small confined space, I found I didn't know what to say. If I were honest, we never really spoke much to each other before either. Mom was always preoccupied with her latest boyfriend, and when there wasn't one in the picture, she'd spend all her time going out while she tried to find a new one. From the age of ten, she'd frequently left me alone in that trailer while she trawled the local bars for her latest victim, but I had never minded as it meant I could stay up late and watch whatever I wanted to on the TV. I also learned how to make a mean mac and cheese in the microwave.

To fill in the silence, Mom had tuned into a radio station. The music played now, a pop number that was really familiar, but for some reason, I couldn't think what it was. I had a photographic memory so forgetting song lyrics happened to me literally never. I frowned, trying to concentrate.

What the heck was this song?

I leaned back into my seat when I noticed that I was feeling drowsy, which was weird as I had only recently got up. My head started feeling heavy, like it was too big for my neck. I glanced behind me to see that Bandit was nodding off too.

And suddenly I felt a cold feeling in my stomach.

Sweat broke across my brow as the fear hit. I looked at my mom and saw the way her hands gripped the wheel. Her shoulders were tense, and she kept her eyes on the road ahead as if she was determined not to look at me.

I knew without a shadow of a doubt that she had drugged us.

"What did you put in the food?" I managed to exclaim, even as my tongue felt like it was pinned to the roof of my mouth.

She looked at me then, guilt all over her face.

"I'm sorry. I had to do it."

Anything else she said I couldn't hear.

Blackness took over, and I felt myself sinking into oblivion.

54

THE SCIENTIST

The call came right on cue.

The woman, Tracey Blueman, phoned to say the girl and dog were leaving with her as planned. She would drug them and meet us at the arranged location. The Scientist felt his excitement build as he waited for her car to arrive. For more than six months he had carefully set out his chess pieces, planning for this moment, and now that it was almost here, a warm feeling spread through his body.

"This is so exciting, Xavier!" Dick said.

He tried to hide his flicker of annoyance. Dick was Xavier's assistant, a student he had picked up in his science class. There was one like him every year. Quiet, shy, and lonely, he sat at the back of the class, never raised his hand, ate alone in the canteen, and had no friends to speak of. He had noticed him straight away. Every time he had seen him in passing, the boy had had a nose in a textbook. It was his armor against a world that had yet to notice him.

But notice him it hadn't.

And that wasn't really surprising. Of medium height, he had a slim build. His hair was not quite blond yet not dark enough to be brown. He wore thick glasses to correct heavy short-sightedness, but the lenses enlarged his eyes to comical effect, making him seem like an owl in appearance.

It hadn't taken much to turn him. All Xavier had to do was notice him and toss out a kind word here or there. Within a few months of Xavier implementing his plan, Dick had become his willing accomplice.

Raised by a family who didn't understand him, Dick wasn't close to his parents, who seemed happy that their son was now across the country at college. They were so far away that it made no economic sense for Dick to go home, even for the vacation season. It was during the summer vacation when Xavier began his plan in earnest. Throughout the semester, he had invited Dick into his home under the guise of helping with his science experiments, but the reality was, Xavier was grooming him. But Dick was too stupid, too desperate for approval to notice. He started lightly, using hypothetical questions to see how far he could push the boy, and Dick had lapped it up like a dog, never suspecting a thing.

It was Dick who had sent Sullivan that message on his phone using an application that made it look as if it had come from his dead wife's phone, and Dick who had disturbed the grave. This part of the plan was actually Dick's idea, and Xavier had found it quite devious and brilliant. He would never tell him that, however. To keep Dick under his control, Xavier only ever complimented him when absolutely necessary; it was part of the brainwashing process. Dick was so starving for approval he would do all that Xavier wanted without complaint.

Dick smiled at Xavier now, causing splotches of red to appear across his neck and cheeks, which only made his acne seem ten times worse. Xavier tried not to let the sight of them disgust him as they always did. *Had the boy never heard of Proactiv?* He nodded. "Let's not get too excited until she actually gets here."

They waited in his Prius, in the car park of a Walmart, as Xavier thought back to his first visit with Tracey Blueman.

He had initially learned of her identity through the reports Forbes' mercenary had compiled. Though Hector wasn't someone he liked or ever had dealings with himself, he had to admit the man excelled at his job — up until the very end, anyway.

In Hector's files, Xavier had learned who the girl Chase was, who her parents were and what kind of life she had lived. Her mother was a person of low moral fiber. Reading about her relationship with the alcoholic and seeing how cheaply they lived, Xavier knew she could be bought, so he wasn't at all surprised when she had agreed to his deal so willingly... Some people just didn't make good parents. He himself knew that better than most. His own had never wanted a child. They were partygoers, selfish to the core and only ever wheeled him out as a freak to be admired or feared. They couldn't wait to send him away to boarding school, where they no longer had to deal with the inconvenience of his being there.

Xavier hated them with a vengeance.

The plan had come together quite simply with the only hiccup appearing when Tracey Blueman had called, worrying over how she would be able to separate the girl and the dog away from the rest of the family. Again, it was Dick who had come up with the idea for the fake robbery. He felt that for Chase to help her mother — who she was clearly resentful of — something bad would need to happen to her. There was too much history between them, but having studied footage of the girl at home, Dick had seen that the girl was inherently kind, and they had quickly used that failing against her. If Xavier actually cared one bit for the Dick, he would have encouraged him into the field of psychology, as science was very clearly wasted on him. As it was, Xavier didn't waste energy on simple emotions such as like or dislike.

A car turned into the parking lot. A beaten up Toyota with a woman behind the wheel. Xavier sat up a little taller.

"Is that her?" Dick asked in his nasal voice.

Xavier leaned forward in his seat, straining to get a better look. "I don't know."

The car parked, and the woman got out. Xavier recognized her cheap clothes and desperation immediately. "That's her."

They got out of the car and crossed the parking lot to meet her. She tossed a nervous look in the direction of her car where they could now see the dog and girl sleeping soundly. Wringing her hands, she greeted them. "I did my part, now where's the money?"

Though this was the agreement, her lack of concern for her own child disgusted him. Xavier's gaze hardened as he gestured to Dick. "Please hand Ms. Blueman her payment."

Dick went to the trunk of Xavier's car, opened it and took out a large canvas sports bag. Inside, divided into blocks of five hundred, was one hundred thousand dollars in cash; Xavier had counted it all himself. It had taken a lifetime to save up that much money. Despite his parents' wealth, they had never shared any of their fortune with him, neither had Forbes, and Xavier had always been too proud to ask either for help. And now, here was this trailer trash, selling off her child for only one hundred thousand dollars. His mouth curled into a sneer that he didn't bother to hide.

Tracey Blueman snatched the bag out of Dick's hands. She yanked down the zip to check the contents inside. When she saw the bills, her eyes went wide with greed. "It's all here?" she asked.

"Of course it is," Xavier replied, annoyed. "I do not go back on my word."

She took the hefty bag from them and tossed it into the trunk of her car. Then she opened the door to the back seat.

"Dick, if you would be so kind..." Xavier said.

Dick jumped to attention. Leaning in, he slid his arms under the unconscious dog and carried him to Xavier's car where he set him down inside a cage on the backseat. Next Dick went over to the girl and carried her to the car where he positioned her next to the cage. The woman looked at her daughter, her guilt and shame obvious to see.

"She's going to be okay, right? You said she wouldn't be harmed?"

"Now you are concerned for her well-being?" Xavier asked, one brow arched in question.

"You told me she wouldn't be hurt. You said you just wanted the dog for your science experiment," she replied.

"And I meant it. The girl will be returned to her family." Xavier put an emphasis on the word "family."

The woman flinched as Xavier intended for her to. She bit her lip, unsure then and looked at the girl again. Her hesitation and mistrust began to grate on him. He'd had enough of this woman now and was itching to get away.

"We had a deal, Ms. Blueman. You have your money now, so please leave or we will be forced to take it all back."

The threat worked as expected. She recoiled physically from him, moving quickly to the driver's seat. Climbing in, she put her hand on the key in the ignition.

"I'm sorry, Chase," she whispered.

Casting one last look at the daughter that she was leaving behind, she turned the key. And as the engine roared into life, she pressed down on the gas and drove away.

55

THE SCIENTIST

They headed west, away from this Godforsaken pathetic town.

Xavier had already packed away Erik-the-IT-man's things, leaving no trace of him behind. For several weeks before his initial "move" here, he had scoped out the town, making copious notes as to the family's routine. As he had hoped, it was fairly consistent. The Sheriff worked eight to five on weekdays most weeks, doing the occasional weekend shift as and when it was required. The young boy — a new hire to the town's garage — worked nine to six. Sullivan seemed to spend a majority of his time just doing things around the ranch, or rehabbing his leg under his father's watchful eye. Which left Chase, who came into the town daily with the dog to pick up the day's groceries. It was all so mundane, so uninspired, Xavier wondered how they didn't all kill themselves from boredom.

When the mechanic's previous tenant moved out during his stakeout, he knew it was a blessing in disguise. While he had no desire to live here, he knew he would never have a better opportunity to get so up close and personal. So, with just a handshake and a few hundred dollars cash deposit, Xavier had found himself living above the mechanic's garage, where he could observe Chase and Gideon's daily comings and goings.

It was masterful, really. He had been right under their noses, but they never suspected a thing. A laugh bubbled up in his mouth, which he tried to hide under a cough. He preferred that Dick never knew his true feelings. It kept the boy on edge, which is how he wanted it.

To truly control someone. It was best to keep them on an uneven footing. They should never feel comfortable or be able to predict your reactions. Like chess, this was another game Xavier excelled in.

While Dick drove, Xavier climbed into the back of the car and performed his inspection of the specimen.

Even to his naked eye, he could see the dog was in excellent health. His coat gleamed and his eyes — well, what he could see of them — were bright. Clearly, this dog was not lacking in any physical comforts. The girl and her friends had served him well.

Xavier moved the fur around the dog's head until he felt the raised scar behind his skull. This was where Forbes' doctor had opened him up. When she had removed the tumor that had originally been placed inside his brain to stimulate trauma.

When Xavier had first learned of this plan, he had thought it ludicrous, but it amused him now that his own breakthrough required the use of this one small dog. He needed what the dog had to complete his own experiment.

He was so close to making history he could barely contain himself. All he needed was to see how the dog's brain had reorganized itself, how it had healed itself, and he could get his experiment to do the same. In addition to seeing into his brain, he wanted to investigate the dog's DNA helix and find what code might be added or missing in order for his body to be as it was.

If what he was proposing worked, he would become the most famous man in history.

Not that fame was what he was after, of course. He only wanted the world to recognize his genius and treat him accordingly. Once he made history, he knew his parents would come crawling back to him — and he couldn't wait to tell them where to go.

If it wasn't for their precious cargo, he would instruct the hapless Dick to drive faster. As it was, Xavier willed the boy to drive more carefully than he had done in his entire life.

56

SULLY

I don't know how long I stood there under that damn tree.

Sam had said her piece and just like that, she was gone. I was left reeling. Despite my turmoil of the last few days, I was in love with Sam and had planned on our future together. Now, not only had that future vanished in a cloud of dust, it looked like I wouldn't even have her in my life. I couldn't collate what had just happened with my life. Only yesterday we were looking at baby clothes, but Sully Jr was now a distant dream.

I forced my feet to move. On autopilot, I walked back to my car and climbed in. Somewhere in the back of my mind, I remembered my phone had rung during our conversation. I took out my cell to see a missed call from Chase. She had left a voicemail. Numbly, I listened as her voice came over the line. She was saying something about going with her mom to a woman's shelter. If this was any other day, I would have called right back and said exactly why that might not be a good idea, but I could barely get the fog that was clouding my mind to lift long enough for coherent thoughts to surface. Bandit was with her and I was sure they were fine. All I could think about was getting home. What if Sam were packing right now? Maybe I could persuade her not to leave.

Energized by the thought, I gunned the engine and drove home as fast as I could.

When I got to the ranch, I couldn't see Sam's car, but she parked it around the back at times so it didn't necessarily mean she wasn't here. I knew my brain was in complete denial of events, but I didn't care. I was holding onto whatever thought I could to get by. Getting out of the car, I didn't bother shutting the door. I just bolted inside.

The ranch was deathly silent. I listened for signs of any movement, but all was suffocatingly still. "Pixie?" I called out. My voice echoed around, sounding strange and desperate to my own ears. I had no idea what I was doing. Even if the dog knew her name, it wasn't as if she would answer me. She wasn't Bandit.

With a sinking heart, I turned towards our room. From the corner of my eye, my mind registered a fact that seemed a little odd. I glanced into the living room to find dad's wheelchair in the corner of the room. Of the man himself, he was nowhere to be seen.

Strange.

Frowning, I changed course and headed into the living room. As I grew closer, I saw the glass on the floor.

The decorative bowl that usually sat on the table had smashed and now lay in several pieces on the scratched floorboards. The coffee table that previously housed the bowl was askew, like someone had bumped it. My heart started to race as it suddenly came to me that something was terribly wrong. I fished out my phone, preparing to call the others when I saw a boot sticking out from behind the sofa. Made of a tan leather, it had the mismatched laces that Chase often laughed about.

It was my dad's boot.

57

SULLY

Sprinting forward, I finally saw him. He was lying on the ground. Unconscious.

"Dad!" I cried.

He didn't move.

There was an angry gash on the side of his head where I suspected it had hit the floor. I felt for a pulse and was relieved to find one. Quickly, I ran my hands over his body to see if I could find anything broken or out of alignment. As far as I could tell, the only injury he had was the one to his head.

Unless of course there was something wrong with him on the inside.

The thought filled me with dread.

I was wondering if it would be safe to move him when I saw there was something gripped in his hand. Prying it open, I found some kind of gadget inside. It took a while before I realized I was looking at a spy cam, the kind people put inside toy bears when they left their child at home with a new babysitter.

What the hell? Where had he gotten that from?

I didn't have time to worry over the spy cam, however, I needed to get him help.

"Gideon? Sam? Are you here?" I yelled out, hoping desperately that one of them would answer my call. Only silence greeted me.

Carefully, I picked him up and carried him to the back of my truck. I didn't put him in the passenger seat as I had no idea what damage he might have inside of him. I couldn't risk there being an issue with his neck or his unconscious body falling forward and hitting the dashboard.

Running back inside, I grabbed several of the quilts my mom had made when I was a kid and ran back out with them. Rolling them into tight rolls, I wedged them securely around him as best I could.

I could call for an ambulance, but the nearest hospital was a forty minute drive away, and I knew I could get him there faster if I drove myself.

Forgetting all about Sam and Chase, I shot off to Memorial Hospital.

58

SULLY

I sat in the waiting room anxiously tapping my foot on the ground.

It had been at least an hour since I'd arrived at the hospital and the doctors had taken over. I watched as they placed my dad onto a gurney and wheeled him away. Although I had checked with the front desk multiple times, there was nothing to report. The receptionist, a woman with unruly hair and eyes that looked too big for her face, assured me that as soon as there was any news, I would be given it. I knew that was crap. It was the line they gave people to keep them away. Florence had used it herself back at the clinic to spare me having to deal with concerned parents. There was nothing I could do but wait.

Suddenly the doors crashed open as Gideon thundered through the entrance. Spotting me in the waiting area, he ran to my side. "Where is he?"

The kid was still in his work clothes and hadn't even bothered to wipe the grease stains from his hands. He must have come straight from the garage when he picked up my message. I shrugged helplessly.

"Still being checked out by the doctors. They haven't told me anything."

Gideon marched straight up to the front desk and demanded to be given a status update on Dad's health. Despite his aggressive stance, the receptionist was calm and comforting, having faced endless desperate and frightened family members before. She fed him the same line she had given me and gestured that he should wait by my side.

Defeated, he came back over and sat down. "What the heck is taking them so long?"

I shook my head, not really wanting to think about what the reasons might be. In my experience as a vet, the faster you knew what the problem was, the less serious it was. Gideon's eyes searched the area, looking for something to focus on until they landed on a vending machine. "You want a drink?" he asked.

"I'm fine, thanks," I replied, though the reality was far from the truth. My throat felt dry and thick with mucus from not having drunk anything all day. Sam's thermos with the coffee was still in the truck untouched though I couldn't summon up the energy to get it. Despite feeling like I'd spent a week in a desert, I didn't want anything. The only way I would feel any better was to know what was going on with Dad.

The doors ahead of us opened and the doctor who had assisted my dad came over to us. His expression was grave, but I couldn't tell anything else by his demeanor.

Gideon and I both jumped to our feet. The doctor, whose name was Dr. Edmund Lyman according to the name badge on his shirt, offered a small smile.

"Your father has received a serious head trauma and is still unconscious. At this point, I can't tell if he will come out of it or not, so, unfortunately, all we can do is wait. All other vital signs are good. It's just the head wound that seems to be the issue. Do either of you know what might have caused it?" he asked.

I shook my head. "No. I was out with my... with Sam, but when I came home, I found him on the ground like that. I have no idea what happened. And Gideon was still at work, so he doesn't know either."

"Zeb was home with one of our dogs, Pixie," Gideon offered. "I left the two of them alone when I went to work."

A puzzling thought occurred to me. "Thinking about it, I didn't see Pixie when I got back. The house was silent, I didn't see her anywhere at all."

The doctor tried to piece the puzzle together. "If something scared her, she might have run off. We'll keep a close watch over your father. I'll let you know if anything changes. Obviously, if you find out any information in the meantime, please call and let me know immediately as it might help solve the mystery of what's happened to him. Other than that, you might as well go home as there is nothing you can do here."

Gideon and I looked at each other, both of us wanting to argue our reasons to stay, but the Doctor was obviously prepared for this.

"Fella's, even if you stay, he won't know you're here. I suggest you go home, get some rest, and wait for my call."

His tone brokered no argument. Having instructed us, he went to the receptionist to check for messages and then was gone.

"I know he's treating Zeb and all, but I don't care what he says. I'm not going home. Where're Sam and Chase?"

His innocent question hit me like a knife to the heart. With all that had happened, I had forgotten my conversation with Sam this morning, but now her words and actions invaded my head. "Sam and I are taking a break," I said slowly.

Gideon couldn't have looked more incredulous. He almost laughed, thinking my words ludicrous until he saw that I was serious. The shock left his face to be replaced by concern.

"This is for real? What the hell happened?"

I shrugged. What could I say when I didn't understand it myself? I bit down on my lip, not trusting myself to speak any further. Seeing that I wasn't willing to discuss the subject any longer, Gideon dropped his line of questioning and moved to another.

"Does Chase know?"

"No. I need to call her back, actually. She's gone with her mom to some woman's shelter."

Gideon froze at my words. "What are you talking about? She didn't say anything about that this morning?"

"I gather it's something that only came up today. I was with Sam when she called, so I didn't actually speak to her."

Taking out my phone, I dialed Chase's number. Instead of the ringtone I expected, however, the call went straight to voicemail. There wasn't even the few seconds delay that would signify bad reception. For the call to go through to voicemail so quickly, it meant only one thing.

The phone was turned off.

An uncomfortable feeling started inside my stomach. Seeing my face, Gideon spoke. "What is it?"

"Her phone's off."

59

CHASE

Darkness surrounded me.

My head felt foggy and my mouth was parched. I felt like I hadn't had a drink in days. I must have had the worst sleep of my life to be feeling like this. My body ached, and I shivered, unexpectedly cold. I reached over to stroke Bandit, but instead of his soft fur, my hand touched something cold and damp. It took a few moments for me to realize what it was.

Dirt.

Confused, my eyes flicked open. Instead of the ceiling I expected to see, there were a canopy of leaves suspended above me. Beams of light struggled through the dense foliage, but they had such a long way to go that the area immediately around me was dark and unwelcoming.

Where the heck was I?

I pushed myself to my knees and looked around me. There was nothing but endless trees as far as my eyes could see. Straining my ears, I listened for sounds of civilization. Voices, a car, anything that would signify I wasn't a million miles away from

people, but there were just the birds screeching over me, and the
wind rustling through the bank of trees. This was like a terrifying
dream that I hadn't woken up from.

What was I doing in the middle of a forest?

Where was Bandit?

I tried to call for him, but the words stuck in my throat. I swallowed painfully and tried again. This time I was able to yell out
his name, although my voice sounded weak and fearful.

There was no response.

I screamed his name, louder this time, more desperate, but
still, there was nothing. No answering bark or the joyful sound of
him crashing through the forest towards me. Wherever he was, it
wasn't here.

I stood up, frantically trying to remember where I had been
before I woke up here. I was in a car, wasn't I? I remembered
watching mom drive to the shelter. Bandit was in the backseat,
and we were both eating breakfast.

The muffins.

It all came suddenly crashing back to me. We were both
eating the muffins mom had given us, and that was the last thing I
remembered. Was there a car crash? Had we been in a crash and I
somehow crawled here to safety?

I looked down at myself but couldn't find signs of any injuries
and my clothes were undamaged, so my theory had to be wrong.
Had Mom taken off with Bandit? But she didn't know anything
about him. She had no idea he was special, so that made no sense
either.

My heart was beating in my chest and I felt hysteria rise up
inside me. Where was he?

Suddenly I remembered my phone. I just had to call Sully,
and he'd find me. Sam used phones to locate people all the time, I
knew that from experience. I reached into my pocket only to find

that my phone wasn't there. Growing increasingly desperate, I patted my pockets, but it was no use, my phone was gone.

And then the panic really took hold.

60

SULLY

G ideon and I rushed home to the ranch.

We were hoping desperately that when we got there, we'd find Chase and Bandit in the kitchen eating us out of house and home, but only oppressive silence greeted us. We searched the place but couldn't find signs of them or Pixie. I had drilled into them the importance of being contactable at all times, so this vanishing act was a bad sign.

A really bad sign.

I punched in a number on my phone. It ran countless times without being answered. Just as I was beginning to think it never would, Sam's voice came on the line.

"Sully, I don't think we should be talking right now."

Hearing her voice almost broke me, but I forced myself to focus, my concern over Chase and Bandit overriding even my own turmoil. "I'm not calling about us. Listen, some things have happened: Dad had an accident, he's unconscious and in the hospital, and Chase and Bandit are gone."

"Wait, what did you say?" Her concern and confusion radiated down the line.

"I got home after our talk and found Zeb on the floor uncon-scious. And there's something else — he had a spy cam in his hand. It looks like he found it under that glass bowl in the living room. I think he was attacked because he found that camera. There's a nasty bump on his head and he hasn't come to yet. I tried calling Chase after I got to the hospital but her phone went straight to voicemail and she knows better than to turn it off."

"That's... OK. When did you last hear from her?" Sam asked, her voice suddenly taking on a professional tone as the sheriff in her kicked in.

"Not since this morning when she left. She left me a voice-mail, which I only picked up after we spoke this morning. She said she'd gone with her mom to a woman's shelter. She wanted to help get her checked in. Her mom said she was going to leave that guy she's with, so I guess Chase thought it was her duty to go with her."

"Duty? Chase doesn't owe her a thing." Sam said firmly.

"You and I know that, but Chase, despite everything she's been through, she's a sweet girl. She cares about people even when she shouldn't."

"I know, it's one of her best and worst qualities," Sam said immediately concerned. "I'm assuming Bandit is with her?"

"Yeah," I replied.

"Come to my office, I'll see what we can do to find her."

"Thanks," I said relieved and grateful for her help.

"Of course," Sam said. "Whatever is happening between us, she's still my family, Sully. You both are."

There was a lump in my throat the size of Texas, so I didn't trust myself to answer. I nodded, even though she couldn't see the gesture.

"We'll be there in ten minutes."

61

SULLY

Less than thirty minutes later we were pacing Sam's office.

Brad, her deputy, was putting a trace on Chase's phone. At my appearance, he had given me an apologetic smile, knowing that Sam had found out about my personal request. He even apologized before I shrugged it off. The man hadn't done a thing wrong. Besides we had something much more worrying to contend with right now.

I wasn't sure how the trace worked exactly, but it wasn't anything near as exciting as they made it seem in the movies. The process was long and laborious, and as yet we had come up with nothing.

"We're not getting a read on her phone, but that's because it's off. We'll only be able to get a hit once it's turned back on again. Unfortunately, the last known location was here. We have to wait to see if the trace picks up anything again."

"I can't believe she's gone off with her, what could she be thinking?" Gideon exclaimed, fury masking his concern. "I knew we shouldn't have let her into the house that first time. We're stupid for trusting her!"

"What's done is done, let's not torture ourselves over things we can't change," Sam said evenly. "We don't know that her mom has done anything. There could be a simple solution to this, like her phone has run out of charge. Still, I've put out an alert, just in case. If she hasn't gone far, we'll find her."

I couldn't help but hear the disclaimer in her sentence. "If she hasn't gone far?" I looked at the clock, then checked my phone for the time of the voicemail message. It was at least six hours since any of us had spoken to Chase. Six hours could give someone quite the head start. "What about that spy cam, can you get anything out of it?"

"I don't know. I've given it to our tech guys. They've already explained that it's an internet IP wireless camera, which basically means that it broadcasts what it sees to an online storage facility. They're going to see if they can find out where that is. If we can get in, we'll be able to see what they've seen. If we get really lucky and they haven't decrypted their IP address, we may be able to find them that way."

"But we're never lucky though, are we? If they're smart enough to get into our home and wire it up without any of us knowing, they've probably got that area covered." I didn't like how I was channeling Negative Nancy, but the odds seemed so against us.

"What about Bandit?" Gideon said. "What about the tracker you put into him?"

Sam frowned at me. "What tracker?"

"After what happened with Forbes, I put a tracker inside Bandit!" I had completely forgotten about the thing. "Gid, I could kiss you right now!"

He grinned at me, suddenly relieved. "Please, don't. Just find them that'll be good enough for me."

I ran to the computer and called up a website. It was a network that we vets used when we were trying to trace missing animals. It was a little like having a microchip that also functioned in a similar manner to the locate your iPhone facility Apple provided its products. I opened a second window and logged into my email, scrolling through the messages until I came to the one I wanted. When I had put the tracker inside Bandit, I had registered it with this website. As part of the service, the website had emailed me Bandit's reference number, the one I would need if he ever went missing. I typed in that number now and hit enter.

We waited anxiously as a timer spun around on the screen. Finally, a map loaded with a beeping icon. "That's it!" I said. "That's Bandit!" I hugged Gideon, yelling into his ear. "Well done!"

After our brief celebratory moment, I leaned in closer to see where he was and heard Sam gasp over my shoulder.

"Back there, that's Harrisburg in Pennsylvania. This means he's past it already. That can't be right, can it?"

I had no answer for her question. Instead, I listened to Chase's voicemail again. Paused, then rewound the part where she mentioned the name of the women's shelter.

Without my even asking her, Sam opened another window on the computer, searching for a woman's shelter in Pinewood, which was just over an hour's drive from here, but Google returned an error. There was no such place in Pinewood.

The shelter didn't exist, which meant Chase was being lied to.

Sam and I looked at each other, horrified.

62

CHASE

The facts were undeniable.

    I had blacked out only to wake up in the middle of a forest with no dog and no phone. None of that was good news or an accident, *and we already knew what I thought of coincidences...* While I had no idea how I came to be here like this, I did know one thing — I had to get out of here; I had to find Bandit. My Muttface was likely in danger.

With an aim in place, I scanned the area around me. There really was nothing but trees and leaves and dirt. A hysterical laugh threatened to make its way out before I choked it back down.

No, you will not panic. Get a grip.

Then I saw a dark shape on the ground around ten feet away from me. It was too small to be Bandit — thank God — still; I approached cautiously. I was alone and defenseless so I felt vulnerable; even the least threatening forest creature had the potential to be dangerous if disturbed. When I drew close, I realized it was a bag, the kind you wear over both shoulders. It was navy in color, with a bright orange label that I would have noticed right away if there was a bit more light around it, and there was something else about it that was odd... it looked brand new. I reached for the bag, noticing that it was made of a cheap polyester fabric. It actually reminded me of the ones Sully had gotten excited over in the Dollar Store. This thing wasn't exactly built to last. I pulled open the drawstring holding it closed, then tipped the contents of the bag onto the ground.

A bottle of water fell out, followed by three bargain basement energy bars and a flashlight. I inspected the side pockets hoping for more, but that was all there was... basic supplies that would only last me a day, possibly two. Looking at items, I came to two immediate conclusions. One, whoever had dumped me out here — and it was clear now that I had been put here on purpose — they didn't want me to die. And two, let me revise what I had thought just moments ago... Muttface was *definitely* in danger.

I shoved the items back into the bag and stood up, determined to get out of here so I could find my buddy.

Think Chase, what do you know about navigation?

I turned around slowly until my eyes settled onto a light in the distance. The sun! I could use that to work out my location. It hung low in the sky, which I knew meant I didn't have long before night fell. I had to get out of this dense forest before it got dark or I would be screwed.

Positioning the sun so that it was directly in front of me, I started walking.

Please, please let me get out of here before it gets dark.

63

SULLY

By now it had become clear to us, Chase's mom had kidnapped them both. I had no doubt in my mind. Though I desperately hoped it was just a case of her wanting Chase back, her disappearance added with the discovery of the spy cam made me suspect that it had something to do with Bandit.

And that terrified me.

If her mom knew he was special that opened up a whole host of questions I did not want to ask. Was it possible that someone else out there knew about him?

I focused on Bandit being the reason for the kidnapping rather than Chase, as there was a large part of me that refused to believe her own mother would hurt her. In all the stories Chase had told about her childhood, her mother was selfish and not particularly nice, but she had never hurt her. She seemed a victim herself. I desperately hoped Chase was okay. She had to be.

Sam yelled down the phone. She was trying to secure a helicopter that we could use to get to Bandit's location faster, but unfortunately, this required some red tape and her hands were tied. She couldn't reveal the helicopter would be to rescue a minor as that would instantly become an FBI issue, or mention anything about a super-smart-dog-that-had-been-created-in-a-lab either. It was looking more and more like we were on our own. We'd have to jump in the car and go after them.

It was a terrible idea, and we all knew it.

As they had a six or seven hour head start, we could be playing catch-up forever. Unable to get anywhere, Sam slammed the phone down and marched over to me.

"I tried, but there's nothing I can get us. There isn't a way to get help without telling anyone what we are doing." She sounded as desperate as I felt.

While Sam had been on the phone, Gideon had been impatiently watching over my shoulder while I kept my eye on the beacon announcing Bandit's current location. He grabbed my arm and started pulling me away from the desk.

"We're wasting time! Let's just go after them ourselves." He looked at the two of us, pleadingly. Sam grabbed her gun and slid it into its holster securely as she nodded in agreement.

"You're coming with us?" I asked her, shocked.

"I told you, you're family," she said.

I was so relieved by her answer that I almost broke down.

The three of us rushed outside and started after them.

64

CHASE

I had been walking now for what seemed like hours.

My feet screamed from pain and I was sure I had developed blisters the size of ping-pong balls. Branches tore at my arms, covering me with scratches that itched one minute, then stung like crazy the next. Wind whistled through the tears in my thin cardigan, and I knew it was only the exertion from the exercise that kept me from feeling the cold. I could still see the faraway sun, but it was barely a dot on the horizon. Night was fast approaching, and I had made no headway out of the forest.

Knowing it was highly unlikely that I was going to be rescued anytime soon, I had to seriously consider my options for camping down for the night. There was a part of me that wondered if I'd be able to navigate by flashlight, but twisted tree roots shot up from the ground all around me, not forgetting those freaking branches. If I tried walking at night without being able to see much around me, I would run the risk of hurting myself — and that was the best-case scenario. I was pretty convinced that, knowing my luck, I would end up dead in a ravine or blunder my way into the path of a bear, which they probably had in these parts, if only I knew where these parts were.

So no exploring in the dark. I would be sleeping here tonight.

I found myself a tree, one with a thick trunk, and started gathering leaves beside it. It wasn't much, but that trunk would offer some shelter in case of rain or wind. From my time on the streets I knew when sleeping rough, one of the worst things you had to deal with was the ground. If you didn't insulate yourself from it, the cold would creep into your bones causing a restless night so my priority was to find whatever I could to create a layer between myself and it, but seeing as there were only leaves and dirt and twigs, I didn't have much to work with.

Back at the ranch, one of my favorite hobbies was watching survival shows on television. You know, the ones where they left celebrities on an uninhabited island for a couple of days or weeks where they have to survive with nothing but a knife? Those were one of the few shows I loved to watch so I knew that finding water was of uber importance, as was creating shelter, and if I was going to be here more than one or two days, making a fire could be the difference in saving my life. While whoever it was had left me here with a bottle of water, a fire would give me the light and heat that I would most likely need to see me through the night. I also knew that a fire helped psychologically, lifting the spirit so you wouldn't give into despair.

I went through all the ways I knew of starting a fire without matches or a lighter. I could use the sun if I had a magnifying piece of glass of some kind, which of course, I didn't. Trust me to be in the one wood where nobody littered. But when I glanced back at the sinking sun, I realized that even if I had a magnifying glass, the sun wouldn't last long enough for me to get something started. I knew I could use batteries and aluminum foil or a cell phone and steel wool. While I was thinking along those lines, the right chemicals could also work, but I had none of those either. In the end, I realized my only possible option would be friction-based fire starting, in other words, rubbing some sticks or stones together which — going by what I remembered from those shows — was also the hardest way to do it, which was just great. I needed another challenge.

Feeling sorry for myself, I dug around the ground looking for a couple of sticks that might work.

If you're wondering how I knew all of this, I've that enormous photographic memory, remember? After searching for a while, I finally found two sticks that seemed like they would do the job. I was intending to use a technique called a Friction Drill where you have one stick standing vertically in the other stick, which would lay horizontally and have a groove cut inside. I was going to use my shoelaces to wrap around the vertical stick, which I would use as a spindle. As the spindle rotates under the correct speed and friction, it should cause embers to appear. Feeling hopeful, I started rotating the spindle, but within seconds, the thing kept sliding out of place or the shoelaces would slip off. I reset it time and time again, but I couldn't even get it to stay in place long enough to get any friction going.

It was hopeless.

Rage surged through me as I flung my hard-found sticks away. Inky blackness inched towards me as the sun began to set. I fixed my eyes on that sun, memorizing that glowing image, hoping that that would be enough to get me through the night. As it finally dipped out of sight, I found myself in a well of terrifying darkness. I fumbled for the flashlight, fingers sliding blindly around it until I was finally able to flip the switch on, but the beam that appeared was weak and only lit the area immediately before me.

By now, I was shivering from the cold, but that wasn't why I was scared. Now that the sun had gone, it seemed the forest was *alive*. All around me I could hear rustling as creatures trod over leaves. Invisible things stirred in the branches overhead, causing the hair to stay permanently raised on the back of my neck. I was terrified that at any moment a scorpion or snake might drop down on me. Briefly, the thought that scorpions provided a decent amount of calories entered my head before I almost retched. I'd die first.

I emptied out the bag and folded it before setting it down on the ground. Sitting on it, with my back against the tree trunk, I wrapped my arms around my legs and rested my chin on top of my knees. Only my butt touched the ground, so I hoped the rest of me would stay warm.

As I fought to fight the panic creeping along the edge of my mind, my thoughts drifted back to Bandit as a desperate gnawing ache appeared in my stomach.

Where was he?

Were they hurting him?

BANDIT

C old.

Why was it so cold?

Bandit opened his eyes to find he was in a place he had never been before. There were vertical lines in front of his eyes that he didn't understand, and the air smelled dusty. And old. Like this place, wherever it was, had not been cleaned in a century or more. His tongue felt thick with dryness and he smacked his lips together, looking for a water bowl. He shook his head, trying to clear away the fog that clung there.

He sniffed the air anxiously, desperate to locate Chase's smell, but there was just that dust. It was so thick that he could not find his friend. Forcing himself onto his trembling paws, he tried to make out where he was. As he examined his surroundings more, he came to a terrible conclusion. The vertical lines in front of his eyes were bars.

He was trapped in a cage.

Bandit began to pant heavily as memories surfaced of his time spent before in places like this, and with them came the fear. How had this happened? How was he back in a cage?

He backed away from the bars but took only a few steps before his rear hit the back of his prison. This was a small cage, smaller than any he had been in before, back where he was from.

Unable to control himself, he whined, a sound of pure fear as he turned around and pushed at the bars with his forehead.

"Now, now, none of that," came an annoyed voice.

Bandit looked up to see a man in front of him. He was not interesting to look at and he smelled like the liquids Sully liked to clean the bathroom with. It wasn't a nice smell and irritated his nose. Bandit pawed at it, disgusted when he suddenly realized that he had seen this man before, at Gideon's workplace — and he hadn't liked him much then. He had tried to warn Chase that something about him was *wrong*, when she and Gideon had been on the fire escape helping him move into the apartment above the garage, but as they had been out in public, he didn't have his iPad on him at the time. And as the two had left the man soon after, Bandit had forgotten to tell them. Bandit whined now, feeling bad. Maybe if he had remembered to warn them, he and Chase would still be together now.

Wanting to speak, Bandit went for his iPad before he remembered it wasn't in the pouch he wore around his neck: it was in Chase's bag. He barked, deeply unhappy by this turn of events.

The man watched him in fascination. "My name is Xavier. You are probably wondering what you are doing here, yes? I am a scientist, a world-class scientist if you must know, and you are the key to my greatest experiment."

Bandit had heard this kind of talk before. Where he was from, people often spoke of him like he was a thing to be used, so this did not frighten him. No, what frightened him was the manic gleam in the strange man's eyes. Bandit barked at him, frustrated that the man could not understand him. *Maybe if he could speak to him, the man would let him out?* However, Xavier shrugged, unconcerned.

"I'm sorry, I do not understand what you are saying."

Bandit's eyes scanned the room until they found his iPad lying on a table in the far side. It wasn't in Chase's bag after all! He barked again, pawing in the direction of his iPad. Xavier saw the motion with interest and smiled.

"You want your iPad? You want to communicate with me?"

Bandit barked once for yes, but Xavier shook his head. "Despite how intelligent you are, I don't care what you have to say. I am only interested in what lies inside your head. I believe you knew my old partner, Sebastien Forbes?

Hearing his name caused frightening memories to assault him. Bandit saw Forbes command the white-coats to do terrible things to his friends, things that had them foaming at the mouth and wetting themselves. Sometimes, after a Forbes visit, his friends wouldn't be able to stand for several days and had to crawl around on their tummies.

Bad man. Bad man. Bad man.

Bandit shook, unable to stop the chill that raced through his body at the mere mention of the man who had tortured him for most of his life.

"I see that you do. Don't worry, he and I are very different people. Sebastien was obsessed with healing his own illness and cared nothing of the world, unlike me. What I do will change humanity forever. What I do, I do for all of mankind. So you see, Alpha, I'm not like him at all."

A sound came from the next room and with it, the smell of burgers and the sweet drink Chase liked called Coke. A young man came into the room. He was thin and there was a nervous air about him. Bandit could see he was younger than Xavier, and he seemed excited. He bounded over to the cage and stared at Bandit.

"He's awake! He doesn't look that smart, does he?" he said to Xavier.

"And how is a smart dog supposed to look, Dick?" Xavier said, barely able to contain his patience. Dick shrugged.

"I don't know, I just thought he would look more special." He wandered towards Xavier and stopped at the bench where the iPad sat. "Pretty clever of them to teach him how to speak using an iPad." He stared at the tablet as if it were a mythical creature that would come alive at any moment.

Frowning, Xavier crossed the distance to him, snatched a heavy metal bar from the bench, then violently smashed it onto the iPad. One, two, three times! The glass screen cracked and smoke rose from the destroyed tablet. Dick jumped back, startled... and a little afraid.

"Why did you do that? I was looking forward to using it with him!"

Xavier fixed cold eyes on him. "The last thing I need is for you to be communicating with this dog. I don't want him filling your little head with any of his big ideas."

Bandit had watched the two in silence, but now he barked louder and louder, until Dick covered his ears, cringing. "Why is he doing that! Stop it!"

Xavier studied Bandit shrewdly. "He is probably concerned for the girl, Chase?"

"Woof!"

"The girl is fine. We dumped her in a forest, but she'll be OK so long as she figures out how to get out of there. We weren't going to harm her. She was collateral damage, and we needed her out of the way."

Hearing this, Bandit felt some of the panic lessen. She was safe! Chase was fine. Or at least, she would be. Squashing himself into a corner of his prison, Bandit sat and tried not to let the fear overwhelm him.

Chase would come for him.

He knew she would.

66

SULLY

Hands gripped on the wheel, Sully watched the needle flirt dangerously towards eighty. It was against the law to drive any faster, but Sully wondered if that still applied when one of its own representatives were in the car.

Gideon had fallen into an exhausted sleep on the backseat. When they had first left, Gideon had insisted upon driving. Wired with all that had happened, he'd had no other outlet, so Sully had stepped aside. He'd let the younger guy drive for several hours until they stopped for a restroom break. It was Sam's idea to switch drivers then, as she had seen the younger boy's eyelids drooping from weariness, now that his initial adrenaline had faded.

The three of them didn't know what they were more concerned about. Having to leave Zeb while he was in intensive care at a hospital almost caused Gideon to break. The kid considered the old man his own father, and in the six months that they had lived together as a family, Sully thought of him as a younger brother though Sully wasn't quite as ready to adopt him like he had Chase and Bandit. Although Bandit was only a year or two old, his brain and intellect were on par with those of a teenager. Sully was only in his thirties and didn't feel old enough to be a father of three grown kids. He felt a sudden sob rise in his throat and had to force himself not to give in to it. His own panic would not help the situation. He looked over at Sam, sitting stoically in the passenger seat, and shot a prayer of thanks that her calming presence was here for this.

Her eyes were fixed on the screen on her phone, which was tapped into the tracking website. The entire time we had driven, Sam called out instructions although as they had gotten quite far ahead of us, the directions mostly consisted along the lines of "stay on this road for another four hours."

It was impossible to believe that, even with all her contacts, there was no legal way for us to catch up to them any faster. Every option we brainstormed led to alerting the authorities, which was just too dangerous. I even toyed with the idea of stealing a helicopter like Chase had, but Sam had put an end to that fast enough. Licensed helicopters needed to file flight plans and get clearance, all of which took time that we didn't have. Sam warned us that if we tried to fly without them, we'd be caught soon enough. Chase had gotten lucky that the one aircraft she hijacked had been a stealth machine that didn't play by the rules. Unfortunately, we couldn't rely on the same good fortune.

Sam looked up from her phone and I could feel her eyes fix on me.

"You want me to take over?" she asked softly.

I shook my head. I needed the physicality of driving. Going through the motions grounded me and made me feel like I was doing something to save them.

She accepted my response but kept staring at me, something clearly on her mind. "Since we're stuck here anyway, I suppose we should talk about us?" she began.

Before she could say anything else, I stopped her with a hand.

"I don't want to be a jerk, but I can't do this right now. There's only so much I can take, so can we drop this for another day when my family aren't in danger?" I probably sounded more bitter than I wanted to, but to hell with it. My heart was already broken. She didn't need to stampede all over it too.

She nodded and fell silent.

I continued to drive.

67

CHASE

I was up by the crack of dawn.

Even with all my preparations, I had barely slept at all. I hadn't felt that icy, deep-in-my-bones-cold since when I had first left home. It was just after winter then and I had survived by sleeping huddled in archways and doorways, burning fires in trash cans to keep warm. But last night there was no fire or shelter from the cold, and the sounds of the forest woke me every time I had almost drifted off to sleep. I was exhausted and felt like the dead, but I knew I had to push on.

I reached up and felt my lips with my fingertips. They were dry and peeling, which seemed astonishing considering it hadn't been that long since I had last had a drink. Despite my best intentions, I had finished that bottle of water a few hours ago. I still had an energy bar left, but the stuff was cloying and made me even more thirsty than I already was. A picture of a cool, refreshing glass of water invaded my mind. I could almost feel the liquid moving down my throat. My mouth even made the motion of swallowing before a sob escaped.

I shook myself. *Get a grip, Chase. Bandit needs you, so stop crying over no water.*

I got up and stretched my weary body before I started moving once again using the sun as my navigation tool. At some point, if I just went far enough, it should lead me somewhere different. That's what always happened on those shows, anyway.

I walked, barely feeling the branches now as they scratched against me. In the back of my mind, it was yelling at me that my body could be going into shock, but as there wasn't much I could do about it, I pushed the warning aside.

It wasn't important, only Bandit was.

I conjured up an image of him in my mind and held it there as I continued forward.

68

BANDIT

Bandit woke to feel cold steel beneath his paws.

He had barely slept all night and had only finally managed it when he collapsed out of pure exhaustion. The man, Xavier, had gone, but Bandit could still smell him. He knew he was never too far away. There was another room close by that he liked to stay in. Bandit didn't know what he did in there, but he heard Xavier talking to himself sometimes. Bandit didn't like him. He frightened him almost as much as the bad man had.

The other boy, the younger one who smelled of burgers, was closer. Bandit could hear him now approaching softly. His footsteps were quiet and considered... Bandit knew from experience that people only walked that way when they were being sneaky. Chase did this sometimes when they played hide and seek. He could always hear her breathing or her footsteps, but he never told her. It amused him not to. Thinking about her now, a whine escaped his lips.

He missed her so much!

He was thinking this, wondering if she were safe when Dick came in. He was holding a blanket as he approached the cage.

"I thought you might like this to sleep on. That cell must be cold."

Bandit barked once, softly. He didn't want the other man to think that he wasn't grateful for his kindness, he wanted him to know.

"Now I'm going to open the door, but please don't attack me or try to escape. Xavier has this place rigged with cameras and you wouldn't get far."

Reaching the cell, he pressed a button on a remote that he found on the workbench, then as the door unlatched, in one quick movement he tossed the blanket inside before slamming the door shut again. Bandit grabbed at the blanket and spread it out as best he could. He stood on it, feeling relief from the cold metal on the pads of his paws. He circled the blanket before sitting down. For this one little moment, Bandit felt a little less terrified than he had been since he had first woken up in this prison.

But that all changed with the sound of hard shoes pounding the hallway outside, followed by a strange clinking sound.

Whimpering, Bandit moved to the back of his cell as Xavier stormed into the room carrying a giant syringe and some heavy looking chains. Seeing Dick, however, Xavier stopped dead.

"What is that? A blanket? The animal will probably soil it and then there will be germs. What were you thinking! He could catch something from the filthy thing. Get it out of his cell!"

Dick shot Bandit an apologetic look as he opened the cage door and pulled the blanket out, dislodging Bandit — who still stood on it — in the process. Bandit made a sound of pure desperation as Dick whispered *"Sorry."*

Xavier pulled on a pair of rubber gloves as he picked up that wickedly long syringe with a giant needle attached and approached the cell.

"Now Dog, this will hurt far less if you don't struggle."

Bandit looked up at the roof of his prison and howled.

69

CHASE

I had been walking now forever, it seemed.

My head thumped with a headache caused by both tiredness and lack of water. The world spun around me at times, which I knew was another symptom of dehydration. It didn't matter how fast or slow I went; the forest was ever looming and there was nothing on the horizon but those trees and branches. I started to wonder how long a person could survive without water, food or sleep. I was pretty sure the figure was a couple of days so I had a good twenty-hours or so left inside me. Whatever happened, I knew that I would find Bandit or I would die trying. My buddy needed me.

I know that my need to save him — which overrode my concern for my own well-being — might seem impressive, but if I were being honest, I was also driven by overwhelming guilt. The fact that this happened at all was my fault.

If I hadn't been stupid enough to trust her, Bandit and I would be together, in our room right now playing our Jeopardy game and eating junk food.

Last night, while I had been trying to sleep but couldn't, my brain had kept going back to all the things that had happened, until it became clear as glass that this was my mom's doing. Somehow she had planned this and had separated us on purpose.

But why? For what reason?

Tears pricked at the corners of my eyes, which caused a disbelieving laugh to escape. How could there be enough liquid inside of me to cry when my mouth felt like there was a desert inside of it? It made no sense at all. As my vision misted over with tears, I heard a sound coming from ahead of me. And for once it wasn't a bird or a squirrel or those possible snakes. I stopped dead and listened to something that bubbled and moved. I blinked, dazed but suddenly hopeful.

Was that the sound of running water?

I picked up my pace and started running towards it. As I got closer, the sound of water became louder until I broke through a bank of trees to find a small river in front of me.

I sobbed with relief, yet still felt half terrified that this was a mirage. Falling down into it, the water seeped in through my clothes, soaking me as I laughed in delight. It was real! The water was so clear I could see the stones lying on the riverbed. Cupping my hands, I scooped up water and drank blissfully. It was the best thing I'd ever tasted in my whole life. Impatient with the small amount I was able to scoop up, I shoved my whole face into the river and gulped it down like a fish.

When I had drank at least a gallon and my tummy felt swollen, I stood back up. Now that I had quenched my thirst, I felt so much better. The headache that had been plaguing me the last few hours vanished almost instantly and energy surged through me. Staring at the river as the fog started lifting from my mind, I realized something else: I could just follow the river now instead of wandering aimlessly in the forest.

Rejuvenated, I started downstream.

I'm coming, Bandit. I'm coming.

70

SULLY

We didn't stop all night.

When I got tired Sam took over and when she was too tired to continue, she swapped with Gideon. We drove that way until the blinking lights of Pittsburgh were behind us. Sam hadn't tried to talk about our relationship again. The rational part of me knew I had been harsh by cutting her off as I had done, but I was barely holding on. I could not think about our broken relationship on top of everything else.

Gideon had barely spoken since he had been up. It was like he didn't know what to do without the other two around him. As soon as he woke, he called the hospital to check up on dad, but there had been no change — he was still out for the count. At least his vitals were stable. The doctor had every hope of a recovery. We still didn't know what had caused his accident, but I was pretty sure that someone had attacked him and frightened Pixie off. That little dog would not have run otherwise. I was terrified to think that it might have scared her away.

"You think Pixie is okay?" Gideon asked, his voice cutting the silence like a knife. I glanced at him in the rearview mirror.

"I'm sure she's fine. She's managed to get away before, I'm sure she didn't go far. When we get back, we'll probably find her waiting for us on the porch." I didn't really believe this, but I wanted the boy to stop hurting. There was enough pain in our hearts without him worrying about the dog, too.

Sam shot a look at me from the corner of her eye. She saw straight through me but didn't say anything. She knew, as well as I, the unlikelihood of my words. Rummaging through her bag, she pulled out two bottles of water.

"Here, drink, the two of you." She handed the bottles to us. I declined, despite how thirsty I was. "You're tired and stressed. If you don't drink, you'll pass out and that won't help any of us, it certainly won't help Chase or Bandit any."

It was difficult to argue with her logic.

Like a pair of schoolboys that had just been chastised by their teacher, Gideon and I took the water she offered. I opened the bottle, gulping it down greedily, then felt immediately guilty.

What if Chase and Bandit were thirsty? They'd been gone almost twenty-four hours now. What if they were hungry?

Putting the cap back onto the bottle, I sat the bottle in the drinks holder, deciding that I wouldn't eat or drink another thing until I had them both back in my sights, no matter how ridiculous that sounded.

Sam would just have to deal with that.

71

CHASE

The river twisted and turned as it made its way downstream. I followed the water, taking care not to slip on the moss-covered rocks and stones that littered my path. Buoyed from escaping the woods and re-energized by my drink, I moved quickly and it wasn't long until I saw the gray line that signaled a road was ahead of me.

Relief washed over me so fiercely, I broke into sobs again. I had done it. I had hit civilization.

Not until that very moment had I really believed that I was going to get out of this alive. But now that I could see the road, I knew I was safe. Using the last of my energy, I ran for the road and reached it within minutes. Turning back, I marveled at the distance I had crossed — sports had never been my thing and I had never run that fast before in my life. But like the woman who finds herself suddenly able to lift a burning car to save her baby, it was amazing what you could do when the ones you loved were in danger. Looking at the empty road, I knew I just had to wait for a car to pass.

I was planning on flagging it down. Ordinarily, I wouldn't

recommend hitch-hiking. The world was filled with weirdos and it was my motto never to be trapped in a confined space with one, but it wasn't like I had a choice. I had to get to a phone to call Sully and warn them. By now they must have realized that the two of us were missing, but only I knew we weren't together.

As my feet pounded the road, I looked at the sky, still pink from its recent sunrise. Besides my footsteps, the only occasional sound came from a bird flying overhead. This wasn't a main road, and it seemed I was in the middle of nowhere. With a sinking heart, I realized that it might be some time before a vehicle turned up, and even then there was no guarantee that they would stop. Steeling myself for more walking, I squared my shoulders, trying to ignore my screaming feet.

I hadn't been going long when I suddenly heard the welcome sound of an approaching vehicle. I spun around to find a lone car turning the corner. It was pretty old looking. As it approached, I saw that there were many scratches to the paint job and several dents that it had accrued over its lifetime. An old man sat behind the wheel, a woman — his wife, I guessed — beside him. They must have both been in their seventies as to my eyes, they looked older than Zeb. I started jumping up and down, waving my arms. The car came to a stop a few feet in front of me.

I bolted to the driver's door.

He wound down the window, looking startled to see me. "What is a young girl like you doing out here at this time of the morning by yourself?" he exclaimed.

"I need your help. Do you have a phone I can use?" I looked at him and his wife pleadingly. The woman, whose face was made up immaculately with tightly wound curls piled neatly on top of her head, nodded.

"Why yes, of course," she said, elbowing her husband. "Harold, what are you waiting for, give the girl your phone!"

Harold reached into his pocket and took out a Samsung phone

that he handed to me. It was the sort of basic phone that Gideon would have mocked. No frills or internet access, I took it gratefully and was punching in Sully's number before they could change their minds. After a few seconds, it started to ring and Sully's wary voice came on the line. "Hello?"

"Sully! It's me!" I cried, almost bursting into tears right there.

"Chase?" He sounded so relieved that my eyes started to tear up. "Where are you?"

I looked at Harold. "Where are we?"

He blinked, confused by my question, but answered it anyway. "You're right outside Dresden, Ohio."

I repeated the location to Sully. I heard him repeat that to someone, probably Sam. "What happened, Chase? What are you doing there?" he asked, concern making his voice harder than normal.

I stared at the old couple, watching me wide-eyed. "I can't talk about it right now, but she lied Sully. My mom lied. I'm not exactly sure what happened, I must have blacked out because I woke up in the middle of the woods on my own."

"You're not together?" Sully asked, incredulous. I heard him curse then, several words I'd never heard him say before.

"You need to find Bandit, I think she took him," I said this softly, hoping Harold and his wife wouldn't hear.

"We're on our way to him. We have his tracker, so we're trying to get to him now. Wait, whose phone is this?" Sully demanded suddenly. He must have seen the number on his phone and not recognized it.

"I flagged down a car. It belongs to this old couple who were driving."

"Let me speak to the driver," Sully said. I didn't even question his command, just did as he requested. I handed the phone to the old man. He took it without question.

"Hello?" he said to Sully. I couldn't hear what Sully was

saying, but the old man's expression changed from questioning to surprise. "Why yes, it's MAJ-124. My full name is Harold Benjamin Bartlet and my wife and I live in Wilmington, Delaware, around two hours south west of here." The whole time he was speaking, his wife watched him with varying degrees of perplexity on her face. Eventually, she just snatched the phone from him and started yelling into it.

"Who are you that you would leave your daughter in such a state? How dare you ask us all these questions when we have nothing but concern for her? Why, she's not any older than my grandchild! The nerve!"

Hearing her outrage must have put Sully's mind at rest. I guess he rationalized that they weren't anything other than they seemed. It wasn't likely that they were in on some evil plan with my mom. Gently, Harold took the phone back from his wife. Sully said something to Harold that got the old man nodding in agreement.

"Yes, I can take her to Red's place. It's an eatery a few miles from here. She'll be safe with us until you can come and pick her up." He listened as Sully said something else to him. "Why yes," Harold answered sounding surprised. "That's the address, that's the one. How did you know?"

Whatever Sully said next caused Harold's eyebrows to raise. His face turned stern, as did his manner. "Young man, I know you are concerned about your daughter but there is no need to make threats at me. We will take her to Red's diner and wait for you there. I'm giving your daughter the phone back now, I assume you won't be making threats at her too?"

I took it from him. "What's happening?" I asked.

"We're going to come and get you and then we can all go after Bandit," Sully said.

"No. You've got to get to him now! You don't know what they

might be doing to him!" I had to fight the urge to scream the words at him.

"Well, I'm not leaving you with two strangers in the middle of nowhere," said Sully, his voice brokering no room for argument. I was surprised, having never heard Sully use that tone with me before.

"I'll be fine. I just found my way out of a forest, didn't I?" I replied, somewhat testily. I didn't want to be a brat, but I could handle myself. Bandit, however... I couldn't bear it if anything happened to him.

Sully didn't respond straight away. I heard Sam and Gideon speak heatedly with him but couldn't make out what they were saying. When he came back on the line, he sounded resigned.

"New plan. Gideon is coming to get you while Sam and I go after Bandit. When Gideon arrives, the two of you will meet us at whatever location we find Bandit. I'll send you the details, but Chase, you have to promise not to go anywhere. Do not go off with anyone, understand? And when you get to this pit stop, you call me from a landline there. Sam will run a trace so we can see exactly where you are. I don't think Harold or his wife are lying, but let's be cautious all the same."

"Okay," I said. "I'll call you soon as we get there. You just make sure you find him, Sully."

"I will," Sully said. I expected him to hang up then, but he didn't. "Be careful. I can't have anything else happen, okay?" He sounded so wary, so broken, that I picked up on it immediately.

"What else has happened?" I asked, scared at what he might say next. There was a moment's pause.

"Don't worry about it now. Let's just get you back to us." He tried to sound reassuring, but I could hear the strain in his voice.

"Sully, is everyone OK?"

"We're fine. You just make sure you're safe, you got that?"

"I promise," I said and hung up.

72

SULLY

I handed the phone to Sam to find her watching me with a funny look on her face.

"What?" I asked.

"I'm impressed with the way you handled that. You sounded... well, you sounded like her dad."

I felt myself get a little embarrassed. "Yeah, well, I'm nowhere near old enough." She didn't respond, but kept on looking at me with that funny expression.

Now that we knew what we had to do, we had a new problem — we were missing one car. Seeing that we were nearing a gas station, I pulled in. "We need to acquire an extra vehicle," I said.

Gideon nodded, and as soon as I stopped the car, he jumped out. Sam frowned, staring at the cars. A young family sat waiting for their dad in one, but the other two were empty, their drivers inside the gas store.

"How is he going to get us a car? It seems unlikely that anyone would be willing to sell one to us, even if we had the cash. They'd be stranded here if they did and there doesn't look like there's going to be a taxi firm for miles?"

I avoided her gaze, feeling suddenly uncomfortable. "I don't think that's what he has planned." She frowned at me, unhappy with my response, then spun around in her seat to see what he was up to. I cringed inwardly, guessing what her next reaction was going to be.

"Oh my God, is Gideon breaking into that car?"

Before I could reply, she jumped out of the car and marched over to him. Feeling helpless at what was coming next, I quickly followed her.

"What do you think you are doing?" she hissed at Gideon over his shoulder. He froze, a lock pick already jabbed into the car lock. Apparently, he always kept some with him for just such an occasion.

"It's okay, I've done this before," the hapless boy responded. Her eyes flashed dangerously, but he didn't see it. Focused as he was on the car, he also didn't see me shaking my head behind her.

"When?" she demanded, hands on her hips. "When have you done this before?"

Gideon gestured behind her at me before I could stop him. "When we were escaping Platinum Industries. We didn't have a vehicle, so I stole one. Sully said it was fine."

Sam's eyes hardened as she spun around to glare at me. "Oh he did, did he?"

I felt it might be time I spoke up for myself. "Well, I did that one time on account of the fact that I had just been shot and Bandit was almost dead. We sort of had more pressing things to contend with. And the truck we took was a rust bucket. No one would miss it. The owner probably made more out of the insurance than he would have done the actual car." The more I spoke, the bigger the grave I was digging for myself. I forced my mouth shut, knowing that Sam would have a lot more to say to me about this later.

"Gideon, please remove that lock pick and step away from the

car. I will acquire one for us myself, except I will do it legally."
With that, she stormed into the gas station. I heard her make
some sort of announcement, then she waved her sheriff's badge in
front of a guy's stunned face. Moments later she came out with a
set of keys and pointed at the car Gideon had been trying to steal.

"Not everything has to be a crime," she said somewhat testily.

"We don't all have a badge we can wave around," I replied, "so I
wouldn't get too high and mighty over this."

She gave me a withering look that had me wishing I had kept
my mouth shut.

73

CHASE

I got into the car with the elderly couple.

They let me hang onto the phone, which I found comforting. If anything happened, I just had to hit redial and Sully would know.

We drove for another five minutes or so before the eatery appeared. Despite how early in the day it was, cars packed the parking lot. The diner was made to look like it was made in the 50s or 60s and was quaint and charming.

"Margaret and I eat here all the time," Harold offered. "They do great pancakes."

At the word pancakes, my stomach suddenly growled. Hearing it, Margaret laughed. "I guess we'd better get some food into you, when was the last time you ate?"

"I had a couple of energy bars through the night" I responded. "Before that…" I trailed off as my thoughts returned to those muffins and Mom. I couldn't believe that it had only been 24 hours since I was in her car with Bandit. So much had happened, it felt like weeks had already passed. An image of Bandit doing his version of a smile as he stared out of the window on the back seat flashed up in my mind. Seeing his face, I felt a stabbing pain in my heart and my arms ached to feel his furry body in them. Harold saw my expression and mistook my need for hunger.

"Let's get you warm and fed while we wait for your dad," he said.

Inside, country music played on the radio, though it wasn't loud enough that I could make out the song. The place was heaving with customers, most of whom I noticed were around the same age as my hosts. Apparently, this place was a major hit with the oldies. The smell of coffee and freshly baked waffles hit my nostrils, causing saliva to flood my mouth. Although I wanted nothing more than to sink my teeth into doughy, sugary layers of goodness, there was something I had promised to do first. My eyes swept the area until they found a phone along the bar area — but it wasn't a payphone. Margaret saw my consternation and spoke. "I'm sure they'll let you use their phone. Go ahead and ask nicely."

I nodded and approached the man who stood behind the counter managing orders. He looked up at me when I neared, even as he barked out an order to the cook behind him in a steamy kitchen. "Haven't seen you before, young lady?"

I climbed up onto a stool. "No. I'm from out-of-town. Um... I need to use your phone. Margaret said it would probably be OK to ask?"

He scanned through several receipts, mind already elsewhere. "Sure. Go ahead. Just no international calls, please. Some of you kids seem to think it's funny when I get my phone bill."

He turned away from me, setting down the receipts onto a spike that was already a third full, and focused on refilling the coffee machine. Picking up the phone, I dialed Sully again. He answered straight away. "That you, Chase?"

"Yeah. I'm here," I replied.

"She's there. You want to run the trace, or are you happy with just the number? It's come up on my phone?" His voice was further away, as he spoke with Sam. "Hang on, Chase. We're just checking to see where you are."

It went quiet as Sam did whatever she needed to do. Moments later, Sully came back on the line. "Got it. We know where you are. You think you'll be OK to wait with these people?"

I looked across the room at Harold and Margaret. He had pulled out a chair for her and was now tucking her under the table and laying a napkin across her lap. It was clear that he loved her very much and that he took very good care of her. "I'm safe here, Sully, don't worry. Harold and his wife seem like nice people."

I heard him let out a long breath. "Excellent," he said. "Gideon is getting ready now to come and get you."

"Okay. Did Zeb and Pixie stay at home, I haven't heard them in the car with you," I asked.

There was a long, long silence. When Sully spoke again, his voice was strained. "Zeb is in the hospital. He had an accident. He's unconscious."

"What?" I cried out, shocked. "What happened?"

"We don't know. I found him unconscious and Pixie was gone. Zeb had a spy cam in his hand... I think someone rigged up the ranch and has been spying on us for a while." He fell silent as the full force of his words came to me.

"But that means they know about Bandit," I said, unable to keep the fear at bay.

"Yeah," was all he could say.

I swayed on my feet, reeling. Who were these people? I felt totally unsafe suddenly and stared at the sea of faces surrounding me, realizing that any one of them could be behind Zeb's attack and the cameras in our home.

"Chase, we have your location now. So I am going to get off the phone and send Gideon to you. Anything happens, or even if you just want to talk, you call me okay? I'm right at the end of the phone."

"I will," I replied. "Just bring him back to us so we can go home."

"I'm working on it, Chase. I'm working on it."

CHASE

I made my way back to the couple.

On my approach, Harold gestured at a chair opposite him. I sat down as Margaret handed me a menu.

"Thanks," I said. Although I was relieved that Sully was on his way to Bandit, I couldn't shake the numbing fear that had flooded me since the moment Sully had told me about the cameras in our home. I felt so hopeless here, being so far away from him.

"Since your dad won't be here for a few hours yet, you should order whatever you'd like. You must be starving if you spent the night in the forest by yourself."

"I am, but I don't really have any money on me," I replied hesitantly. I wasn't fishing, but I didn't want them to think I could pay for a meal either. These people had already been so nice to me, the last thing I was going to do was eat and run.

Margaret gave her husband a look as her eyes softened. "Well, of course, we're paying child, what kind of people would we be if we didn't help you after your horrific ordeal?"

I looked at them gratefully and saw the kindness in their eyes. I gave them a smile, my first in forever it seemed.

"Oh, Harold, look. Isn't she pretty when she isn't scowling?" Margaret said, eyes twinkling. My smile grew a little wider at her comment.

A waitress came and poured coffee in our cups. She obviously recognized them both by the welcome she gave them, but didn't know them well enough to address them by name. I filed this away in my head, adding it to the pile of evidence I was accruing that the Bartlet's were good, honest folk.

I grabbed my cup and started gulping the scalding liquid down. It burned my mouth, but I didn't mind, desperately craving its heat in my stomach. I glanced down at the menu, which had all the usual items you'd expect in a place like this.

"Can I have the stack of pancakes with bacon and eggs? And some toast, too. And orange juice?" I said this to the waitress but my eyes were on my breakfast mates as it would be they who would be paying for the meal. Harold nodded as if he were happy with my choice.

"Margaret and I will just have some scrambled eggs, I think. We don't usually eat much in the morning, but we'll keep you company."

The waitress nodded and went off quickly. She was nice enough, but seemed rushed off her feet. Looking around the place, I could only spot two waitresses, which seemed silly given how busy they were. *Must be short-staffed.* I gulped down the rest of my coffee quickly when I suddenly noticed how filthy my hands were. I didn't want to think about how the rest of me must have looked. Embarrassed, I stood up. "I should probably go wash up."

Margaret pointed to the restroom. "Last door on your right past the counter." I nodded my thanks and followed her directions.

The restroom was like the rest of the place, quaint and clean. Catching sight of my reflection, I was shocked to see how crazed I looked. It wasn't just the streaks of dirt over my forehead either which added to that illusion, but I found not one, but two leaves in my hair, not to mention I looked as if I were back to my dumpster diving days. Taken as a whole, I was amazed Harold and Margaret hadn't thought I was a feral beast. Pretty sure I wouldn't have let myself into my car if I had one. I pumped a handful of soap from the dispenser and started scrubbing. It took a while, but after several rounds of washing and rinsing, I almost resembled myself again. Realizing this was about the best I could do without an actual shower, I went back to join the others.

The food had arrived and now covered the table. The smell of buttery pancakes wafted into my nose as the sight of the crispy bacon caused my stomach to clench in anticipation. I sat down quickly and grabbed a piece of bacon, meaning to shove it in my mouth when I suddenly remembered what had happened the last time I had eaten. I hesitated, lowering the hand holding the piece of meat.

"I know this is going to sound strange, but, could you eat a mouthful of all the food on my plate first?" Harold's eyebrows raised in question while Margaret just looked confused. "Please," I continued. "I can't eat until you've had some first."

They looked at me funny before giving each other a perplexed look, however, they each grabbed a fork and took a nibble of everything.

Relieved that the food wasn't drugged, I crammed the piece of bacon into my mouth, forgetting all about utensils. Although Harold and Margaret seemed a little taken aback by my lack of etiquette, neither of them said anything. I chewed fast, inhaling everything in sight while they picked at their eggs with a fork. In no time at all, my plate was empty. Harold must have sensed I could still eat as he signaled the waitress. "Tess, can we have the same again? Thank you."

With horror, I heard myself making a strangled sob and had to physically choke it down. I would not break down in here, not in this nice place with these nice people. I would not repay their kindness by embarrassing them like that. Harold looked away respectfully while Margaret's own eyes crinkled over with sympathy as she stretched out her hand and patted me on the arm.

They sat silently across from me, sipping out of their cups of coffee while I demolished the second round of food. Finally, I leaned back against my seat, hands across my swollen stomach. I had expected to feel satiated, but instead, I just felt sick. Turns out sleeplessness and exhaustion coupled with worry and food don't mix.

"Can you tell us what happened to you?" Margaret asked, concern etched over her face. "Do we need to call the police?"

I shook my head warily. "Trust me, there's nothing they can do. I just need to regroup with my dad and we'll be able to sort this out. But thank you," I said, finally remembering my manners. I took a gulp of OJ and waited for the waitress, who came back and cleared the table. After she filled up our drinks once again, she disappeared off.

"If you don't want us to call them, you're going to have to explain why that is," Harold said kindly but firmly. "I don't want to intrude, but these are not normal circumstances and I need to know that we are doing the right thing by you."

I looked at them, knowing that I owed some sort of explanation, even if it couldn't be the real story.

"My mom and dad have been fighting for years. They've never gotten along, but dad had finally decided to get a divorce, only my mom wasn't happy about it as dad pays for everything. So, anyway, one thing led to another and when she found out that I didn't want to live with her she went crazy. She got drunk and must have drugged my food because when I woke up, I was in that forest. Our court day is today, so I think she had this crazy idea inside her head that if I couldn't make it there to stand against her that she would win somehow. I don't know. It's messy."

Normally I can lie without blinking, but I felt bad about doing it to them. Still, it wasn't like I could tell them what was really going on. Margaret squeezed my hand.

"That's a terrible thing your mother did, I'm so sorry dear." Harold nodded in agreement, but he looked more stern about it. "Are you sure we shouldn't tell the police? I would have thought this would help your father's court case?"

I shook my head. "No. Despite what it looks like, we have it under control now."

"And what about Bandit?" Harold asked. "I heard you mention his name a few times."

I looked him square in the face and hoped that he was buying my story. "He's my dad's dog. She knows he loves him — he's had him for years — so she took him out of spite."

Margaret shook her head, making clucking noises even as her eyes turned hard. "Some people just shouldn't be allowed to have children or pets."

She would get no disagreement from me.

75

SULLY

The tracker had finally stopped moving a few hours ago and was fixed at a location just outside of Cleveland, Ohio.

Google maps showed that it was a disused school. I suppose as evil headquarters went; it was a pretty clever choice. No one would be poking around, and they — whoever our enemy was — would be free to do whatever it was they were doing.

The building flashed up before us as I slowed the car to a crawl, coming to a stop by a dense bank of trees. I didn't want whoever was inside to be notified of our arrival. I was getting a sense of déjà vu except the last time I had hidden a vehicle behind trees; it was a crop-duster, and Gideon and I had just arrived by Platinum Industries. This deserted place was a far cry from that high-tech behemoth, however.

The school was old and sprawling and made up of several one-story buildings. At some point, this must have been a fun learning establishment going by the faded painted calculations and symbols that I could still make out beneath a blanket of ivy. A good number of the buildings were boarded up, but that still left five or six possible buildings where Bandit could be housed, which seemed a lot of ground for the two of us to cover.

"We need to get to him quickly since they've already had him for some time. God knows what they're doing to him. We should split up."

Sam gave me a look that showed she clearly disagreed with my suggestion. "Nope. We stay together." Her voice had no room for argument, but I tried anyway.

"Come on, Sam, I know how to take care of myself." I knew she wasn't worried about herself, so her insistence on staying together must be out of her concerns for me, and my ego didn't like this one bit.

"Yeah, well, last time you thought that you were shot so..." She left it hanging, but I filled in the dots.

"I wish Chase hadn't told you that," I grumbled under my breath. "Not everything needs to be shared."

Although the place wasn't being used (other than by these bad guys), it was still owned by the government or some such entity as they had done a decent job of keeping the school free of vandals, although they didn't go as far as to fork out for wired security alarms — I could find none of the usual blue and white signage that signaled an ADT presence. It looked like the buildings had basic water and power supplies, however, as I couldn't see a generator anywhere, unless one was tucked away around the back.

Huddled together, we approached the first building. A giant rusty chain wrapped around the handles on the front door. Even if we could get the door open, we would never get through that chain. I looked over the brickwork until I came to a window, almost hidden behind a curtain of ivy. "We get in through there."

Sam nodded and pulled her gun from its holster. As I parted the ivy, Sam held her gun by the handle and smashed it against the glass. The window cracked, then broke into a thousand pieces, raining glass around us. I cringed at the sound, impossibly loud in the near silence.

"I hope they didn't hear that."

Sam shrugged. "If they did it's too late, and if they didn't, we have the upper hand."

"I like how you think, even if it is strange logic that got you there," I replied.

Sam shot a smile at me, eyes flashing with life. It was at that moment that I realized how she thrived on this kind of excitement. Seeing how bright her eyes were and how red her flushed cheeks were, I realized just how much I loved this woman. When we got through whatever this was, I was determined to win her back.

76

SULLY

Climbing through the window, we found ourselves in a dark corridor. Light slanted in at angles that illuminated patches of ground ahead of us, but left the rest of the corridor shrouded in darkness. Dust covered every inch of surface, giving the place a musty, unpleasant scent that had me scratching my nose. Unperturbed by any of this, however, Sam put her analytical eyes to work.

"The dust hasn't been disturbed, I don't think anyone's been in this wing for a while," Sam said.

"Yeah," I agreed. "Let's see where it takes us though, hopefully, it connects to one of the other buildings. It'll be a lot quieter than trying to smash through another window."

I turned on the flashlight on my phone, using it to highlight the way ahead. Sam went to walk before me, but I pushed her behind. "Single file. Me first, you after. Got it?"

She looked at me, unimpressed with my bravado. "Really? We're doing this now?"

I nodded, not messing around. Whatever she thought of my capabilities, I was going to do my damnedest to protect her. I expected her to put up more resistance, but her eyes suddenly softened.

"Okay, tough guy. Lead the way."

We walked down the corridor, eyes and ears peeled for any movement or sound, but other than a mouse scrabbling past when it saw us, all was silent. We walked until we reached a set of double doors. Grabbing the handle, I turned and pushed, but there was something on the other side of the door, wedging it closed. "Give me a hand with this," I said.

Sam came up behind me, put her shoulder to the door and waited for my count.

"Ready?" I asked. She nodded. "Three, two, one... push!"

Together we shoved the door hard and got it open about a foot before we stopped, unable to move it any further. I could see the corner of what looked like a steel cabinet lying horizontally behind the door. Either it had fallen down of its own accord or someone had put it there to dissuade visitors. I was pretty sure I knew what the answer might be.

We squeezed through the gap and found ourselves in a gymnasium. Empty bleachers loomed eerily, the ghost of past crowds haunting the place. Although the room can't have been used in years, I could almost hear the sound of a whistle blowing followed by a stampeding team as it raced up and down the court. It'd had been over a decade since I'd last stepped foot in a place like this, and truth was, I hadn't missed it, never having been a fan of school, remembering how stressful it was when I realized early on that I wouldn't become the surgeon my parents had expected of me. This had eventually led to our estrangement. So much time wasted because the two of us were too stubborn to pick up the phone. Thinking of my dad now, lying in the hospital bed alone, I felt the guilt torment me, even as my head knew that he would want me to save Chase and Bandit first.

Hold on, dad. Be the usual stubborn goat you are, and just hang on...

We moved through the sports hall towards another set of double doors at the opposite end when I heard a sound. I stopped as hope flared up in me. The sound was small but distinctive, and one I recognized immediately.

It was the sound of paws.

"Bandit?" I asked softly.

Sam stared at me quizzically. "You heard him?"

"I think so," I said.

Re-energized, I sprinted towards the double doors and pushed them open to find myself in another endless corridor. This one wasn't as dark as the last, however, so I could see very clearly the dog standing in front of me.

It wasn't Bandit, but it was a dog I recognized.

Pixie.

77

SULLY

S hock and disappointment tore through me.

I couldn't believe my eyes. "Pixie?" She tilted her head at me and listened as if she was trying to understand what I was asking of her.

"You think whoever took Bandit and hurt Zeb, kidnapped Pixie?" Sam asked.

"It seems likely though I've no idea what they would want with her?"

Sam looked thoughtful as she studied the dog. "Maybe they were just told to grab a dog and didn't know what Bandit looks like?" Sam offered. "Until we found her, we only had the one dog."

"They had a camera in the ranch though? Shouldn't they have seen her through that?"

"I don't think we ever had Pixie in the living room. She stayed mostly in the den or with Gideon. And you know she didn't like Bandit, so if he was around, she usually wasn't."

"But why is she roaming around on her own?" I wondered aloud.

"Maybe she snuck out from wherever they had her contained. She's done it before, after all," Sam replied logically.

Her explanation made sense. I crouched down until I was eye-level with the dog. "Pixie, do you remember me? I got you that nice food and toys. Gideon would be really excited to know that you're okay." The little dog didn't react until I mentioned Gideon. At his name, her ears pricked up.

"That's right. Gideon's your friend." Pixie did a little dance with her paws that let me know she had understood at least some of what I had said. "You know who else is your friend? Bandit. Can you take us to him, Pixie? Can you take us to Bandit?" She tilted her head the other way. For a moment, I thought she didn't understand, but then she barked three times and started moving away. She stopped a few feet away, then turned back to look at me.

"She's going to take us to him!" I said excitedly.

"Good girl Pixie, good girl!" said Sam.

We took off after the little dog. She led us through twisting corridors and empty classrooms, never hesitating in her direction. She barely even sniffed at her surroundings, so I knew there was no doubt that she knew where she was going. I could feel the edge of my panic lessen, knowing that any minute we would be reunited with Bandit. I hoped to God he wouldn't be in the same condition as the last time I had found him when he was lying across the operating table with his head cut open. The Doc wasn't with us this time and I wasn't sure I would be able to save him without her help.

We must have been going for some ten or so minutes when Pixie turned to look at us, barked three more times and then started racing forward.

"This must be it!" I sprinted after her as she ran through a doorway, Sam following close behind. We were still running when I found myself skidding to a halt. There was a barrel of a shotgun in front of me and it was pointed right at my head.

A man in a white lab coat with long hair and a younger guy, who looked just a year or two older than Gideon, stood ahead of us. They both had shotguns that were trained on us. In that brief first moment of seeing him, the man in the lab coat reminded me of those scientists we had seen at Platinum Industries, except this man didn't bustle about like those did. He was calm and considered, clearly in control. Despite our circumstances, he had a mild-mannered air about him. He seemed perfectly ordinary, like someone you would never give a second glance at. It was either a cunning disguise or something that he'd need to spend a lifetime discussing with a shrink.

I looked past them to see a cell — and trapped inside was Bandit. Seeing me, he jumped to his feet and barked excitedly.

The scientist looked down at Pixie. "Well done, Dog. You brought them right to me."

Shocked by her betrayal, I could only stare as the scared and sweet little dog I had come to know suddenly changed demeanor completely. Her eyes turned cold as she bared her teeth at me, snarling viciously. She looked wild and ferocious and utterly terrifying.

I could have kicked myself. We should have listened to Bandit when he had warned us she was strange. Looking at her and the man, the truth came to me. "You're a spy. You were working for him the whole time," I said to the dog.

"You're not as dumb as you look," the scientist said to me.

"Oh I don't know, I'm feeling pretty stupid right now," I replied.

I stared around our surroundings, hoping to find something to help us out of our predicament. There were a row of windows set high into the wall but they were tiny, put there just to let more light in. An odd assortment of scientific apparatus covered the benches — I had no idea what they were used for. The young guy who I guessed must be his assistant, came at us with cable ties that he tied around our wrists.

"Not so tight unless you're deliberately trying to stop the blood flow," Sam said through clenched teeth. Immediately the boy looked apologetic.

"Sorry, I've never done this before."

"You don't say," Sam said, peeved at being caught.

After he had restrained us, he started backing away when the scientist stopped him. "Aren't you forgetting something, Dick?" He stared pointedly at the gun still in its holster around Sam's shoulder.

"Right," Dick said as he relieved Sam of her weapon. "Do you want me to put them in the utility room?"

The Scientist shot him a withering look. "I don't want them in the same room as the dog, so what do you think?" It wasn't really a question if his scathing tone was anything to go by. Dick flushed, embarrassed, then gestured with the gun at us. "Follow me, please."

I gave Bandit one last look as we were lead away from him, into another area that contained several small metal tanks — around the size of a dog I realized — that were connected up to a complicated system of liquids and gases. The tanks had long been empty, however, and I couldn't see any signs of what they might have once contained. My mind flicked back to Pixie suddenly, who had stayed in the room with the Scientist. For her to be as deceptive as she was, required abnormally high intellect... of Bandit proportions, essentially. But that wasn't all she would need. Despite Bandit's cleverness, like all dogs, he was a straight shooter. The kind of deviousness Pixie displayed was alien to their kind.

I had been silent a while now, and Dick finally noticed. Worried that I might be up to something, he stopped suddenly and looked at me. "Whatever you're thinking, it won't work. Xavier would have already thought of it before you."

"Xavier? That's his name?" I asked. Dick nodded, not the least bit concerned that we now knew his boss's identity.

"I was thinking about Pixie. How she behaves isn't normal for a dog," I began.

"That's because she isn't a normal dog," Dick replied. "She was created, right here."

"Created?"

Dick hesitated, possibly wondering if he should let me in on the big secret, but then he shrugged. "Well, I guess it doesn't matter if I tell you now since neither of you will be getting out of here. Pixie was genetically grown, cloned from the DNA of a regular dog but then adapted into the creature you know now. Xavier created her out of nothing but a few minuscule cells. When she became fully grown, and Forbes was making headway with his Alzheimer's research, Xavier copied the placement of the tumor that is inside Bandit and put it into Pixie. It's why she's as clever as he is."

Sam and I looked at each other, reeling by what we were being told. "But that's not all he did, is it? He did something else to make her so devious?"

A grudging respect grew over his face. "Yes. During Forbes' research with the tumors, they found that if they placed the tumors on different parts of the brain, there were differing results. For example, placed in one area, the tumor made the dog very aggressive, in another, the dog became very controllable."

I pictured Pixie changing her personality like Jekyll and Hyde, and the horrific answer came flooding to me at once. "He put multiple tumors inside her brain, didn't he? That's why Pixie is the way she is?"

Dick nodded. "Yes. Her head's riddled with the things. We think that the many tumors might also be tampering with her personality, causing her mood to swing, but that suits his purpose so they have been left as they are."

Sam had been watching the two of us closely while we spoke. I knew she was looking for the right moment to stage an attack, but before she could do anything, we arrived at a metal door. The old metal sign on it had lost a screw and now hung precariously on one end. The writing was faded, but I could make out the words "Utility Room". Dick opened the door and moved us inside ahead of him.

Barring a few boxes of old files with past school kid's names that someone had forgotten to deal with. It was empty.

"But Bandit was suffering from convulsions with just the one tumor, Pixie must have physical side effects?" I asked, unable to stop feeling concern for the dog, particularly now that I knew her behavior was through no fault of her own.

"Oh, she's dying for sure. Probably doesn't have more than a few weeks left, but she's already served her purpose so it isn't a great loss to Xavier, especially now that he has Alpha back."

Sam suddenly spoke up, her voice filled with concern. "Has him back... he had him before?"

"Oh, sorry, I thought I'd already explained that. Alpha was created here too via the same cloning process. He was actually Xavier's greatest success until Forbes took him away when he was barely a pup. Xavier's thrilled to have him home."

The boy's eyes turned bright thinking of the scientist's happiness, and I realized at that moment, just how much Xavier controlled this kid.

"Xavier is a lunatic. I've met his partner and Forbes was no better. Do you have any idea how brainwashed you are?"

Dick's eyes glittered angrily. "Don't you dare talk about him like that! Xavier is a God amongst men. You have no idea how important his work is!"

"So important that he kidnaps little girls and conducts unethical experiments on the powerless? Don't be so stupid." I didn't bother to hide my disgust. He needed to hear the truth, no matter how much it hurt.

"Stupid?" Dick said. "You're the one who thought his wife was messaging him from the grave. If anyone's stupid, it's you!" He stopped, waiting for my reaction, convinced that he had won over me. And he was right. I felt like I'd been punched in the gut.

"That was you?" I asked, my voice barely above a whisper.

"Xavier wanted you preoccupied, so I came up with the idea to mess with you. I knew you were going back to visit your wife's grave — hell, the whole town knew — so I dug it up a bit, and left that hair clip for you to find. Then I messaged you using an app that makes it seem like the message came from a particular phone line. You were so hung up over your wife that you lost your mind over it completely. So who's the stupid one now, huh?" Dick gloated. He turned to Sam next, determined to stick the knife in. "If I were you, I certainly wouldn't be marrying this guy, not when he's still so in love with his wife."

I couldn't breathe, knowing what this idiot child had done to me. It was all I could do not to kill him: my hands might be bound, but I could still wrap them around his scrawny neck. I counted to three in my head, desperate for the rage to quieten. I had to keep reminding myself that this boy was under the thumb, that he didn't know any better. I couldn't take it out on him, no matter how badly I wanted to. Through the haze of red, I saw Sam looking at me, her face filled with sorrow, regretful now that she knew I hadn't made up the message.

Dick marched us to the corner of the room, then backed away. He kept looking at me, hoping that I would say something he could use against me, but I was numb. Disappointed, he left. Moments later the door closed in front of us and I heard it lock.

We were trapped.

Silence enveloped us. Trying desperately to regain a small sense of myself, I turned to Sam. "Told you we should have split up."

She shot me a withering look.

BANDIT

Sully was here! Oh boy oh boy oh boy!

Bandit knew he would come. He knew they wouldn't leave him here like this. But seeing them, Bandit was also worried now. Dick had taken Sully and Sam away with a gun pointing right at them, which Bandit knew were terrible things. He was there when Chase had used one on the bad man. After the loud sound when Bandit thought his ears had exploded, the bad man had died and Chase had cried. They could not die — not only did he and Chase love them, Sully was also their pack leader.

Fueled by the knowledge that they needed his help, Bandit ignored his own fears and threw himself at the cell door. He slammed against the metal, using the full force of his body. The doors rattled — they did not seem to be that well made — but the door remained firmly closed. Ignoring the pain that shot through his body, Bandit moved to the back of the cell to get a running start and *HURLED* himself at the door again.

The cold metal hit him like a wall but stayed locked. He landed hard on his feet. Whimpering, Bandit held up an injured paw and licked it when a sound from across the room caught his attention. He turned to find Pixie staring at him. Her eyes glittered as she flattened her ears onto the back of her head. Prancing up to the cell, Pixie nudged the door with her nose.

Bandit barked, yes! She was helping him!

Though they had never liked each other before, Bandit was thrilled that Pixie was now his friend. Excited, he chuffed in encouragement and lowered down onto his stomach. He barked instructions at her, letting her know that the way to open the cell was on the bench. He described the object as best he could as Pixie went over to investigate. She jumped up onto her two front paws so she could see onto the counter.

Daintily, she picked up the metal bar Xavier had used to destroy Bandit's iPad. Bandit barked twice. No *that isn't right*. She dropped it down with a clang, then nosed around the bench with Bandit barking more. The closer she got in their version of "hot and cold". Finally, she picked up the remote Bandit had seen the others use to open his cell. He bounced up and down on his paws, ignoring the pain that shot up his right front leg.

Yes! That was it!

Pixie moved her nose over the button but stopped short of pressing it.

Bandit barked at her to do it, but she deliberately set the remote back on the bench and made a noise that sounded like laughing.

Bandit froze, shocked to the core. She was taunting him! She had no intention of helping him at all!

Hurt and confusion flooded through him. What was wrong with her? Why was she such a bad dog? He never got the answer to his question, however, as Xavier came into the room. Seeing Bandit limping in his cage, he frowned, displeased.

"What have you done to yourself, Dog? Have you been trying

to get out? I hope not. I can't have you hurting yourself — I need my specimen undamaged."

Seeing Pixie across the room, Xavier shot her a look. "You best not have been upsetting him, or it's back into the tank for you."

At his words, Pixie cowered and shook, backing away from him. She seemed genuinely scared, causing Bandit to feel even more confused. *Why did she help him if she was scared of him?* Nothing about her actions made any sense.

Xavier scanned the room until his eyes settled on those heavy chains he had brought in with him before. Grabbing them now, he came towards Bandit with them.

Moments later, Bandit found himself with one heavy chain around his neck and four around each of his paws, each of which were now secured to the ground. Bandit could only stand, sit, or lay down, but other than that he could not move. Whimpering, he hung his head in misery.

Xavier nodded, satisfied with his work. "There. You can't move, therefore you cannot hurt yourself."

Dick came into the room carrying the drink called coffee that Bandit knew Sully liked, but he stopped when he saw him. Seeing that he looked uncomfortable with what he had done, Xavier took the coffee from him and took a sip before speaking. "He's fine, besides it's the only way to make sure he won't hurt himself. It looks far worse than it is. I did the same to Pixie for years while I was training her and look how well she turned out."

Bandit suddenly realized that these were the very chains that had caused the scars on Pixie's body. Even in his despair, he felt sympathy for her. No dog should ever be chained up like this, no matter how bad they were.

Xavier drank more of the coffee as he studied scans and charts as Dick watched Bandit from across the room guiltily. Having seemingly forgotten his threat of only moments ago, Pixie now wove herself between Xavier's legs, desperate for affection, but the older man grew tired of this very quickly and kicked her out of his way.

Hurt, Pixie slunk off into a dark corner as she watched Bandit with those angry black eyes.

79

SULLY

Well, on the plus side, Bandit was safe. In a big cage, essentially, but safe.

Sam and I were stuck in our own prison, with those cable ties that were clasped pretty tight around our wrists. Thankfully Dick had left our hands bound in front of us so it wasn't as uncomfortable as it could have been. Still, we were in quite the predicament and I wasn't sure how we were going to get out of this.

I had been trying to wrap my head around what we'd been told. Not the Emma thing — that I had bolted down and filed away for another time. I knew if I focused on what Dick had done, the anger and resentment would bubble over and consume me. I could not afford for that to happen, so I willed myself to move past it. I would deal with that when I had the luxury to.

And so it was that I now found the vet in me taking over. What Xavier had done to Pixie defied all natural laws and was madness at best. In spite of Dick's grand talk, Xavier wasn't any better than his old partner had been. As far as I was concerned, they were both as deluded as each other, though Xavier was worse in my book. At least Forbes had been suffering from a disease which would have soon debilitated him. From what I could see, Xavier was wrecking lives and torturing animals for his own ego... he had to be taken down.

There was a pipe in the room Sam had been staring at for close to a minute now. I tried to think how it could possibly help our situation, but failed completely. After Dick had left, she had sat quietly beside me. I figured she must be pissed at being caught out like this, what with being a sheriff and all.

"Don't be so hard on yourself, you didn't know this would happen," I said, I thought, helpfully. She looked at me, an exasperated expression on her face.

"You think I'm concerned about our situation here?" she said.

"Well, sure. We're tied up and locked in a room. They took your gun and everything else we had of use. I don't see how anything short of a miracle will get us out of this."

She moved on to her knees and stood up gracefully, one brow arched in challenge.

"A miracle, huh? How's this for a miracle?"

With that she raised her clasped hands high over her head, then she swung down fast and forcefully... With a snap, the cable ties broke loose and clattered to the ground. And just like that, Sam's hands were freed. I gaped at her, astonished.

"How the hell did you do that?"

Sam shot me a triumphant grin. "Gravity and physics, my friend. When you swing your hands down with so much force and pull them apart on the downswing, the cable ties can't take the force and snap. This is survival 101 training. Haven't you seen the Youtube videos?"

"Like you ever watched Youtube until Chase got you doing that." A thought occurred to me next, causing me to frown at her. "So the whole time he was tying us up, you knew you could get out of it. No wonder you didn't seem afraid."

She gestured at me. "You try. Just get them as high above your head as possible and swing down fast and furiously while trying to pull your hands apart."

I tried to get up onto my feet, but I wasn't half as graceful as she was when she had done it. I staggered to my feet clumsily was probably a better description of what I did. Once I was up, however, I did as she instructed and goddamn if it didn't work.

I was amazed.

"It's lucky he didn't tie our hands behind our backs. Then we would have been in trouble," she said.

"We're not out of the woods yet," I replied. "We still need to find a way out of this room."

"Well, let's get searching."

80

CHASE

After we'd eaten, we sat there at the table drinking coffee and chatting.

Once I had given them my creative explanation of events, Harold and Margaret hadn't bothered me with any more questions about my life. Instead, they seemed happy to just talk about theirs.

They were childhood sweethearts, I learned, having met at high school. They were married young and had five kids by the time they were in their 30s. Sadly, one of the kids had died at a young age. Some horrible illness, they had said. They explained that their son, Stephen had been sick his whole life forcing them to spend their entire fortune on his medical bills, as they desperately tried to find something that would help him. A cure never materialized, however, and eventually they lost that nice big home they had saved their entire lives for.

After Stephen had died, they downsized and moved to Wilmington, where it was cheaper — though far less safe — to raise their other kids. They were heartbroken and had never really recovered from it. It wasn't the physical bricks and mortar aspect of losing their house that they missed, but the memories they had shared with him there. They could never be replaced and this being before the time of phones with video cameras, they only had pictures of him. I remembered how Sully had been when I had met him. He had been clinging on to his wife's memory by hoarding her things. I can't imagine how it must have felt for Harold and Margaret to have let go of the only home they had known with their son.

Seeing as I had started to feel down by their story, they quickly explained that though their funds had diminished greatly, they considered themselves blessed to have seen their remaining kids grow into happy and healthy people who went on to have kids of their own. Margaret had been so proud when she took out her purse and showed me several photos of their whole family that she kept in her purse.

I was amazed not just by the sheer number — there must have been at least forty of them — but by how close they all were. Here they were at Thanksgiving, then Christmas, then at one of their grandkid's birthday parties. The family even threw summer get-togethers at a campsite where folk flew in from all across the country. These were highly organized affairs that included scheduled events like a performance show and sports. They even made itineraries for them. *I mean, who were these people?*

I'd never met my dad or anyone from his side of the family. My mom didn't get on well with her family either, so I had only really met one aunt a few times. She lived in Arizona and had a lot of pets, was all Mom would tell me. She didn't mention her often, but whenever she did, she had this look on her face. I knew what it was straight away, even if she could never admit it — she was jealous of her sister. From what I knew of her, she had a happy life and a loving husband. Apparently that was all my mom needed to know to be envious of her enough to cut her out of our lives.

I had looked down at Margaret's family, at the army of people that she called family, and wondered what it must be like to be surrounded by people who loved you.

Suddenly I realized what I was thinking and felt immediately awful. Sully loved me and Bandit too. Even Gideon... probably. And of course, Sam and Zeb. I felt bad for my moment of ungratefulness. You know how they say if you are never grateful for what you have, you will never have enough? I saw it on an Oprah rerun once, and it had stayed with me ever since. I mentally reminded myself that my life was very different now, and that I should be grateful every day for that.

We'd been in that diner for hours now. I had told them I didn't need a babysitter, but they refused to leave until my family got here. Harold said they had been coming back from visiting their daughter who only lived a couple of hours drive away near Cleveland, so they were in no hurry to get home. Her oldest was just heading off to college and they had gone to give him money towards his tuition. They had just sold Margaret's car — which was much nicer and newer than Harold's — to pay towards his school costs. As they had told me this, I regretted all the food I had put away. I took in their appearance, finally able to see how their clothes were patched several times over. Here I was eating like crazy when money was a concern for them.

Although the time passed as pleasantly as it could under the conditions, my mind kept drifting to Bandit. Until he was safe, I couldn't relax. I found myself drumming my fingers on the table in agitation.

When both the breakfast and lunch shift had gone to be replaced by the evening staff, the door finally opened as Gideon came rushing in. I shot to my feet, so ridiculously happy to see him. I leaped up from the table and threw myself at him before I even realized what I was doing. His arms went to encircle me and he squeezed me right back. We were holding each other for a few

seconds before I suddenly got all embarrassed. Gideon and I
hung out all the time, but we didn't really touch, so this was kind
of a big deal. We stepped away from each other; me blushing furiously while he looked suddenly awkward.

"And this must be your brother then, as it obviously isn't your
father," came Harold's voice. It sounded like he was trying hard
not to laugh.

"No, I am her... brother," Gideon said unconvincingly. "Our
dad couldn't get here because of..." He stopped suddenly, looking
at me for help, not knowing what cover story I had given them. I
rushed in to fill in the gaps.

"Court. Dad's in court. That's why he couldn't make it, but my
brother is here now so that's great and we should get going."

I turned to Harold and Margaret then, suddenly feeling
desperately sad that I would never see them again. They really
were decent people in the world I was learning this every day. I
threw my arms around the two of them, much to their shock, but
they hugged me right back. "Thank you so much," I whispered to
the two of them. Margaret had tears in her eyes as she patted me
on the shoulder and smiled.

"You get on back to your family, dear. I'm sure your dad, or
whoever he is, is looking forward to having you back." She had a
twinkle in her eye. It was the first time I realized that neither of
them had been buying my story, yet still they had sat with me and
paid for all that food, even though they knew I was lying the
whole time.

My mind was literally blown.

I turned to Gideon. "Do you have any money? I ate a ton of
food so we need to pay them back."

Harold and Margaret shook their heads, aghast. "Oh no, dear,
we don't need your money. You keep it. It was a pleasure to help
you."

"But," I argued, "what about your grandson? You just said you sold your car to pay for his schooling."

"We'll be fine Sweetheart, we always have been, and we will again. The Lord has a way of providing. Bless you for offering though, child. Tell your dad he raised you well."

I smiled at them, feeling myself tear up. If only they knew.

"We better go," Gideon said.

I nodded. "Thank you again, for everything. Bye."

I followed Gideon out the door when I suddenly turned back around. "Wait, what's your surname again?" I asked.

Harold looked surprised and curious, but he answered. "Bartlet. Why?"

I shook my head. "No reason, I just wanted to know who I owed this kindness to."

And with a last smile that I flashed at them, Gideon and I left the diner.

81

CHASE

The car Gideon had brought with him was in better condition than the Bartlet's. It had leather seats and AC, something I usually adored but barely appreciated right now. I wanted to know everything that had happened since I had left that morning.

Gideon explained what they knew, but it wasn't until he came to Zeb that I started asking questions. I was stunned by what had happened to him, but most of all I felt guilt, guilt that I wasn't there in his time of need. Since I had arrived at his ranch, Zeb had been there for me the whole time. From Forbes' death, Zeb had never complained about Bandit and I suddenly living in his home, not once. Instead, he had become the grandfather I'd never had so the fact he was in a hospital unconscious with none of us by his side, that killed me. I tried to be strong, however, because despite how awful I was feeling, it couldn't compare with Gideon's pain. His initial relief at seeing me had faded somewhat. Now I could see just how stressed and tense he really was.

I borrowed his phone and called the hospital to check on Zeb's progress, but nothing had changed. It took some convincing to get them to give me any updates since they said family only and I had no proof that I was until I described Sully and Gideon to them.

After I finished with the hospital, I tried calling Sully, but his phone went straight to voicemail. I felt a moment of panic as this wasn't usual. What if the bad guys had gotten to them? I was about to say just as much to Gideon when I realized that it was more likely that Sully had turned his phone off so it wouldn't ring if the bad guys were searching for them. You always saw this in the movies when people were trying to be stealthy, but suddenly their phone would start ringing at just the worst time possible. I knew Sully and Sam were smarter than that, however. At the first sign of danger, they would have switched it off. Still, I wanted to get a message to them to let them know I was safe, so I sent Sully a text message that simply said, "left the diner."

I figured, worst-case scenario if someone had gotten hold of their phone that message wouldn't mean very much to them and it would not warn them that we were on our way.

Having done as much as I could with the phone, I studied Gideon's profile. His jaw was clenched tightly, and I was getting really concerned that he would literally bust a gut or something. "You want me to drive?" I offered. He looked at me skeptically.

"I didn't drive 5 hours to save you only to die now, so no thank you."

"If we crashed it wouldn't be my driving but your teaching that would have done it," I retorted. It felt good to bicker. It felt normal, like we weren't driving towards our impending doom. But the conversation died down as quickly as it started. It was too much effort to joke around, especially when we were both so concerned for our family.

Turning to the window, I stared at the scenery blurring past, praying silently in my mind that we would get there in time.

82
——————

CHASE

We pulled up at the rundown school a few hours later. I saw Sully's car parked by some trees and we pulled up alongside. There was no sign of either him or Sam, not that I really expected one. I stared out at the sprawling buildings, suddenly overwhelmed by the scope of our search. *How were we going to find them? How were we going to get to them before the bad guys?* Gideon must have thought the same as me as he stopped dead in his tracks, his eyes surveying the scene around us.

"Where do we start?" he asked me. I was about to hazard a guess when something glinted in front of me. I zeroed in on some pieces of glass on the ground and continued up until I found the window that had recently housed them. I pointed. "There. That's where Sully and Sam got into the building. That glass looks freshly broken. And look how clean the frame is: they knocked all the glass out of it so it wouldn't cut them when they climbed inside."

Gideon studied the window and nodded, agreeing with my assessment. "Before we go," he leaned into the trunk of the car and retrieved a flashlight and a wrench.

I stared at the items in his hands, unimpressed. "What, no gun?"

"Sam already has one, plus she figured this would be enough."

"But she isn't with us," I pointed out.

He looked at me exasperated and rolled his eyes in that way that always half irritated and half amused me. "Thanks, Captain Obvious."

"You didn't tell her you're a crack-shot? Doesn't she know what you did before when Forbes' men attacked us?" I asked, unable to get my head around it all. Gideon was the best shot out of all of us. It seemed stupid not to arm him to the gills.

"Sam feels very strongly against us using weapons of any kind. I think she still considers us kids."

"One day, we need to sit her down and tell her every little detail, even if it means getting Sully in trouble," I replied glumly.

We headed over to the window and climbed inside, careful not to cut ourselves on the remaining bits of glass that the others had missed in the frame. Gideon switched on the flashlight as the beam spotlighted the way ahead. He swung the flashlight around, searching for any signs of them when the light picked up some footprints on the ground. "One big set and one smaller one," I said studying the imprints in the dust.

With their trail set easily in front of us, we followed their footsteps down the corridor and into a sports hall. Here the dust wasn't as bad as in the corridors, so the footprints trailed off, but Gideon spotted doors at the end of the room. One was slightly ajar, as if someone had gone through but hadn't closed the door completely behind them. "They must have gone through those doors," he said. I nodded and the two of us moved quickly through until we found ourselves in another corridor. Here the flashlight picked up another set of prints, but these were smaller and distinctively doglike. My eyes flared open in hope.

"Bandit's paw prints?" I asked.

Gideon lowered into a crouch to study them. He frowned, uncertain. "I'm not sure, I can't really tell, but it seems likely."

I moved beside him to examine the prints myself when we heard a sound from down the hall.

Panting.

I was so familiar with that sound, I knew instantly that it was caused by a dog breathing through it's open mouth. I looked at Gideon, meaning to tell him when Pixie rounded the corner.

I blinked, my shock mirroring Gideon's own.

"Pixie? What on Earth?" Gideon asked. Seeing him, Pixie froze for a few moments before her tail started to wag vigorously back and forth. She ran up to Gideon and jumped up against him as she squirmed and barked with delight at seeing her long-lost friend. Gideon was thrilled to see her safe and bent down to pet her. But I didn't move, thoughts racing through my mind.

Something was very wrong with this picture.

She was the last to have seen Zeb before he was injured, but she had disappeared only to reappear here now. At the location where Bandit had been taken to. Now, I'm not a girl who believes in coincidences at the best of times, so I figured the bad guys must have brought her here. But why wasn't she locked up somewhere, like I assumed Bandit was?

Gideon must have sensed my hesitation as he stopped to look at me, but before he could voice anything, I shook my head at him. I bent down and gestured at Pixie. "Hey girl, do you know where Bandit is?" I asked her.

She cocked her head and considered my question. Then she spun on her heels and did several loops in a circle with excitement. She barked three times, darted away, then came back again, paws dancing across the ground with impatience.

"She wants us to follow her! She's going to take us to him!" Gideon said, pride and excitement in his voice. "Lead the way, girl," he said and started after her.

I didn't move, thinking about the things that had been happening lately, and a niggling doubt went through my mind. Bandit — wonderful, loving Bandit — could not get along with this dog and I hadn't listened to his reasons why, but I'd always trusted my Muttface before, and even though this might be too late in the day, I decided to trust him once again. Instead of following Pixie, I lunged forward and picked her up in my arms.

Immediately her head snapped around as she snarled and barked viciously at me. The change in her was absolute and terrifying. It was all I could do not to let go of her. I moved my head away from those snapping jaws.

"Chase, what are you doing?" Gideon asked. But even as he asked, his expression went from bewildered to concerned as he saw how violently Pixie was reacting. Quickly, he clamped his hand around her mouth, squeezing her jaws together so she couldn't hurt me. "I've never seen her like this, it's like she's turned feral."

I looked at him, shaken, straining to hold her still. "Or maybe this is who she really is," I said quietly. "Bandit kept trying to tell us about her but we wouldn't listen. And the thing with Zeb, you know Pixie was probably the last person or animal that saw him before he went unconscious, right? What if she had something to do with it? What if she's working for the bad guys? It would explain why she's running around this place on her own."

Gideon frowned, trying to take it all in. "But how is that possible? She's just a dog, what would be the purpose of leaving her with us?"

I shrugged. "I don't know, but everything started to happen around the time she turned up. All I know is, Bandit didn't trust her and he must have a reason for that, and now we find her here where it's all happening. Yeah, we can't trust her."

As I said this Pixie bucked wildly in my arms, trying frantically to get away. It was getting harder and harder to restrain her. My muscles spasmed, having to fight against the dog. "We need to put her somewhere, I can't keep holding on to her." Gideon looked around, then nodded towards a room at the end of the hall.

"In there," he said. Together, we moved towards the room as fast as we could, while we held tight to Pixie who still hadn't stopped thrashing in my arms. I had no idea how she had any energy left.

Gideon kicked open a door and we went through into a small restroom and placed pixie into a cubicle as Gideon quickly shut the door behind her. Then he took out a coin and flipped the lock closed from the outside. Trapped, Pixie went *insane*. Growling and snarling, she started flinging herself at the door.

Smack! Her whole body connected with the door with a loud crash. I had no idea how she didn't break all the bones in her body, but Pixie fell down to the ground then launched herself at the door again. She was making such a horrendous noise that even though it seemed obvious, she was working for the other side, I was still concerned about her hurting herself, but we had no choice. There was nothing we could do for her so we left her there and hoped that the others — the bad guys — were too far away to hear the racket she was causing.

We moved away until her barking was a faint sound in the distance. "Give me your phone," I said to Gideon. He handed it to me without question. Although I didn't expect him to answer, I called Sully's phone again, but this time the phone was on. My heart flared up with hope. After a few rings, it was answered by a man's voice that I did not recognize. And with that, my hope was quashed.

"Where's Sully?" I demanded of the unknown answerer.

The man's voice came down the line, weedy yet triumphant. "Would that be Chase by any chance? I'm impressed, I never thought you would find your way out of the woods so quickly."

His words made me think about my mother as another jolt of fear raced through my body.

"That was you? Is my mom with you?"

He laughed, although it was without any mirth. "She's probably drinking away the money I gave her. You really have been very unlucky with your parents. Absolute trash, the two of them."

Although I had suspected that she was in on whatever this plot was. To hear it straight from his mouth hurt like hell. I didn't reply immediately, not wanting him to hear my pain.

"I take it you are here to save the dog, Sullivan and Sam? Well, I will make it easy for you, if you come to me now I will spare their lives."

I don't know what possessed me to do what I did next, but I didn't think about it — I just reacted. I ended the call and switched off the phone.

Gideon looked at me aghast.

"Why did you do that? What have you done?"

83

XAVIER

The dead dial tone sounded in his ear.

Xavier stared at the cell phone in his hand, shocked. "I think she hung up on me," he said to Dick. His assistant's face became concerned. "Well, that seems a stupid thing to do, doesn't she want to see her family alive?"

"I guess not," Xavier replied. "Bring them to me. Now that the girl is here, I'm not happy knowing that our two captives are in the other room. Bring them here so we are all in the same place. And do it quickly before the girl gets here."

Dick nodded and rushed to do his bidding.

In his cage the dog suddenly shot up, having heard the conversation. Although he couldn't speak, Xavier had no problem understanding the hope that now shone from his eyes.

"Yes, your friend Chase is here, but she is walking into a trap and there is nothing you can do to save her."

Furious at him, the dog howled in desperation even as the chains kept him immovable.

84

SULLY

We'd been searching the room for anything that would aid our escape, but other than those ring binders which contained some very boring reports, the room yielded no treasures. It looked like the only way out was the way we had come in. As luck would have it, though the buildings were worn around the edges, this door was solid and nothing was breaking through that lock short of a bullet. Unfortunately, as Sam's gun had been taken along with the rest of our personal items, I couldn't see a way out of this room. There would be no miracle a second time around. I was about to admit as much when I heard footsteps approaching.

"Quick," I whispered. "Get on the other side of the door, someone's coming!" Without a word, Sam darted to the other side while I waited with my back pressed against the wall, trying to make myself as inconspicuous as possible. Seconds later, a key slid into the lock and the handle turned until the door was cautiously opened, but when the person — I couldn't tell yet whether it was the assistant or the scientist — saw that the room was seemingly empty, he threw open the door and marched inside, pointing a shotgun ahead of him.

Immediately, I jumped on him, wrapping my arms around him, dragging him into the room. The assistant — I recognized it as him now — struggled against me until Sam pressed some fingers into the back of his neck. Presumably, he didn't know that she didn't have another weapon on her. He froze as Sam took the weapon off of him and patted him down, searching for anything we could use, but on his entire person, he seemed to only have the keys to this room, some cable ties, and his phone.

"Tie him up over there," Sam said as she pointed to a thick column holding up the ceiling when the hapless assistant spoke. "You're too late, you know. Even if you leave now, you won't be able to save her."

I stopped dead. "What are you talking about?"

"The girl, Chase? She's here. And my boss is going to get rid of her."

The blood started rushing through my head and I took great pleasure in punching him in the face. The boy's head snapped back as the shock of the blow sent him reeling. As I waited for him to regain his faculties, his future use of the sentence sank into the furious fog in my brain. "She's too smart for him."

He swung his head around to refocus on me. Blood dripped from a cut on his lip, but his fevered eyes showed no pain, such was the force of Xavier's hold on him. "I doubt it," he said. "Xavier's the smartest man I've ever met."

I thought quickly, trying to come up with a plan. "If that's the case then I guess you're coming with us."

Sam shot me a startled look, obviously wondering if I'd lost my mind.

"If he does have Chase, then we're going to need a bargaining chip."

“Right,” she replied. “I guess we don’t have a choice.”

“Nope,” I said pushing Dick ahead of me as we followed him.

I wasn’t ashamed to admit that I felt some vindication in using Dick against his beloved boss. *Karma always comes round to bite you in the ass.*

85

CHASE

Okay, so I had no real plan.

I just knew that if I had stayed on the phone, he would have said something and I wouldn't have been able to get out of there and then we would all be screwed so basically I panicked and hung up the phone. I rage-quit as Gideon, who played a lot of video games, would say. All I knew was that we wanted to avoid that guy. If he really did have the others, then we had to make sure we didn't add to his little arsenal.

"We need to call the police," Gideon said to me, but I shook my head violently against the idea.

"No. We need to find Bandit first. We can't involve the police until we get him safely out of here." Gideon looked like he wanted to argue, but he knew I was right. We hadn't come this far to wreck it all now.

We were about to turn down a new corridor when we heard someone quickly approaching. We tried to go the other way, but we ended up at a dead-end, and the footsteps were getting closer. Suddenly Gideon grabbed me by the shoulders. "I'll lead him away, but when I do, you get out of here. You find Bandit and the two of you get out of here and then you call the police to save the rest of us."

Every nerve in my body shrieked no. There was no way I was doing this. Who knew what they would do to him once they caught him? Not to say the idea of being alone in this place didn't thrill me in the least. "There must be another way," I began, but Gideon shook his head.

"We don't have time for this Chase, we have no idea how many of them there are. Just do as I tell you. Go!" He handed me the flashlight and before I could say anything else, he took off towards the footsteps.

And as he vanished around a corner, I found myself alone.

I felt small and suddenly very, very scared.

86

CHASE

After Gideon left, it took a few moments before I could move. The silence was overwhelming and I could suddenly hear every tiny bit of sound. It was like my senses were in overdrive, heightened as they were for any sounds of danger. I had been the same way before that night in the forest. I couldn't believe I was feeling like that again, and so soon after.

I waited forever it seemed, but there were no footsteps coming my way so Gideon must have successfully lured whoever it was away from here. I was hoping desperately that he was safe. But I knew I didn't have the luxury of worrying about him.

I had to find Bandit.

Backtracking through the one-way system I soon found myself at a crossroads, but I took the one path we hadn't taken before. I moved swiftly, light on my feet, a skill that I had learned during my time on the streets. I wasn't a big girl and although I liked to think I could handle myself: flight was always better than fight, and better than all that was if they never saw you in the first place.

I followed the network of twisting corridors until I passed through old classrooms and the cafeteria. I almost missed the door set way at the back of the room, but what I noticed was the dust was disturbed on the ground by it. And it hadn't been kicked up by just one person. There was a definite arc left in the dust that suggested that the door swung back and forth on a regular basis. Feeling excited, I hugged the walls and kept myself low to the ground as I moved behind tables and chairs, just in case someone came through the door — if they did they might miss seeing me so long as I didn't move.

Reaching the door, I pushed it open just a gap so that I could see through to the room beyond. It looked like it used to be an office in here, a pretty big office but an office all the same. A wooden bench wrapped around the room hugging the wall and there was a bank of flat-screen monitors on one side. Some of the screens showed different areas around the school, but with horror, I realized that the rest were inside our ranch. I even recognized my own room. From the vantage point on screen, I worked out that the camera would have been on my shelf, which was covered with all sorts of junk, so it wasn't surprising that I had never noticed it before. There was a crudely drawn poster on the wall. I ran my eyes over it to discover it was a map of the school and on it, someone had noted down every trip wire, alarm and camera that was in this place. I was horrified to see that there were quite a few. It made it seem very unlikely that Gideon had gotten away.

Feeling sick to my stomach, I tore my gaze away from the monitors to see a room beyond. From a small porthole window, I could see what looked like scientific apparatus, but my eyes weren't interested in any experiments being conducted. They were focused on a cell in the back of the room where inside, standing up, his tail whipping back-and-forth was my best friend, my Muttface and he could barely contain himself from seeing me. I wondered why he wasn't moving, however. Usually, you couldn't keep him still, especially if he was excited. I snuck over to the window and peeked through.

It was then I saw the chains.

Bandit had been chained in place! Fury burned through me. How dare they do that to him! Seeing his reaction, I knew that there was no danger in the room so I rushed inside. Bandit whined and tried to shove his nose through the bars of his cell, but he couldn't reach.

"What have they done to you!" I cried, reaching through the bars to stroke his head. His tongue snaked out, and he managed to lick my hand.

"We need to go now OK, how many guys are we up against?" Bandit barked at me twice. I blinked, surprised by the low number.

"Two, just two guys?" Bandit barked once for yes. I suddenly felt much more hopeful. Two guys we could handle. We'd taken out an army before, so yeah, I was liking the odds.

I fumbled around the outside of the cell looking for a latch or something where I could open it, but there was nothing. Instead, there was this weird automated lock on the door, but unlike the rest of the place, this lock looked high tech. Whatever the guy was spending money on, this was it. Bandit whined and pawed on the ground. I turned around, worried that maybe someone had snuck up behind me, but there was no one.

"How do I get this open?" I asked. Bandit pawed the ground again.

I scanned the room quickly, trying to figure out what had caused this reaction in him. Across the way, lying on a bench, I could see the remains of what was probably Bandit's iPad but even from here the cracked screen was obvious. I looked back at Bandit who was still doing his funny paw movement, almost like he was pointing.

Wait, that's what he was doing, he was pointing!

I ran over to the bench to investigate. All manner of scientific stuff was spread over the bench. There were documents and xrays and scans and graphs and I didn't know what any of it meant, but I knew they wouldn't be helpful for opening Bandit's cell. Grabbing the papers, I started shoving them out of the way when I suddenly found a little remote control. There were only two buttons on it, but Bandit suddenly started shaking with excitement. Bingo. Grabbing the remote, I pointed it towards the cell and pressed both buttons.

The doors swung open! But he was still chained up inside. I ran into the cell to find that the chains were clipped together using carabiner clips, the kind that rock climbers use. It consisted of a simple D shape but instead of a spring-opening gate — which would have been quite easy to open — it had a screw-lock, something which Bandit's paws and jaws would not be able to work.

Luckily, I had my hands.

Quickly, I unscrewed each of the carabiners that were keeping the chains in place until I had him free. He leaped up and wrapped his paws around either side of my neck and then licked my face all over. I stumbled back from the weight of him and would have fallen if it wasn't for the cell wall behind me. Hugging him close, I lay my face against his fur as I listened to his heartbeat, thankful that my friend was back with me again.

"We're not safe yet. Do you know the way out of here?" I asked him. He barked once again and started moving away. I followed, quickly.

87

XAVIER

While his hapless assistant went to secure the prisoners, Xavier went hunting on his own. Though he didn't have the kind of money and manpower that Forbes had had at his disposal, Xavier knew enough to place alarms around key points at the school. This was how he had known Sullivan and his girl-friend had arrived, and how he knew to send Pixie to lure them into the trap.

It was this same alarm that allowed him to know that they now had two extra visitors. It was a simple system, consisting of an invisible beam that ran across the floor of the corridor. He was notified each time someone broke the beam as a silent alarm would flash by the monitors. One of these alarms had been tripped just minutes before.

His hand twitched down by his side, the hand that held the sheriff's gun. He didn't like weapons as he found them Neanderthal, but it would not do to go up against these children alone — he had read the reports and knew that at least the boy was good with firearms. Xavier wasn't worried about his own life, however, knowing that they would not hurt him until they secured the dog and their adoptive parents.

Xavier knew he had the upper hand, so the gun was for show more than anything else.

Once the children had tripped the alarm, Xavier had sent Pixie to trick them as she had the others, however, she still wasn't back and it had been a while now. Xavier knew something had gone wrong, though his security system would not show him what that might be. He walked now, towards the spot where he had last seen Pixie on the monitors.

He hadn't gone far when he heard them close by. Hugging the wall, he shrank into the shadows until he was completely hidden from sight. Holding his breath, he waited. A figure materialized in front of him. It was the boy, Gideon. Xavier didn't move, expecting Chase to also appear, however, it seemed the two had gone their separate ways. Not a problem, Xavier thought to himself. One was better than none. Pointing the gun in front of him, he took a step out of the shadows.

The boy must have sensed him before he saw him as he spun around, but he had no weapon and Xavier had the advantage of surprise.

"Whatever you are thinking, stop. There is nothing you can do that will be faster than my finger pulling on the trigger of this gun."

Gideon stared, recognizing him immediately. "You're Erik, the IT man. You were there, the whole time?"

Xavier smiled. "Yes, right under your noses. It is amazing how complacent people can be once they believe themselves out of danger."

"You won't get away with this, we'll stop you!" The boy couldn't help but make the threat.

"Oh, I highly doubt that. Now, I do not want to hurt you so just tell me where the girl is."

Gideon glared at him, defiant to the end, and almost spat the words out. "I don't know. She went another way."

"Well, she won't go far, not once she knows that we have you all."

Carefully, keeping his eyes pinned on Gideon, Xavier took out his cell phone and hit one on the speed-dial. The phone rang and rang and was finally answered just as Xavier began to feel a hint of concern.

"You have something more pressing to do than to answer the phone?" Xavier asked testily.

"Well," came a voice that was clearly not Dick. "That depends on whether you consider being tied up and gagged more pressing."

Xavier felt a moment of shock before it faded into grudging respect. "Mr. Sullivan. I see you have managed to escape, how commendable."

"Yeah, well, I was getting pretty bored in that room, wanted to stretch my legs. Now, much as I don't want to sound rude, I make it a habit never to speak to people I don't like so how about we cut to the chase and strike a deal. Release Bandit and in exchange, you will get your assistant back?"

Xavier didn't answer straight away as his mind furiously calculated several possible outcomes. Finally, he decided on one. "Follow the signs to the science lab. I will meet you there."

Before Sully could respond, Xavier disconnected the call.

Xavier knew Sullivan thought he had the upper hand... and he was happy to let him think that.

88

SULLY

I turned to Sam, a triumphant smile on my face.

"Well, that was easier than I thought it would be."

She gave me a look that revealed she wasn't quite as convinced of our success as I was. "I wouldn't be counting your chickens yet," she said.

Despite what I had said to Xavier, his assistant Dick wasn't gagged, but I did find some twisted pleasure in binding his own wrists together with some spare cable ties that we had found in his pocket. It was the least I could do to repay what he had done to us. It was nice, a full circle moment, as Tony Robbins would say.

I pointed the shotgun at the kid, who was only a couple of years older than Gideon. I wondered how a boy like him got involved with this kind of thing but knew it all boiled down to bad parenting; nearly everything did. He was probably missing a father figure, which is how he fell under Xavier's grooming. I realized how easily Gideon could have become this boy. As the thought played on my mind, I determined that I would do better by him. Gideon would not end up like this.

With Dick leading the way, we reached the science block in

just a few minutes. The dark and twisting corridors of this place were a lot easier to navigate when you had a guide. I pushed open the door, gesturing for Dick to enter first. While I didn't think there were any traps, I wasn't taking any risks. Dick strode confidently in, Sam and I following close behind.

The room we found ourselves in used to be an office but had now been equipped with a bank of monitors lining one wall. The first nine monitors seemed to display areas around the school, but the last nine were focused on an entirely different location.

It took a moment before I recognized the ranch, at which point the puzzle came crashing together.

The camera I had found in Zeb's hand — they were hooked up to the monitors here! With growing horror, I took in the familiar sight of our home. When I realized that there was a camera in Chase's room, however, a white-hot fury rose inside of me. Sam must have reached the same conclusion as I felt her suddenly tense beside me. What sick animals were they that they would spy on a teenaged girl's room? And then another thought came to me, of my dad, lying unconscious in the hospital. It seemed likely now that Pixie had attacked him after he had stumbled upon one of their hidden spy cams. The only time they would have had the chance to bug the place was during our trip back East... I couldn't believe their plan to unhinge me and split us apart worked so well. Even Chase's Mom, they had bought her assistance somehow. My mind felt like it was going to explode.

We moved past the office, into what was once a large science lab, but now housed research more than anything else. The walls were covered with diagrams and notes that I could not make out from my position by the door. I suspected even if I could read them I wouldn't understand a thing they said. There were many complex symbols and what looked like code. Amongst the scribblings, I caught a glimpse of diagrams of an oblong tank. It looked a lot like something you'd find in an X-Men movie.

Across the room, there was a sound as a second pair of doors that were nearly hidden in shadow, opened. The two of us tensed as I aimed the weapon on the two figures coming inside. As they stepped out of the blackness and into the light, my world spun. It was Gideon, and he was being marched inside at gunpoint by Xavier. Seeing me, Gideon's face turned apologetic. "Sorry Sully, he came at me from nowhere..." He trailed off, mad at himself for being captured.

"It's fine, we have his assistant so we're one-for-one right now."

The scientist looked at me. "I suppose I should introduce myself as it would be rude not to. My name is Xavier. You've already met my assistant Dick there."

I held my hand up, cutting off any further conversation. "We don't have to do the evil-man-explains-his-grand-plan thing. I just want my family back. I'll give you your assistant, you give me Gideon and Bandit, and we will go on our merry way."

The half smile that had been on Xavier's lips suddenly hardened. It was the smallest change, barely perceivable, but I saw it. In one instant, he turned from mild-mannered scientist to cunning nemesis.

"Unfortunately, you have made a mistake in your calculations. Dick knows what is at stake here. He knows how important my work is, as such, he wouldn't hesitate to give his life."

He looked to Dick for confirmation. Dick nodded, sticking out his chin proudly. "Xavier's work is all that matters."

Sam let out a hiss of breath. "You can't mean that. Neither of you." She turned to Dick. "You can't give up your life for this madman!"

But Dick shook his head at Sam sadly. "You just don't get it, do you?"

"And they never will," finished Xavier. "What I have created is something that could change humanity as we know it. I have spent my life working on this particular project and it is almost complete. What I do, I do for all of mankind and in the grand scheme of things, isn't that worth one boy's life?"

"You don't know that your experiment will work. There's no guarantee, an innocent being could be killed for nothing," Sam cried.

Xavier looked at us, almost apologetic. "I don't expect you to understand. Throughout history, the people with the greatest creations, the ones with the biggest effect on the human race, were always mocked and never believed. I have long accepted that this would be my fate."

"You're talking in riddles and haven't explained a thing!" I said. "Why can't you just leave Bandit alone? You already know about the tumor placement, what more could you need him for?"

Xavier explained patiently, as if to a child. "The tumors are nothing. Alpha has other properties which we don't yet understand. Have you ever seen him sick or hurt? If so, has it ever occurred to you that he recovers incredibly fast? That kind of accelerated healing is the final element I need for my project. Once I have that, there will be nothing in this world that I can't cure."

I wanted to tell him he was crazy, but a memory surfaced of the time I had operated on Bandit myself, only for him to come out of the anesthetic far faster than he should have done. Then there was the stab wound itself, which healed very quickly, even under conditions that would normally cause stitches to tear, or at the very least, an infection to occur. And then I thought of the head trauma caused by the Doc removing his tumor. Bandit's brain had rewired itself in record time afterward. We had been so relieved he was fine and hadn't lost his intelligence, none of us had really questioned it.

Xavier saw the look in my eyes and smiled. "I see that you do know what I am talking about. So you see, I am not quite the madman you first thought of me. Now, Mr. Sullivan, unless you are willing to kill Dick and risk Gideon's life, hand me the weapon please."

I looked at Sam, then Gideon, feeling helpless. Despite all that he had done, I couldn't harm Dick; the kid was under Xavier's twisted control after all, shooting him would be like shooting a person who was suffering from a mental illness. Sam gave me a small nod to let me know I had her support. Reluctantly, I handed the shotgun to Xavier.

"Regardless if Bandit has that ability or not, what you're doing is still wrong." I was determined to have my say, even if it proved detrimental to my health.

"At the end of the day, I do not care what you think, and while I don't like hurting people, I will if I deem it necessary."

"Like it was necessary to hurt my dad? It was Pixie, wasn't it?" I said. "You got her to attack him."

He nodded, emotionlessly. "When he found the bug, I instructed Pixie to take him out. I let her use her own creativity how. It was she who decided to do what she did. Speaking of the dog where is she?"

Gideon looked at him, hatred spilling out from his eyes. "Locked in a room where she can't hurt anyone anymore."

"What about Chase? You think I haven't noticed that she's not here. Where has the girl got to?"

Gideon glared at him. "You'll never find her. You can kill us all, but you'll never find her."

Xavier's eyes narrowed, the only sign of his displeasure. "Is that a challenge? Because I do love a good competition."

Keeping his eyes on Gideon, Xavier leaned over the bench and retrieved a familiar -looking phone. My phone. He scrolled through until he came to a listing that I couldn't see from over here. Pressing the button, he must have also hit speaker as the ring tone started echoing around the small room.

Moments later, Chase's desperate voice answered. "Sully, please tell me that's you?"

"No. This is Xavier. I have your whole family with me right now, Chase. If you do not come to the science lab within five minutes, I will kill them all, starting with Mr. Sullivan here."

89

CHASE

The call came just as Bandit and I were approaching the exit. Light streamed in through the doors ahead. I actually had the phone in my hand, ready to call the police like Gideon and I had planned, when the phone rang.

Seeing Sully's name flash up on the screen, I hadn't hesitated at all. I just answered the call. Now I was wishing that I had thought twice about the call before answering it. It's true what they say about hindsight.

If I had ignored the call, I could pretend that I didn't know about his ultimatum, but now, we were in a bad way.

A really bad way.

I looked at Bandit, desperately wishing that we had his iPad so that he could communicate with me. I had around four minutes to come up with a plan that would save us all. What could I do? I looked at Bandit again, his furry face staring up at me, mirroring my concern in his green eyes.

What could we do?

90

CHASE

Think, Chase... think!

With every second that passed, I was horribly aware that it was another second closer to the death of my family. I had to come up with a way to save them, but how? Bandit whined beside me, feeling helpless. Even if he had an idea, he wouldn't be able to communicate it to me with our basic system of yes and no. While I tried to keep the overwhelming panic at bay, a mental clock ticked down inside my head, making me feel like the pressure would cause it to explode.

I shook my head to clear the fog. I couldn't let them down. I had to figure this out now but with millions of worse case scenarios flying at me from all angles; it was hard to focus, much less think of a doable plan.

Three minutes, Chase! THREE MINUTES!

OK... let's do this in steps.

The guy had the others trapped somewhere. I wouldn't be able to take the two of them on without any weapons... so my only option was to get them away from the others!

Thrilled, I now knew what I needed to do. My mind went

through several possible options, but as they ranged from unlikely to impossible, I shot them down fast. I stared around the corridor I was desperate for something to jump out at me. But there was just the dust and dirt. Nothing tangible that I could use. I was about to give up when I saw it. The small red flower-like shape of a sprinkler attached to the ceiling... and with it, the bank of TV monitors and the map of the camera locations that I had seen in the office flashed up in my mind. With my photographic memory, I could see every single one of the locations.

And suddenly, I knew exactly what I needed to do.

"Bandit, I've got it!" He danced around me excitedly as I quickly explained my plan to him. After I had run through the details, I checked that he had understood them all.

"Woof."

He dashed down the corridor while I ran into each of the small rooms leading off from the corridor. The first was completely empty, but in the second, I found a few textbooks, covered with an inch of dust. *Perfect*! Grabbing them, I sprinted out of the room and went into the next. But this room had nothing I could use. Trying not to freak out over the time, I bolted into the next few rooms until I found myself in a classroom. And here, with relief, I saw some tables and chairs stacked in the corner.

Dropping the textbook, I grabbed a table and dragged it across the room until I could position it under one of those sprinklers. I stacked a chair on top of the table, then hurriedly tore pages out of the book. With the loose pages in my hand, I ran outside, almost colliding with Bandit, who returned with a rusty bin in his mouth.

"Good boy, that's exactly what we need!"

Taking it from him, I dropped the torn pages inside, set the bin on the ground, then we searched for the final missing piece. It was Bandit who saw the beer bottle first. He barked and grabbed it.

Bringing it to me, I smashed the bottle on the ground, then grabbed a shard which I held over the bin.

It was the early afternoon, and a sunny day, so I was desperately hoping that it would be enough to start a fire. As I waited impatiently, I suddenly wondered how, for the second time in recent days, my life relied on my ability to start a fire. It would have been funny if it wasn't for the fact that a madman was about to start shooting my family down, one-by-one.

The two of us stared at the paper in the bin, silently willing for it to catch alight. I had lit fires using this method several times while I was on the street, but I had never been timed for it, plus it worked much better when it was a magnifying glass, but as I didn't have one on me, it was this or nothing.

Please, God. Please make this work.

By now, I'd lost any idea of time, but I knew we must be coming close to his deadline. Deathly afraid, I tensed, my body on full alert for the gunshot that would announce that all was lost when a black mark appeared on a piece of paper! It started to scorch then sizzle as the sun's ray focused through the glass to form concentrated light.

"It's working, boy!"

"Woof!" He cheered me on. And suddenly, the rest of the paper burst into flames! We'd done it! We sprinted back inside even as Gideon's phone started to ring again. I snatched it up without hesitation as we ran into the classroom. I set the bin on top of the chair, just beneath the sprinkler and the two of us immediately run back out into the corridor then answered the call, breathlessly. Before I could speak, the man's irritated voice came down the line.

"Time's up young lady, yet I don't see you here?"

"Wait!" I yelled desperately. "We're on our way! Don't hurt any of them! We got a bit lost, but we're almost there now!"

"If I don't see evidence of your imminent arrival, you can say goodbye to Sullivan."

He hung up, but I was beyond relieved that they were all still alive.

"Quickly, Boy, onto the next part of the plan!"

He took off fast as I prayed that my idea would work...

It just had to.

91

SULLY

I sat on the ground, in a line with the others.

Our hands were chained behind us, locked up tight and secured with padlocks. Having learned their lesson, there were no cable ties that we would be able to easily escape from this time. I looked at Sam to find her genuinely scared. Seeing the fear on her face made me realize that the danger was very real. Unless Chase could come up with a way to get us out of here safely, we were going to die.

When we were previously in danger, everything had happened so fast, I had no time to think of anything other than trying to survive, but now I found myself reflecting over everything that had happened. I ran my eyes over Sam's face, desperately trying to memorize every beautiful freckle and line. Even as fear would have crippled lesser people, her eyes never stopped working the room. She would be trying to find a way out of this for us until there was no time left.

I should have married her the instant we had met. What a fool I was for waiting this long.

An image of Zeb flew into my mind, pale and unconscious, lying there on his hospital bed.

I'm sorry I failed you.

Tears blurred the edge of my vision even as my eyes moved to rest on Gideon. The boy who had initially greeted us with a shotgun, so determined was he to protect my dad. Gideon sat there quietly — very unlike him — with a focused expression on his face. He kept his eyes pinned on Xavier and Dick, who had their eyes peeled to the monitors on the wall. Their weapons lay within reach, but neither had their hands on them. I tried to get his attention, to let him know my regret at failing him too, but Gideon never looked away from them. As I watched, he slowly changed positions, shifting his right leg and bending it back so that the heel of his boot was inching towards his hands.

What was the boy doing?

Slowly, carefully, I saw Gideon remove a thin piece of metal from the inside of his boot, and suddenly I realized what it was. His lock picks! My eyes flared open as I realized what he meant to do. I had to buy him time. Neither Dick nor Xavier could see what he was up to.

What could I do to help him?

92

SULLY

Getting up on my feet, I ignored the terrified looks Sam cast my way as I suddenly barreled into the two men. I smacked into Xavier, knocking him into the monitors where his head hit them with a satisfying thud. He stumbled back, stunned, touching his head where it must have been throbbing something bad.

"Sully! What're you doing?" I heard Sam scream in the background, but I didn't have a chance to answer. Furious that I had dared touch his idol, Dick roared as he came at me with his bare hands, too mad to even think about snatching up a weapon. With my hands bound behind me, I made an easy target so that even this weedy boy was able to sucker-punch me in the face. I dropped down, reeling from the blow. Dick shook his fist, hurt from hitting me, and grabbed one of the guns. As he pointed it at me, Sam suddenly darted forward, blocking his shot with her body.

"No! Please don't hurt him. You don't have to do this!" she cried.

"Sam! Get out of the way!" I shouted at her. This was disastrous and the last thing I wanted. I had wanted to buy Gideon some time and was willing to risk my life to do it, but Sam's actions had me facing the death of another woman I loved. The fear almost suffocated me.

Dick's finger hesitated on the trigger. Whatever he felt about me, he obviously didn't feel the same about Sam. "What do you want me to do?" he asked Xavier.

Still seething from the blow to his head, Xavier glared at me. He opened his mouth to give the command to end me, but then his eyes were drawn to the monitors as Bandit raced across one of the screens. On another screen, Chase appeared, desperately chasing after him. A light blinked on a monitor, drawing his attention. Xavier smiled.

"It's too late, Sullivan. It seems the dog has made his decision to sacrifice himself for you."

Turning to study the chart on the wall, Xavier located Bandit's position. "He's by the junction between the library and the gym. He just tripped the alarm by the boy's locker room. Get there quickly before the girl does," he instructed Dick. The boy nodded, grabbing his shotgun. Shooting one last filthy look at me, he went to do his bidding. Holding onto the remaining shotgun, Xavier pointed the weapon at me.

"As soon as the dog gets here, you are a dead man, Mr. Sullivan."

And then a miracle happened.

He barely finished speaking when an alarm suddenly shrieked overhead and the heavens burst open.

Water rained down on us, pouring out from the sprinklers overhead. I realized in an instant that Chase must have set them off! *Clever girl!* Xavier froze, unsure what to do. He stood there, watching the water spray onto the paperwork pinned to the wall, turning the calculations into inky blobs. Then panic hit as he saw his life's work becoming ruined.

"No! My work!" he screamed.

Leaving the gun, he ran to the bench, pulling diagrams and calculations off the walls, trying frantically to protect them from the water. Pre-occupied, he never saw that Gideon had broken free of his restraints. Quickly, he unlocked my chains, then Sam's, as chaos and water showered down on us. With the three of us free, I picked up the chain and ran for Xavier.

Scrabbling around with an armful of his work, and with the alarm drowning out all sounds, he didn't see me coming until the chain lashed out at his head.

It hit him with a sickening thud. His eyes flew open in pain before they rolled into the back of his head. He fell down into a pool of water, out for the count.

93

CHASE

Huddled in the dark room, Bandit and I waited.

Having memorized the locations of the cameras and trip wires they had set around the place, my plan was for it to look as if Bandit had run off without me, to make it seem like he was sacrificing himself for the others. We tripped the wire that lead into this locker room here, and we were now waiting for them to leave the others to find us. Bandit hid behind the door while I waited in the shadows close by with Gideon's wrench and his flashlight.

It didn't take long.

Someone thundered down the hallway outside and crashed into the room. It was a young guy, not much older than Gideon and quite a bit weedier. He held a shotgun in his hand, so I knew we had to be careful. I waited until he approached me and I turned the flashlight on and aimed it at his face. Blinded, he instinctively went to cover his eyes when I hit him with the wrench using the full force of my body, and Bandit flew at him from the other side. The guy dropped onto the ground like we'd knocked him over with a demolition ball. Bandit stood over him, snarling into his face while I relieved him of his shotgun.

"Don't move, scumbag!" I hissed into his face.

The guy froze, eyes still glazed from the flashlight. Having scoped out the room before his arrival, I knew there was a small side room in here. Though it was empty, it still carried the scent of chemical cleaners. I prodded the gun at him.

"Get up. Slowly..." I commanded in a voice that was hard from the hatred I felt at this guy who had been threatening my family. I marched him into the side room, shut the door, and wedged the wrench under the handle so that he couldn't get out.

As we started out of the locker room, towards the others, the sprinklers and alarm turned on.

And with it, I knew we only had moments before the fire trucks would arrive.

"Hurry, Bandit, we've got to free the others!"

94

SULLY

Xavier lay on the ground, unconscious.

My hand itched over the trigger of the shotgun, but Sam stopped me. "No. You do that, and you'll never come back from it."

I looked at her, torn. Though I heard the truth of her words, I wanted retribution for the pain this man had caused on so many others. In that moment, I didn't care about the future, whether I would regret this. I wanted nothing more than to blow this man off the face of the Earth.

My finger started moving of its own accord, but I stopped short of pulling it when two familiar beloved faces flew in through the doors.

Bandit barked joyously, while Chase ran in, stunned but relieved to find us safe and sound. "But, I came to rescue you," she said, confused yet happy.

"And you did an amazing job, hun, the sprinklers were genius," Sam said, smiling as she hugged her close. I didn't even blink. I ran over and grabbed the two of them, mashing their bodies against me until Chase's muffled voice sounded from within.

"Sully... I can't breathe..." she said.

Watching us from across the way, Gideon fussed Bandit, grinning. Chase pulled reluctantly away from me, brushing the wet hair from her eyes.

"This is him? This is the guy who's been after Bandit?" Chase looked down at Xavier's prone form. She rolled him over with a sneaker to see his face, but gasped when it flopped into view.

"This is the IT guy who's renting the apartment above Warrey's!"

Gideon nodded, mouth tight from the guilt of not knowing that this was the man who was out to ruin our family. "I had no idea... if only we'd known sooner, I could've done something. Maybe Zeb wouldn't be lying in the hospital now if I had..."

I shook my head at him. "You can't blame yourself, Gid. It happened, but now it's over."

"We're not out of it yet," Chase said suddenly. "The fire trucks will get here soon and there's still all this stuff everywhere." She pointed at the piles of Xavier's paperwork. Though some of it had been ruined, I could still make out his writing on the rest. "And what about him? We can't just leave him there. Remember what happened with Forbes...?"

It was Bandit who came up with the solution. Grabbing the chains Xavier had used on us, Bandit carried them over to Xavier and dropped them onto his prone body, his intention clear as day. Chase nodded and looked to Gideon for assistance. "Gid, help me get him into the cell. Let's see how he likes a taste of his own medicine."

"Woof!" Bandit barked solemnly.

While they dragged him into the cell and chained him up, I looked to Sam. "Quickly, we need to destroy anything that mentions canine anatomy or Bandit. If you're not sure, just tear it up." I led the way, ripping up whatever I could get my hands on.

We quickly destroyed all the evidence we could find that

mentioned Bandit. Xavier had taken copious notes and pictures. Some of the notes I understood, but I had no idea what the end goal was. All I could fathom was he had some sort of living experiment that he was conducting, but it looked like something was wrong with it. He needed Bandit's brain's ability to remap itself and his super fast healing to essentially fix his experiment's damaged organs. In the brief amount of time I had to go through his notes, what I learned filled me with dread. The last time a scientist had played like this he created Frankenstein and we all know how that story turned out.

We got rid of most of his research, though I made sure to keep the most incriminating things I could find. These I stacked under a sheet of plastic where they would be protected from the water. We worked fast, together as a team. With the alarm screeching overhead, I knew we didn't have much time to get out of there before the fire trucks started turning up.

I found a vial of Telazol, a cocktail of two other drugs, which when used together resulted in the sedation of cats and dogs. Xavier had obviously been keeping it in case he needed to use it on Bandit, but I took it now. The plan was to use it on Pixie. I was ready to leave Pixie to the cops to deal with, but even after everything, Chase reminded me that it wasn't Pixie's fault. You don't get bad dogs, she had said. Only badly trained dogs, and that was on the owners. She had pleaded with me, letting me know that if anyone could help her, it would be me. I had mixed emotions knowing that she was the cause of my father lying in hospital, but in the end, I knew Chase was right. I had spent my life saving animals, and I couldn't turn my back on this one.

As we left to find her, we passed by the office Xavier had used as his control room.

"Hold up," I said to the others as I ran into the room. Searching around the monitors, I guess I was hoping for a simple way to disconnect the cameras that they had in our home. I couldn't find one, however. As the cameras were all inside the ranch, though, I hoped the authorities wouldn't be able to identify the location. In any case, there wasn't much I could do about that now. I turned to leave when a movement on one of the screens caught my eye. A figure had moved out of one of the school's corridors, through a door to the outside. I would have thought it a figment of my imagination, but for the fact that the door was closing slowly on itself now. I had no time to guess at who that might be, however, as Gideon called through the door at me.

"Sully, hurry up!"

Nodding, I sprinted out to join them. We found Pixie moments later. It took two of us to hold her down as she had worked herself into a frenzy by now. When the syringe finally sank into her, she yelped and twisted her head around, trying to snap at me with those jaws, but the drug was quick-acting and within seconds she was out for the count. I picked her up and followed Gideon as we met back up with the others. Securing her into the back of my car, we drove off, moments later passing by the fire trucks as they screamed past us on their way to the school.

With that chapter blessedly over, we sped back to Montpelier. Back to my dad.

MR SMITH

He had been tipped off by a detective in the police department.

The company that he worked for, a covert department of the government, had feelers everywhere. It was their job to investigate crimes that were considered unusual in nature, the sort of case Mulder and Scully would have looked into. He glanced into the rearview mirror to check his disguise once again. He had a nondescript face — perfect for this line of work — and was currently wearing the uniform of a forensic investigator. Not that anyone would check his credentials, but if they had, they would discover his name was Mr. John Smith. Good luck trying to identify him with the most common name in America. Grabbing his tool case, he cut through the cops littering the scene and followed the crime scene tape to the room that had gotten local uniforms so worked up.

On his way, he passed by what had been a science lab. The local police had been very disturbed when they had found the man who they now knew was one Xavier Williams, a science professor at a community college in Columbus, Ohio, strung up inside a jail-like cell. He had been chained so tight that he had not been able to move an inch. Despite this, however, when they had found him, all the man had cared about was his research. He was still screaming at them to protect it when they had dragged him and his assistant away.

Mr. Smith arrived in the basement of the derelict school. Water dripped from the sprinklers still. They had been turned off now, however, the occasional one still leaked. He followed the markers set by the police until he reached a strange contraption in front of him.

It was a steel tank shaped and sized like, well, like a coffin. The lid was made of glass and through it, he could see that the tank contained some kind of thick liquid. Lifting the lid, he tried to get a better look at the substance inside but was unable to determine what it could be using the naked eye alone. It had a faintly chemical smell, but he couldn't put a name to it. Opening his tool case, he took a sample of the liquid and bagged it up. It would be sent to their private laboratory, and the results given to him soon after. Focusing on the job at hand, he must have leaned against a switch of some kind as images suddenly appeared on the inside lid of the tank. Sound too came out of hidden speakers along the side of the tank. He stopped to watch the images, which appeared to be a collection of video footage that was somehow being projected onto the lid.

The footage all consisted of one man. He looked to be in his thirties. Athletic build, kind eyes. He smiled and laughed a lot. His voice boomed out from the speakers, saying nothing of interest from what Mr. Smith could gather. It was a jumble of nonsense video, the kind of thing you might find in someone's home video collection before they edited it down. No one else featured in the footage. Running his hands along the tank, he finally found the switch that had activated the footage and depressed it. The footage and sound blinked out.

Curious, he thought to himself. This would need further investigating into.

Until he had the tank drained, there was nothing else he could find inside it, so he turned his attention to a nearby table where a pile of paperwork sat. He went through the pile with gloved hands so as not to disturb any fingerprints. What he could initially decipher, he found of great interest.

It looked like Xavier might not be insane after all.

What he was looking at was a possible way to accelerate cloning. Whether or not Xavier was successful was another thing, but his work would have to be looked into for sure. This kind of discovery could not be allowed into the public eye if, in fact, he had been successful. He had knocked this kind of thing on its head before, and he would do so again. So long as his bosses kept him in employment, it wasn't for him to question their instructions.

He came to an X-ray and stopped, perplexed. While the rest of the documents had pertained to human elements, this scan showed a dog. As he studied the scan, he found more items of concern. He took the scan and slipped it into a protected envelope that he tucked inside a hidden pocket in his jacket. This wasn't for the local lab. His people would examine this in confidence.

It took hours to comb through everything else in that room. He found a few more references to a dog and took all of those. It wasn't until his eyes were becoming gritty and dry from staring so long that he stopped. Looking at his watch, he was surprised to find that so much time had passed. He'd order takeout tonight, so he could eat while he logged everything he had found into the system.

He stood up and stretched his aching muscles when something caught his eye. He crossed the room to the far side and saw a cell had been built there. It looked like the cell that was upstairs in the science lab, except this one had a bed in addition to a toilet and sink.

Turning on his flashlight to UV, he shined the flashlight under the bed, knowing that beds were a haven for forensics. Stains and lint, invisible to the eye, flared up. But there was something else, something golden. Moving in closer, he saw it was a long strand of blonde hair.

Carefully he picked it up with a pair of tweezers and slipped it into a bag.

What puzzles did this hair hold?

He couldn't wait to find out.

96

CHASE

We must have broken so many speeding laws to get back home as fast as we did.

Anytime we were stopped by police (which happened at least three times) however, Sam just flashed her badge and explained it was a matter of life and death. At one point of our journey back, we even got ourselves a police escort. If I weren't as tired as I was, I probably would have enjoyed it a lot more. As it was, I was too exhausted to take much of it in. I just wanted to get back to Zeb to make sure he was okay. I felt like every minute we weren't by his side, was a minute he might not make it.

Pixie had still not come to in the back of Sully's car. We had secured her in a blanket so when she did wake, she wouldn't be out to move or hurt herself. It was the best we could do with what we had. Sully said she'd be fine, so I took his word for it. While Sully drove (Sam was traveling with Gideon — they weren't more than a car or two behind us at all times), I called a friend who we thought might be able to help Pixie. Knowing that Xavier had messed with Pixie physically, we knew there was only one person we trusted who might be able to figure it out.

"Hello," she answered the phone sounding surprised. "Sully?" she asked.

"No, Doc, it's Chase. Sully's driving." I said.

"Chase! What a lovely surprise to hear from you. How are you all?" Doc Robins said.

I looked at Sully, then Bandit lying in the back seat and decided maybe now wasn't the time to get into everything. "I'll fill you in later, but Sully wanted to ask if you could do us a favor? We have another dog here. She's smart too, like Bandit, but not in the same way. Sully said she's got several of those tumors inside her and they're causing her to be mean and aggressive. He doesn't know what to do. Can you help?"

"There's a lot more to the story that you're not telling me isn't there?" came her voice over the line.

"Yeah. We'll tell you all about it in person. Can you get to our place? We should be there in a few hours. We're stopping off at the hospital first."

"Is everything okay? Who's been injured?"

I wasn't able to answer as I found myself suddenly listening to the dead dial tone. Frowning, I stared at the phone to see that it had died and there wasn't a charger in sight. Feeling my consternation, Sully looked at me.

"What happened, is she coming?"

"I think so. I didn't get to find out because your phone died." I started rummaging in the glove compartment, but other than gum and a sponge for the windscreen, I didn't find what I was looking for.

"I think I left it with Sam. We'll just have to make do until we meet up with them again."

97

SULLY

We arrived at the hospital after visiting hours. The nurse in charge wouldn't let us inside at first, especially when she caught sight of Bandit, but Sam used her authority to get onto the ward. That badge was like a magic wand: wherever she waved it, things always happened. I thought we would be meeting more resistance than the one nurse, but as we turned the corner that would lead to my dad's room, his doctor, who was going over a patient's file by the nurse's station, looked over at our motley crew in surprise.

"There you are. I've been waiting all afternoon for you to call me, why haven't you called back?" He demanded. I was taken aback by his tone.

"We were out of town and my phone died. Why, has something happened?" Even as the words left my mouth, I felt a cold hollow build in my stomach, but the doc smiled at me.

"Your father is awake Mr. Sullivan and has been waiting — very impatiently might I say — for you all to get here."

I heard the words, but I was too afraid to believe him, so I didn't move until I felt a tugging on my arm. It was Gideon.

"What are you waiting for?" He ran past me into dad's room. And suddenly, like my feet had a mind of their own, I found myself racing after him. By the time I got inside Gideon was already at dad's bedside holding onto his hand. The old man was propped up against the bed, but other than a bandage around his head, he seemed his usual self.

"Glad you could make it finally. Wouldn't want to interrupt whatever important thing you've got going on."

A smile broke out over my face. I crossed the room in three quick strides and hugged him. I was expecting him to push me away — we'd never been the touchy-feely type with each other. Instead, his arms came up around me and he patted my back before we let go of each other.

"You had us all scared there for a moment," I said.

"We've got the good doctor to thank for that." He gestured at him standing in the doorway. Seeing that we were all fine, the doc smiled.

"I suppose it wouldn't do any good to tell you all to leave because he needs his rest?"

"They just got here! Give them a moment, would you?" Zeb said, peeved.

The doctor smiled and nodded. "Half an hour and then I won't be able to stop the nurse from kicking you out." He left, smiling at us. I waited until he was out of earshot before I started speaking again. As soon as he was gone, Zeb's expression changed, and he became deadly serious.

"It was Pixie. Did you find her? She attacked me after I found a camera in the house. I was just going to call to warn you when she went crazy and started attacking me."

"Yeah. We know," I said. He looked at me in surprise.

"You do? How?"

We filled him in on everything that had happened since his accident. As we talked, his eyebrows raised higher and higher until at one point, I thought they would shoot clean off his head. When we were done, he let out a long, drawn breath.

"That's some excitement you all have gone through. Makes me glad that I was out for most of it."

"When are you coming home?" Gideon asked hopefully.

"I suspect they will want to keep him in for a day or two, to make sure he's in the clear, but he'll be back soon," said Sam.

"And when I do, I am ready for another round of your lasagna you hear? That bump on the head wasn't enough to kill me, but the hospital food might," he said with a glower.

Sometimes, he and Chase were so strikingly similar.

98

CHASE

Birds sang outside my window, signaling all was well with the world.

I woke to a commotion outside.

Bandit wasn't in his usual place on my bed, but I could hear his excited barking outside. Moving to the window, I looked out to see Doc Robins had arrived, and she was playing with Bandit and talking to him. I couldn't hear what she was saying from here, but whatever it was, he liked it, as he started jumping up at her with delight.

When Bandit had been at Platinum Industries, it was the Doc who had taken care of him. Blackmailed into working for Forbes, the Doc was the only person to have ever showed kindness and affection to Bandit... until he met me, anyway. When it was all going down at PI, it was the Doc who helped to save the day. We owed her a lot.

I pulled a cardigan over my PJ's and went out to greet her. When she saw me, a big grin spread over her face.

"Chase! It's so good to see you again."

"Hi Doc, how was Africa?"

"Did you manage to help out there," asked Sully who had joined us. She turned to him and gave him a hug.

"A little, though it is never enough, is it? I'm glad to be back on US soil, though. It seems my work here isn't over with either." She stared past him into the house. "Where is she, the dog?"

"We've got her safely secured in the den. She's managed to exhaust herself after working into such a state yesterday. Now she's just cowering in the corner, although that could be an act. You can never tell with her. She is a very good actress."

The Doc stared at him, her eyes glittering with intrigue. "That is highly irregular for dogs. They usually show all their emotions. Subterfuge isn't common in the species, if at all."

I looked at her suddenly worried. "You are going to help her, right? You're not going to just be doing experiments?"

She looked at me. "Of course I'm not going to experiment on her. Nothing I do will hurt her, I promise. My days with those kinds of experiments are over. No, what I have planned for her is to remove those tumors. Then after that, it's lots of patience and love."

She looked nothing but sincere, and Bandit certainly wasn't acting like he was concerned. I hoped that maybe Pixie could be fixed.

Everyone deserved a second chance.

Bandit and I had gotten ours, so I hoped I could say the same for Pixie in the future.

99

SULLY

While Elora examined Pixie, I'd accepted a phone call from Dad. It seemed he was ready to come home that day. Hearing the news, a great weight lifted from my shoulders. Until he had been given the green light, I hadn't realized how concerned I was that something else would happen to him, but now that I knew he was coming home, there was something pressing I had to do.

I found Sam inside our room where she had spent the night — I had slept on the couch. We hadn't discussed our relationship since we'd gotten back and we were too tired to do anything but sleep last night, so I had taken the couch respectfully to give her space, but now it was time to talk. I was ready.

Sam had a suitcase on the bed and was packing her things when I came into the room. She looked up at me, hesitating for only a second.

"How's Pixie reacting to Elora?" She asked.

"Better than expected, actually. I don't know if it's just exhaustion or if she can sense the Doc means her no harm, but Pixie has calmed right down. When I left them, the Doc was feeding her some treats."

Sam picked up a work shirt and folded it neatly before setting it inside the suitcase. "That's good. Hopefully, she can give Pixie the help she needs." She reached out to pick up a sweater when I took her hand in mine. She stopped and looked at me.

"I know I haven't been myself since the visit East, but I need you to know that what happened was never an excuse. I never behaved that way because I wasn't ready to marry you. I am completely and wholeheartedly ready to be your husband. I love you Sam and I think I'm finally ready to let go of the past. I need you to trust me, to trust us. I need you to marry me."

Her eyes softened and I could see she wanted to believe me but there was that slight hesitation that hint of doubt in her eyes. I had hurt her with my actions, and this doubt was the result of it.

"I don't know, so much has happened..."

I entwined my fingers with hers and drew her in closer. "Exactly. It made me see sense. My life is with you and the kids. You are my family now so let's make it official. Let's go get married."

Her eyes widened as she suddenly understood what I was trying to say. "You mean now? Are you serious?"

"I mean this week. We don't need a crazy ceremony. We can do it in our local church."

She was caving now, I could see it, so I pushed harder. "You were right, I know that now. I was under a lot of stress and a part of me was still getting over Emma's death, but she's gone and you're here, and I'm not interested in waiting anymore. Lets just get on with our lives. So what do you say, Sam?"

She looked up at me, her big beautiful eyes spilling over with tears.

"I do."

100

CHASE

The time had come to say goodbye to Pixie.

The Doc had led her to her car and the rest of us had gathered around them. I immediately noticed that Sully and Sam were holding hands. I don't know what happened between them in the hour that the Doc was getting acquainted with Pixie, but I was so relieved. I loved the two of them together; they had felt right, right from the moment they had met, so when they separated, it felt like my parents had split up, which was crazy I know since I didn't know either of them a year ago.

Time changes so much.

The Doc helped Pixie into her car. She had some sort of grate in between the front and back seats, so if Pixie suddenly decided to Hulk out, she wouldn't be able to attack the Doc. I was surprised to find Bandit coming out to say goodbye, knowing how many issues he had with her. But I was even more surprised to find he had his new rabbit toy in his mouth. Even though Pixie had never been nice to him, Bandit knew it wasn't her fault. He jumped up onto the back seat and carefully laid his toy in front of her. When she didn't move, he nudged it towards her. Eyes wide, she grabbed the rabbit. I was half expecting her to lay into the thing like she had done with his other toys, but she just hugged it to herself for comfort. Satisfied that his gift had been accepted, Bandit jumped back down and came to my side.

"Good boy, Bandit. That was a super nice thing you just did."

He woofed, pleased with himself. Gideon stepped forward and fussed Pixie one last time. She pressed into him, seemingly scared of leaving. She had taken his love for granted and now it was going away. I knew how that felt, having come close to losing Bandit myself. I hugged him close to me as Doc got behind the driver's seat and gave us all a wave.

"I'll be in touch as soon as I have any updates but you can check up on her anytime, I started a private Facebook group for us."

Gideon and I shared an amused look, neither of us expecting the Doc to be a Facebook user. She gave us a quick smile over her shoulder and then they were gone. The others headed back into the house, but I hung back with Bandit. I crouched down until we were eye-level with each other.

"I'm so sorry that I didn't listen to you about Pixie. You tried to warn me but I had my own stuff going on and like Sully, I got caught up in it all. I promise I will never do that again, OK? I'm really sorry buddy."

Bandit leaned over to lick my face. And as the familiar smell of his dog breath washed over me, I figured all was right with the world.

101

CHASE

When the others left to bring Zeb home from the hospital, I decided to stay at the ranch with Bandit. I knew the staff wouldn't be keen on letting him in the hospital, and since I wasn't going to leave him ever again, staying home was the best solution. Besides, I had something I needed to do.

Bandit sat opposite me now, head cocked in question, as he could feel the nervous waves pouring out of me. Grabbing the phone, I dialed a number — careful this time to hide our caller ID — and waited, rubbing my sweaty palms over my jeans. The call was eventually answered by an angry male voice.

"What?" he demanded.

Though I had steeled myself for his voice, hearing it still caused negative emotions to flood my body. I shook them off, determined to see this through. "I'm calling for my mom," I answered, proud of the way my voice remained steady.

"Chase? You're too late," he said spitefully. "She's gone."

"Gone? Where?" I asked.

"Hell if I know. Her clothes are gone, and she took off without a word. Didn't even pay the rent so now I'm being tossed out, can you believe that?"

It was unbelievable that he thought I would feel sorry for him. I realized at that very moment that both Tubs and my mom were very similar people: they were both selfish and too involved with themselves to ever care about anybody else. Though I had a million things I had spent years storing up to say to him, I realized one simple word would convey them all.

"Good," I said, then I hung up.

So she had finally done it... she had finally left him. While I was furious at the way she had used and betrayed me, I had to admit that there was one small part of me that was happy she had finally left him behind.

Maybe now she could be a better person and can go for that life she had always wanted.

102

SULLY

D ays later, I found myself tugging at the collar of my shirt, not used to wearing such confining clothes.

My hair had been newly cut, I'd even had a close shave. All in all, I was looking quite dapper, even if I said so myself.

I could hear a hum of anticipation from the church's reception hall outside. We didn't know that many people here, but it seemed the whole town had turned up, regardless. I hadn't realized how many people liked our small family, in particular, Sam. They had waited years to see her married off and today was the day. Earlier, I had caught a glimpse of Warrey outside, looking like he had stepped out of a copy of Mechanic GQ. A bevy of available women were trying to get his attention, but he scowled at them all. I felt secretly proud that the better man had won Sam's hand.

Take that, Warrey.

There was a knock at the door and in came my dad, looking quite the gentleman himself. I couldn't think when I had last seen him in a suit and was surprised to find he seemed more at ease in one than I.

"Hey," he said to me. "You almost done?"

"Yes," I said, without any hesitation in my voice.

"There's something missing though," he said as he gestured me closer. He held a simple white rose in his hand, which he now pinned to the lapel of my suit. It matched the one on his own.

"Thanks." I checked my reflection in the full-length mirror and caught the uncomfortable expression on his face. "What is it?"

Dad looked up at me, clearing his throat to speak when Gideon came into the room, followed by Chase and Bandit. Gideon wore a suit not dissimilar to my own, while even Bandit had a bowtie around his neck for the occasion, but it was Chase who stole the show. She was wearing a pretty peach dress that showed off her glossy chestnut hair and creamy complexion. She looked beautiful... and truly uncomfortable. I grinned, watching her pull on the dress, fidgeting.

"Do they make these unbearable for a reason? How do people wear these things? And my God, the shoes! I hope you're not expecting me to walk gracefully in them," she exclaimed. Gideon shared my amused smile, which only caused her to glare more.

"Stop being so smug just because you don't have to be strapped and cinched into submission," she complained grumpily.

"Well, you look very pretty if that's any consolation," said Gideon, causing Chase to shut up instantly and blush furiously. She didn't say anything else, but she stopped tugging at her skirt and stood up a little straighter.

"Just like the Princess in Bradley the bumblebee."

This had come from Bandit, who had been given a brand-new iPad. He was referring to the first picture book we had taught him to read. After reading the book, he had compared Chase to the Princess. It was the first time he had paid a compliment to Chase, and she had taken it about as well as she had taken this one. Some girls craved attention for their looks, but Chase wasn't one of them, preferring that people liked her for her smarts instead. It was one of the things I loved most about her. Despite her embarrassment, she bent down to stroke him.

"So, are you guys ready for this?" I asked them.

"Are you kidding me? I just want to know why you hadn't done this any sooner," Gideon exclaimed. By his feet, Bandit barked once in agreement while Chase nodded. Even Zeb agreed. Though he had fallen silent since the kids' appearance, he seemed very much on board with proceedings.

"It was obvious the two of you should be together even during that first meal we had together, you know, when you made spaghetti?" Chase said, cutting into my thoughts.

Her words struck a chord in me. If I were honest, that was the moment that had cemented the deal for me too. Seeing Sam's dimples and her smiling face, I was gone even then, but it was amazing to hear the kids had felt the same.

An usher knocked on the door. "We're just about to start. Can we have the groom's party outside?"

We all jumped to attention. I had been here before, but previously I had felt nervous and anxious. This time, I felt only peace and calm. We had already gone through so much together. What was a little wedding?

As Gideon opened the door, I followed them outside to meet my new wife.

I couldn't wait.

103

SULLY

The ceremony flew past.

Before I even knew it, we had exchanged our vows, and we were now standing on the steps of the church as confetti rained down on us. Through the colored rice, I could make out some familiar smiling faces, among them Florence and Mark, who had traveled here faster than a rocket when I had given them the news. I hadn't realized just how much they cared, or how desperate they were to see me happy again. To have them both here now made the moment complete. I was about as happy as a man could be.

We ran up to my truck, which someone had decorated with a "just married" sign. I helped Sam inside, hoisting up the long hem of her dress and tucking it around her then turned to find Zeb beside me. The bandage was gone from his head now, but he still looked a little pale. He swore sunshine was all he needed, that and good food. Throughout the ceremony, he had seemed a little subdued. While Sam busied herself with well-wishers, he looked at me a little awkwardly. Finally, he spoke.

"Son, I'm sorry I didn't support you in your first wedding. It's clear that Emma was a lovely person, and I'm sorry I never got the chance to meet her, but I'm here now, and I hope I can make it up to you this time around."

I knew how hard that was for him, and I was truly touched. With that simple apology, years of anger and resentment melted away. He reached out and offered me his hand. I shook it as he smiled at me.

"Congratulations, Son, we all love her."

I shot him a grin, then searched for the kids. Chase seemed suddenly shy as she came up to me and gave me a big hug while Bandit pressed against me in his own version of an embrace.

"Enjoy your honeymoon," Chase said. "Bring me back something from Montréal."

"Woof!" Bandit agreed, making us all smile.

"I will," I promised. "You guys be good and stay out of trouble. We'll be Skyping you every day to check in, and remember, Montréal is only two and a half, three hours drive away, tops. We can come back in case of any emergencies."

Gideon rolled his eyes at me. "We'll be fine. Just leave already before Sam goes without you."

As if she heard him, Sam honked the horn impatiently.

"OK, OK," I said as I climbed into the truck beside her. She leaned against me, happily slipping her hand in mine. As I looked into the rearview mirror, at these people who had joined us on the happiest day of our lives, I saw a blonde figure hovering at the back of the crowd. I couldn't make out her face at first, through the waving hands and confetti, but then the crowd parted like a wave and her face stared directly at me.

Looking exactly the same as she had when I had last seen her alive.

It was my wife.

My other wife.

My dead wife.

I froze, but before I could react, a flash of light blinded me as Chase yelled out, "Say cheese!"

When the light died down, and I found my eyes readjusting, Emma had vanished.

I shook my head, knowing it was just my mind playing tricks on me... I had just spoken to my father about Emma, so it wasn't unreasonable that I would see her again now. Having been here before, I was determined not to fall for those tricks again. Smiling at Sam, I focused on my bride as I pulled the truck out of the driveway. She leaned out of the window, waving energetically and blowing kisses, happiness causing her cheeks to turn rosy.

As the crowd of loved ones cheered us on, I drove us towards our future.

Just my bride and me, knowing that whatever came next, the two of us would weather it all.

Thank you for reading HAUNTED.

If you loved this book, then please leave a review to help keep a roof over Jo's head, and also so other readers know to check out Jo's work!

The more reviews she gets for a book, the faster she prioritizes writing more books in that series.

If you know others who might enjoy the series, let them know! You could even tell your local library to get the books so that those on a low or fixed income can enjoy them too.

Keep reading for a synopsis for HUNTED, the thrilling final book in the Chase Ryder series!

HUNTED

*Mad scientists, evil mercenaries, and
a genetically modified dog.
We thought we had survived it all...
but the worse was still to come.*

Two weeks have passed since Sully and Sam were married, but instead of the happiness they expected when they returned from honeymoon, they found the unimaginable sitting on the couch. Before any of us could understand what was happening, we were attacked by a covert government group, but unlike Forbes' men who had wanted Bandit alive, these were sent to wipe us out.

To clean us from existence.

With nothing but the clothes on our back, we fled across the country, our enemy hot on our heels when disaster struck.

Driven insane by grief, one of us goes to strike a terrible deal with the enemy that would defy all laws of nature and bring everything crashing down around us.

As the others raced to stop them from making a devastating mistake, and with the cleaners breathing down our backs, Bandit and I headed off to implement a risky plan — one which would either save us from being hunted, forever...

Or it would get us all killed.

"Best series since Dean Koontz's earlier work." - **Kindle Customer, Amazon**

"Jo Ho continues delivering a heart-pounding, action-packed riveting tale. From start to finish, I couldn't put it down. Jo will bring emotions out of you that you weren't aware you could experience simply reading a book. A master character and world builder." - **Susan P, Amazon**

"Wow, just wow! This is one of my favorite book series ever and I can't stop gushing about the author and the Chase Ryder series. If you read Dean Koontz, this author will make you fall in love with her characters. Chase and Bandit are such lovable and courageous characters." - **Samantha, Amazon**

"One of the best indie written books I've ever read. The only 5 stars I've ever given (seriously)." - **Amazon Customer**

"Though this series is categorized as young Adult novels, I, as an Old Adult enjoyed the hell out of them. If you have ever had a beloved pet ... cat or dog ... you will love the three books of this series." - **John E. Fillhart**

"If you like thrillers you will not be disappointed !!!! If you love dog

stories and this 3 book series will warm your heart !!! Fast paced and exciting you will not be able to put it down." - **Kindle Customer**

"Such a great ending to a wonderful series. Jo Ho took me through every emotion with her writing of this book." - **Candy, Amazon**

"The best ending to the best book series. Please read! I've said it twice and I'll say it again: BRING ON THE MOVIES!!!" - **Lucky Tyson**

Read the stunning conclusion to the series now!

Grab the book HERE

WE'RE NOT DONE YET!

Jo has another series that you might like!
Continue reading for a sneak peek of her new Urban Fantasy
series Twisted.

Fans of The Mortal Instruments, The Vampire Diaries, and Pretty
Little Liars will love this thrilling series!

(Available as ebook, paperback, and audiobook bundle)

TWISTED MAGIC 1: TWISTED BOOKS 1 - 11

Want the magic of Charmed? The romance of The Vampire Diaries? The suspense of Pretty Little Liars? Save 75% off the price of the single books when you purchase this special edition of Books 1 - 11 in the Twisted Magic series - that's almost 1,200 pages of thrilling story!

"I just wanted to be normal, but the day college started a supernatural world opened up. Now I don't know who to trust... or even if I'll survive the night."

Written like your favorite CW or Netflix show, expect thrills, heart-racing romance as well as epic twists and turns that will keep you guessing!

Marley Gray is just an ordinary girl when she moves to a new city to start college. She doesn't know that magic even exists, much less that she is the descendant of one of the most powerful witches to have ever walked the earth. As far as she knows, she has classes to sign-up for, parties to attend, and an over-protective father to avoid.

Along the way, Marley discovers roommate Cassie might just be the oddest - if richest - girl she's ever met. Then there's Eve, the older girl with a mysterious past who hides her true face under layers of make-up and a bitchy attitude. Thank God for Tyler who seems nice even though she's just suffered the worse kind of loss that anyone can.

When a night out ends with them all thrown together for the first time, something happens that no one expected. Something magical. And suddenly they discover they each have been gifted with strange new powers - but why? And who is the mysterious good-looking stranger who seems to know far more than he is telling them?

In no time, the girls find themselves in a desperate race against a powerful enemy who - in his centuries-old quest for revenge - could destroy not only the city of Boston, but quite possibly the world.

Can they work together to overcome their demons before all hell breaks loose?

Saving the world has never been this twisted!

★★★★★ - "OMG. THIS. BOOK. Had me from the first page!" - Kanyonmk, Reviewer

★★★★★ - "Spectacular. The action and adventure start from the beginning and don't let up... Ever." - Susan P, Reviewer

★ ★ ★ ★ ★ – "This series is amazing, each book just keeps getting better." – Nicole Henderson, Reviewer

★ ★ ★ ★ ★ - "I'd give this more stars if I could. I am hooked." – Patricia Eroh, Reviewer

★ ★ ★ ★ ★ - "One of the best series I've read. Must-read." – Derek Williams, Reviewer

★ ★ ★ ★ ★ – "Definitely a series to read if you're a fan of Supernatural, Charmed, Pretty Little Liars and a whole bunch of similar shows." – Jon, Reviewer

★ ★ ★ ★ ★ - "Jo Ho brings everything to this story. If anyone in the TV industry is reading this, YOU DEFINITELY NEED TO MAKE A SHOW OUT OF THIS SERIES!!!!!!" - Candy, Reviewer

This special edition contains the first 11 books in the Twisted Magic series:
Book 1, What Doesn't Kill You
Book 2, Beware The Signs
Book 3, See No Evil
Book 4, The Blood That Binds
Book 5, When Trouble Comes
Book 6, Bad Habits
Book 7, Left Behind
Book 8, Hell Hath No Fury
Book 9, In Her Skin
Book 10, First Date Jitters
Book 11, Grave Matters

Read the first chapter of this suspenseful series —>

CHAPTER 1

Becky Stevens wanted to die.

The sun had set hours ago leaving the sky a purple-black haze and it could stay that way forever for all Becky cared. If she never saw daylight again it wouldn't be a bad thing.

At least then she wouldn't have to listen to the snickering of those around her, laughing as her world was rocked, and her dreams shattered.

Music blared out from the speakers inside Tonic. The new local hotspot had recently been voted the most popular student hangout of the year but the place seemed too loud tonight, the flashing lights headache-inducing. She felt suffocated by the closeness of the heaving club goers.

She couldn't move without being pressed up against a sweaty stranger. Despite what her well-meaning friends thought, this really was the last thing she needed.

All she wanted was to veg out in her pj's in front of Netflix, but they had dragged her out against her will. She had to show *him* they had said! She couldn't give him the satisfaction of letting him know how he had broken her.

He was her boyfriend Mark.

Well, technically, he was her ex-boyfriend now.

Earlier in the day she had caught him with his tongue down another girl's throat. It wasn't what she had expected to see. Especially that early in the morning during her daily coffee run. The two of them had been together since high school where they were crowned prom queen and king. Dubbed the most popular couple, the two had graduated to the same private college together. As far as she had known, they were a team and Becky had fully expected to live happily ever after with him. They had decided where this amazing life would happen — in California among the palm trees and sunshine. They even knew what they would name their kids: Gemma for a girl, and Logan for a boy.

Why would he do that? Why would he encourage talk like that, getting her hopes up if he had no intention of making any of it happen?

As if the cheating itself wasn't bad enough, as if *seeing* him do it wasn't bad enough, it had to happen as Becky stood blindsided, surrounded by a group of her friends all out getting their breakfast shakes. Her humiliation wasn't complete it appeared unless it was witnessed by *everyone*, which was probably why they had insisted on this unfortunate night out. Her friends had figured a few drinks and some twerking later, and Becky would have forgotten all about him.

But although she had tried to enjoy herself, had tried to wipe that picture of him kissing someone else from her brain, there was no hiding that her heart was broken.

She didn't want to be here.

What she needed was a good cry and to drown her sorrows in a tub of Ben & Jerry's.

Pushing past the dancers, Becky reached the exit and turned around to wave goodbye to her friends. They shouted something at her, but Becky couldn't make out what they were saying above the singing of Bruno Mars. Getting the gist of it though, she shrugged apologetically, mouthed "next time," and made her way outside.

Becky shivered, unaccustomed to the sudden chill, as the fresh air hit her. They had been experiencing an unseasonably warm summer so the abrupt cold was a shock to the system. She clutched her cardigan closed over her chest, wishing she had worn her favorite one with the buttons. Shelby had insisted on this skimpier one. It came with a waterfall opening that didn't hide her assets and that was a good thing, apparently.

Although no amount of cleavage had kept Mark faithful, Becky thought bitterly.

Picturing her warm bed, Becky hurried towards the dorm she called home. It was only a few blocks away and if she wasn't wearing these stupidly high heels, she could probably get there in half the time. Unfortunately, everyone knew the price of beauty. The four-inch shoes gave her legs the illusion of length even if they pinched her toes and made balancing an Olympic art form.

Making her way across the square, Becky left the music behind and quickly found herself swallowed up by the silence. As she walked, she noticed that there was something different about the air tonight. She couldn't put her finger on it. There was a heaviness to it that was almost palpable. She could feel it weighing down on her.

Or maybe that was just the sudden realization that she was single again.

She'd have to date again. She'd have to go through all the uncertainties that came with meeting someone new, but this time, it wouldn't be as easy as finding him in the same class. Becky was already in her second year at college and she knew the talent — or lack of it — that existed there. The thought of having to be more social, of having to regularly hang out at places like Tonic filled her with dread. While some lived for going out, partying all the time just wasn't for her.

Her ghostly reflection appeared on the glistening black glass as she approached the John Hancock Tower. She looked away when it creeped her out too much. Her friends always laughed at her for being so jumpy. Becky had grown up with a superstitious mother who always warned her it was best not to look at yourself on shiny surfaces at night, because you might not like what you find there.

It wasn't like she was five or believed in monsters anymore.

Realizing how ridiculous she was being, Becky mentally shook herself. If she hurried up, she could still catch a few old reruns of Gilmore Girls before bed. That show was what she liked to describe as Hug TV. It was the kind of show that always made you feel better after you experienced it — just like a hug — and a hug was exactly what was required right now.

It was as she was clearing the building that Becky heard a footstep behind her.

She noted it in her mind but kept moving, expecting the person to keep their distance or to move away, respecting her personal space.

But more footsteps came... Closer this time.

Too close for comfort.

She stopped, spinning around to see who it might be. A gang of local kids had taken to water bombing passers-by lately. Becky was not going to be amused if this was them now, especially not in this cold. Scanning the area quickly, she could see no one. Still, she felt the hairs on the back of her neck rising, one by one. She couldn't shake the eerie feeling that someone was watching her. Tentatively, Becky called out.

"Who's there?"

There was no answer. No other sound.

Just the tap-tapping of her heels, picking up the pace.

Nervously, Becky fumbled for her bag, hoping to take her phone out. She wasn't sure who she would call, she just knew she would feel better with it in her hand, but in her haste, the bag slipped from her shoulder dropping to the ground. Makeup, and her Tennerson keyring fell onto the sidewalk, sounding as loud as gunfire in the silent night. Having fallen from her bag, her phone lay on the ground a little distance away.

Even from a few feet away, she could see a large crack spider-webbing across the dark screen.

"No, no, no..."

Dropping down to the ground, Becky scrambled for her phone, punching the home button, hoping desperately for it to come on but it stayed stubbornly off. Her fingers reached round to press the two buttons that she knew would reset her phone when...

Something *moved* in the reflection of the glass building.

Startled, her head snapped up to look at it.

What she saw there filled her with such terror that she froze, unable to move...

This ends the preview of TWISTED MAGIC 1. To continue reading click HERE.

ALSO BY JO HO

ROMANCE

Silver Screen Secrets Series

A heart-warming suspenseful romance series for dog lovers!

If you like Nora Roberts and our four-legged friends, then you will love this series!

Until The Stars Don't Shine, Book 1

Until The Sea Runs Dry, Book 2

Until The Last Leaf Falls, Book 3 (June 2020)

Until Color Fades Away, Book 4 (Fall 2020)

YOUNG ADULT

The Chase Ryder Series

Read this heart-warming thriller trilogy to learn the story of a mysterious dog who has escaped from a sinister lab, a lonely homeless girl surviving on wits alone, and a grieving veterinarian still haunted by a past that he can't let go of.

Can they keep their new family together while fleeing from the army of a ruthless billionaire? Will they even survive?

Gold Medal Winner of a Readers Favourite International Book Award

Wanted, Book 1

Haunted, Book 2

Hunted, Book 3

Twisted Series

Between her bizarre roommate, standoffish new friends, and overbearing father who's followed her to campus, Marley's first year at Blackville University is off to a rocky start. But when a strange night out leaves her with magical powers, college starts to look a lot more exciting...

What Doesn't Kill You, Book 1

Beware The Signs (Book 2)

See No Evil (Book 3)

The Blood That Binds (Book 4)

When Trouble Comes (Book 5)

Bad Habits (Book 6)

Left Behind (Book 7)

Hell Hath No Fury (Book 8)

In Her Skin (Book 9)

First Date Jitters (Book 10)

Grave Matters (Book 11)

Plus more to come!

Standalone Books

Who is the boy next door? A thrilling mystery that will keep you guessing until the very last page!

The Boy Next Door

See them all including her special discounted boxset deals at:

www.johoscribe.com

ABOUT THE AUTHOR

A proud geek and video gamer, and champion of complex female protagonists, Jo brings her page-turning screenwriting style to books to weave well-crafted, suspenseful stories with twists you don't see coming. She writes YA books under Jo Ho and heart-warming suspenseful romance under Joanne Ho - most of them featuring dogs!

A self-taught screenwriter, Jo's writing life began when she created the groundbreaking, critically acclaimed CBBC action fantasy television series, "Spirit Warriors," which introduced leading actress, Jessica Henwick ("Game of Thrones," "Star Wars: The Force Awakes") to the screen. Granted the biggest budget ever given to a CBBC show at the time, it was nominated for "Best Children's Programme" at the 2011 Broadcast Awards, with Jo herself, going on to win the Women in Film & Television's "New Talent" Award in 2010. Jo even made history for being the first East Asian person - man or woman - to have created a British television drama series.

Since then, Jo has worked with some of the most acclaimed producers in the world with several television shows and movies currently in development, she also writes for games. When she isn't working on her own stories, Jo helps others with their work - she is one of the BFI's (British Film Institute) recommended script consultants.

Jo suffers from MCS (Multiple Chemical Sensitivities), a debilitating condition she has developed over the last few years which has left her mostly housebound. Unfortunately, it is still not officially recognized in the UK despite the World Health Organisation listing it as a physical disability. There is currently no help for sufferers of MCS in the UK. Unable to travel or attend meetings and writersrooms, she has lost many screenwriting opportunities but has refused to allow the condition to rule her life. Despite the wrench life has thrown at her, Jo started to write and publish books.

Her debut novel WANTED, Book 1 of the Chase Ryder series has been a bestseller in 15 YA categories. It also won top prize in the YA Sci-Fi category for the 2018 Readers' Favorite Book Awards. It is her dream to bring all of her book series to screen and she believes she can make it happen with her readers' help!

Jo lives in London and hopes to travel across America one day in a super kitted out, MCS-friendly, Zombie-apocalypse-ready RV with her lovely fella Matt, and three equally lovely kitties.

Don't forget to **SIGN UP** to her mailing list for updates, book release details, gifts and exclusive offers at www.johoscribe.com

Check out her romance books here: https://www.amazon.com/Joanne-Ho/e/B081QVSCH5